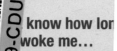

know how lon
woke me…

ed my eyes. The hotel room was dark, with faint
oming from the bedroom. I heard noises—a
g sound like metal scraping against metal, then
a muffled thud. They seemed to be coming from the
bathroom beyond the bedroom, and I thought I must be
disoriented. *Someone is pushing a squeaky service cart
in the hall, that's all,* I told myself, but I couldn't close my
eyes again. The hair on my arms bristled.

I saw a shadow move inside the bedroom. Someone had
entered my suite. I felt the vibration of his footsteps as
he crept over the carpet.

He couldn't see me. The back of the sofa blocked me
from his view. I stretched out my hand and groped over
the coffee table. My fingertips traced objects, and I took
care not to knock over the wine bottle or wineglass. Cold
steel met my fingertips. I lifted the SIG without making
a sound. Rolling smoothly off the sofa, I assumed a
crouched firing position and shouted, "*Freeze!* Don't
move or I'll shoot…."

LADY JUSTICE

ELLEN ELIZABETH HUNTER

W⊕RLDWIDE®

TORONTO • NEW YORK • LONDON
AMSTERDAM • PARIS • SYDNEY • HAMBURG
STOCKHOLM • ATHENS • TOKYO • MILAN
MADRID • WARSAW • BUDAPEST • AUCKLAND

A special thank-you to the Southern Poverty Law Center.

Recycling programs
for this product may
not exist in your area.

ISBN-13: 978-0-373-06268-3

LADY JUSTICE

Copyright © 2012 by Ellen Elizabeth Hunter

A Worldwide Library Suspense/ October 2012

First published by Magnolia Mysteries

www.Harlequin.com

Printed in U.S.A.

LADY
JUSTICE

"I, Ann Maguire Kelly, do solemnly swear that I will support and defend the Constitution of the United States against all enemies, foreign and domestic; that I will bear true faith and allegiance to the same; that I take this obligation freely, without any mental reservation or purpose of evasion; and that I will well and faithfully discharge the duties of the office of Attorney General of the United States. So help me God."

ONE

DURING THE NIGHT, a spring rainstorm battered George-town, a deluge that stripped newly born cherry blos-soms from trees and beat them to death in the gutters. A rain so heavy it would have put out any fire, no matter how fierce. The wind raked bare branches across my second-floor windowpanes. In my dreams, the scratch-ing noises came from the claws of a large bird as its wings beat the house and its talons scored the glass.

I woke with a lurch, trembling and alone in the dark. On my bedside table a telephone shrilled. I snatched at the handset with dread. Few people know my private number, and when they call in morning's numb hours, it is always with bad news.

"General Kelly, I'm sorry to disturb your sleep," said a voice both urgent and familiar. Early-morning calls from my deputy of the National Church Arson Task Force were becoming a matter of routine. Arsonists prefer to work under cover of darkness.

"It's Vernon Young, Ann. I'm sorry to wake you so early, but another church was torched last night."

"Where?" I suspected he would name a town in the Southeastern corridor. Houses of worship—African-American congregations, mixed-race congregations, Jewish temples—were being razed in the Southeast as if on a weekly schedule.

"Charleston," Vernon replied. "My chopper just landed here at Charleston Air Force Base. A full task force has been on the job since midnight. I'm driving out to the site now to join them." Noise from the airfield roared in the background: rotor blades chopping air, ground crews shouting to be heard above the din.

I shoved a second pillow behind my back and drew the blanket up under my chin. In the past year, I'd learned to wake up fast, and Vernon deserved my full attention. "How bad is it?"

"It's as bad as they get. The team leader reports the church was razed to the ground. And…uh…that's not all." Vernon hesitated. "It gets worse. The K-Nine unit found a body in the rubble."

"I knew our luck would run out on that score. So far they've been content to cause property damage." *And spiritual damage,* I thought. "Any idea who the victim is?"

"No. The corpse is burned beyond recognition. Can't even tell if it's a man or a woman."

"Anyone missing?"

"We're checking on that."

"Do the media know about the corpse?"

"No. Not yet."

"Good. Let's keep it that way. Buy ourselves a little time. Have agents move reporters and spectators as far from the scene as possible. Call it a safety measure. Then get a chopper in close and airlift the corpse to Quantico. The docs there work miracles identifying the faceless and the nameless."

"Yes, ma'am, I'll call Quantico right away. I'll report back when I have news."

"Good. All right, then, Vernon, keep me posted."

I looked at the clock: four A.M. Two phones occupied my bedside table: my personal private line and the encrypted wire to the White House. At least the red light on the White House handset wasn't flashing. At least I wasn't being summoned to the Oval Office to crisis manage another terrorist attack or the gunning down of a guard at the Holocaust Museum.

My bedroom was cold with wind rattling the windowpanes, the demons of dreams replaced by the demons of reality. I turned off the light and closed my eyes, but troubling images persisted. Towering flames consumed one-room churches. Agents bagged charred remains and airlifted them away from ashen ruins. I wondered about the identity of the corpse and how it got trapped in the inferno. Was it male or female, young or old? Victim or perpetrator?

In the year since I assumed my post, the Department of Justice had been plagued with a rash of unsolved church arsons. None had claimed a life. Tonight's discovery added a new and frightening dimension to the equation of arsons and hate crimes.

Sleep was impossible. I tossed and turned in twisted sheets. Jack was away on assignment in Afghanistan. I missed the comfort of his long, lean body next to mine, the heat he generated that always felt a degree above normal, the steamy hollow behind his knees where I warmed my feet. Mostly, I missed our pillow talk. Everyone brought their troubles to me. I took mine to Jack. He nurtured and protected the tender feelings my public position forced me to conceal.

My sense of isolation deepened as my very soul seemed to desert me to wander among the stunned parishioners, to share their grief and outrage. Their defeat was mine. It was my job to find and prosecute those committing these hate crimes. Yet armed with teams of agents and millions of dollars, I had made little progress.

Too restless to sleep, I rose, showered, and dressed. I drank coffee at my kitchen window and watched day break without the benefit of sunlight. I made a half-hearted attempt to catch up on paperwork as I waited for a decent hour to call my driver and security detail. I apologized for waking them. "The day has started off badly, and there's no guarantee that it will improve."

Later, I was to remember those prophetic words.

Georgetown was barely stirring as my driver maneuvered our black Cadillac Escalade through cobblestone streets. Quaint bookstores and pricey boutiques guarded their treasures behind chain-mail armor. Twigs littered sidewalks. Our few tantalizing spring days had fled overnight, temperatures dipping into the freezing range once again. Winter was not through with us yet. Chill winds ripped white blossoms from dogwoods and flung them at my windshield like bruised and blood-tinged confetti. Overhead, heavy black clouds rolled in, dampening rooftops and spirits.

Sharing the backseat with me, Agent Lauren Colby scanned the streets for signs of danger. The Bureau provided my security detail, two agents to guard me against a thousand armed felons.

Colby was young and pretty and totally devoted to her job. A woman in a man's world, she could not afford to give off mixed signals if she wanted to survive and thrive. It wasn't fair and it wasn't right, but I'd butted heads with an inequitable system all my life.

Colby dressed in severe styles and colors. Charcoal-gray suit for her; royal blue for me. Rockports on her feet. So she could run, she reminded me, eyes darting askance at my two-inch heels, my one vanity because I'm five feet two. Colby favored boxy jackets that concealed the Glock ten-millimeter semiautomatic weapon she carried in a shoulder holster. Wide-bottomed pants that obscured the second gun strapped to her ankle. She was a crack marksman, the chief reason she'd been selected for my security detail. At the Hoover Building's indoor firing range, she consistently outshot senior agents.

"We're picking up Sam Claiborne," I reminded my driver.

Carlos Perez was trained in pursuit and evasive driving at the Bureau's Emergency Vehicle Operations School in New York. In his youth, he had been a professional race-car driver. Now in his fifties, he worked for the Bureau and, in fact, served as a third bodyguard when I was commuting. He had convinced himself I was unaware of the MP5 assault rifle he kept stashed under the dashboard. This morning the Senate Judiciary Committee was meeting in closed session. Sam Claiborne, hero of the first Gulf War and current U.S. senator, was a powerful member. Sam was sponsoring an amendment to greatly expand the authority of the Hate Crimes Bill. I was to brief the senators on the statistics of church arsons in America, its demoralizing effects on the communities, and to convince them Sam's amendment would give the DOJ and the Bureau the teeth we needed to take a big bite out of the asses of those who were desecrating churches.

I am the daughter of an Episcopal clergyman. I was raised with the knowledge churches are sacred places. These arsonists were attacking all I held holy. Hounding them down had become a personal vendetta for me.

"You're on our way," I had told Sam last night. "I'll pick you up."

Last evening, there had been a sixtieth-birthday celebration for Sam at his home. Naturally, even in the confines of an event as celebratory as a birthday party, the talk had turned to politics, to the difficulty of pushing through Sam's amendment.

I'd played my role, promising the amendment had the full support of the new president, and public sentiment was on our side.

"My father is the new bishop of the Archdiocese of North Carolina," I'd told them. "I grew up seeing how congregations love their churches. I've seen their disappointment when a building campaign failed to reach its goal. I know that watching their houses of worship burn to the ground breaks their hearts. And their spirits.

"I think that's why they do it. Those hateful militias. They know they're breaking the spirits of those who oppose their ambitions to overthrow the government and lead us into anarchy."

Then Jesse Taylor, Sam's housekeeper, had entered, dimming the lights and bearing a huge chocolate cake decorated with six candles. "One for each decade." He had a broad grin. Jesse was kin to Sam. No one could quite figure out the relationship, perhaps a great-nephew, but nonetheless he was family from "down home."

We sang "Happy Birthday" and "For He's a Jolly Good Fellow" loudly and out of tune. Everyone was grinning from ear to ear. So glad to celebrate with our hero.

Someone raised a glass. "To fighting Senator Sam!"

"Hear! Hear!" the others of us cheered.

"Speech. Speech," someone called, feet stamping boisterously under the dining room table.

Sam, his face crumpled in a mouth-and-eyes smile, rose from his chair. I'd grown so fond of that gentle mien, the round, happy face, buzz-cut gray hair, rimless glasses, genuine smile. A countenance that reflected compassion, understanding, intelligence.

He said, "I owe everything to you special folks. I can't fight these battles alone. Without you, I'd be nothing."

He tipped his head and tilted his glass in my direction. "I'm especially grateful for your support, Ann." His eyes twinkled as he turned to the small group assembled around his dinner table. "Because if all the attention goes to my head, this straight-up young lady will set me back on course faster than the tough old granny who raised me."

Chuckles all around, especially from me.

When we left Sam's house at nine, it was raining buckets. Now, again this morning, the heavens threatened to open. Carlos pulled up at the curb in front of Sam's historic Federal residence on narrow N Street. Painted gray with black shutters and a glossy black front door, the two-story house anchored the row of residences at the middle of the block. Abruptly, the door swung open from within and Jesse Taylor stepped out onto the stoop. He seemed distracted and out of focus. Panic distorted his normally serene features as he frantically scanned the street. Seeing my car, he sprinted the short distance across the brick sidewalk, shouting and waving his arms. A sour taste filled my mouth. Something was wrong. Very wrong. Carlos lowered the window.

Jesse cried, "Thank God, you're here. I called nine one one, but where are they?" His eyes raked the length of the tree-lined street, skimming past quaint row houses all the way to the distant intersection. "You've got to help him. He needs help!"

Agent Brad Moore threw open the front passenger door and jumped out.

I reached for my door handle, but Colby restrained me with a firm grip on my arm. "Stay here with Carlos, General, until we check things out."

"No! If something is wrong with Sam, I've got to go to him."

With Colby's warning I might be walking into a trap ringing in my ears, I hurried around the car in the wind, hopped across a puddle at the curb, and followed Jesse and Moore into the house. Colby dogged my heels, and I sensed rather than saw when she withdrew her gun from her shoulder holster.

"Where is he?" I asked urgently.

"Upstairs," Jesse whispered, not meeting my eyes.

"Show me."

"I can't," he whispered again. Rocking on his feet, he made a grab for the newel post. "I can't look at him."

I started up the creaky stairs to the landing. The fanciful moon face of a grandfather's clock beamed down on me with mock cheer. Without warning, the clapper began to strike the hour and I jumped. We scurried up the remaining stairs and reached Sam's bedroom just as the clock struck twice.

Colby pushed past me, shielding my body with her own. Her weapon was drawn and aimed straight ahead. Rushing adrenaline heightened my senses, causing interior details to leap out in sharp relief. Wedgwood blue wallpaper with crisp yellow daisies. Wainscot painted bright white. Sam's rimless bifocals marking the pages of a thick, open book on his bedside table.

Wrapping my arms around my chest, I became aware of the cold. Wet, bone-chilling air flowed through a ten-inch opening under the raised window. The carpet beneath the window was sopping wet.

A four-poster bed dominated the room. An antique, it sat high off the floor, a small step stool pulled up to its side. White linen sheets and pillows still bore the imprint of the man who had lain there. A flowered coverlet was tossed aside. Sam was nowhere in the room.

Moore veered off to the left, Glock pointing the way. He lunged through an open doorway. The clock stopped striking. *Seven precisely,* I thought mundanely, anything to distract me from this terrible foreboding.

We found Sam in the study off his bedroom. Gloomy light filtered through sheers at the windows, revealing a scene straight out of my wildest nightmares. The Honorable Samuel Louis Claiborne sat in a large wing chair where he appeared incongruously small and helpless. He was so close that if I reached out my hand, I could touch him. *Oh, cover him up,* I wanted to shout. Sam, the bravest man I know, the hero of Desert Storm and the survivor of countless savage skirmishes on the floor of the United States Senate, had been felled by a single bullet.

My emotions threatened to overtake my reason, and it was all I could do to remain on my feet. *Hang tough, Kelly,* the seasoned prosecutor inside me warned. *You're at a crime scene. Survey it, evaluate what you see, soak up the details, this instant, before the hordes descend.*

Neat and orderly, the room showed no signs of a struggle. No overturned furniture, no upended lamps. Bookcases organized. Military histories lined up smartly like soldiers on parade. Computer, fax, modem silent. No messages blinked on the answering machine. Maps and documents stacked like paper skyscrapers, for Sam was researching the Gulf War, writing his memoirs.

Everything was as it should be, except for the tell-tale whiff of gunpowder, the sickly sweet smell of clotted blood.

I gripped the edge of the desk as the room spun. I hung on, willed myself to steadiness. I seized my cell phone from my shoulder bag and used its camera to take pictures. A callous gesture, one might think, but not for a seasoned prosecutor. As soon as the detectives arrived, this scene would change, and change dramatically. Shutting my cell phone and dropping it into my purse, I forced myself to view what I had just photographed.

In a scene staged by a director of the macabre, Sam's chair had been moved to a central position in the room. In it, his lifeless form was slumped to one side, his head leaning into the wing as if too heavy for his aging neck to support. Dazzling medals and polished brass decorated the front of his parade dress uniform. A five-star general's helmet dipped rakishly low over one eyebrow. Around his neck, the prestigious Congressional Medal of Honor dangled on a blue satin ribbon.

Civilian life had added extra pounds to his midsection, so the buttons of his jacket did not quite meet. The uniform—immaculate and crisp—appeared to have come straight from a dry cleaner's bag. Some oddity caught my eye. Averting my gaze from his face, I leaned in for a closer look at his jacket. Striped fabric peeked out from under the lapels. Pajamas. My gaze dropped to the floor. His brown feet were bare.

Hot tears stung my eyes. What monster had done this to him? This disrespect for his uniform and his medals of honor made a mockery of everything Sam stood for. With firm resolve, I shifted my attention to his face. A small black hole marked the bridge of his nose. His eyes were shut, and I was spared the sight of their blankness.

Agent Brad Moore stood behind the chair, two fingers pressed against Sam's carotid artery. Moore's worried gaze never left my face. He shook his head sadly. "No pulse, General. I'm sorry."

From a distance, Agent Lauren Colby called my name. "General Kelly, are you all right? General Kelly?"

TWO

THUNDERING FOOTSTEPS SHOOK the staircase. In a flash, I knew what had happened. When Jesse Taylor had called 911, the call went to Metro P.D. Now all hell was breaking loose. Uniformed cops and plainclothes homicide detectives pushed into the small room, surrounding us, eyeballing Sam's dead body.

"We're FBI." Colby reached for her shield. "This is the attorney general."

"Don't touch a thing," I said. "In fact, you should leave now. We'll handle this on the federal level."

One of the homicide detectives started to argue but stopped mid-sentence, his mouth gaping. The doorway filled with a black uniform and all eyes turned in its direction. "There's the captain. He'll tell you."

Looking like a throwback to an SS officer, the Metropolitan Police Department captain strode confidently into the room, sweeping all of us with a cool, appraising glance, taking in the situation in an instant. His eyes fixed on me. I could tell he knew at once who I was and wasn't happy to see me. I was a complication he hadn't anticipated. His frown faded, replaced by a quick, artful smile.

He stretched his hand to mine, saying smoothly, "I'm Captain Rakes, General Kelly. We met last year at your swearing-in ceremony. You were surrounded by people, and I don't expect you remember me."

Captain Rakes was correct. I didn't remember him. I

returned the handshake. "Of course, Captain, I remember you well. We were just about to call CID. Why don't you and I step outside for a moment and talk?"

I nodded to Brad Moore, noting he quickly understood my unspoken instructions. He turned his back to the others but not before I saw him extract his cell phone from his jacket pocket.

With Captain Rakes behind me, I led the way out of the study, passing through Sam's bedroom where cops buzzed like mad hornets at a hive. Moving into a relatively quiet corner, I sized up the police captain. Tall, thin to the point of reediness, chiseled features, sharp eyes that could slice through lies. He wasn't going to be easy. Then, neither was I.

I began with a conciliatory tone. "Captain, we've got a problem here. As you know, the homicide of a United States senator has got to be investigated by the Bureau. If there is so much as a whisper of a breach of national security, there will be a full congressional inquiry. All this is mandated by law, as you well know."

Through narrowed slits, Rakes cut his icy eyes at me. "With all due respect, General Kelly, I know no such thing. Georgetown is my jurisdiction. I am responsible for any crime committed here. Let me assure you, the feds will get a copy of my report. I'll fax one to your office as well. Now, if you'll excuse me, I've got a dead senator on my hands."

"You can't do this. Look, if you leave now, we'll just call it a simple misunderstanding." I was agitated and chopping the air with my open hands. We both knew he was in the wrong. We both knew he'd be forced out of the investigation. Right now, he had the power to mess up the crime scene. Ultimately, the embarrassment would be DOJ's. Was that his motive? To one-up the feds? There was no love lost between federal and district government, and everybody knew it.

"Can't do that, ma'am," he said curtly. "I'd appreciate it if you'd wait downstairs."

"I'd hoped we could settle this between us. Now you leave me no choice. I'm taking this up with the commissioner."

The gloves were off. Rakes' lips pulled downward into a sneer. "Whatever." He signaled a young cop, who trotted over, as eager to please as a puppy dog. "Put General Kelly in one of the first-floor rooms. See that she's comfortable."

To me he said, "I've got some questions for you, ma'am. Be with you as fast as I can."

He turned his back on me. The young cop spoke courteously. "This way, please, General Kelly."

Moore and Colby waited on the stairs. "Did you reach him?" I asked.

We started down. "Spoke to the AAG himself," Moore replied. Moore referred to the director of the Criminal Division, Assistant Attorney General Edgar Cross. It is the responsibility of the Criminal Division to enforce federal law, and the murder of a U.S. senator fell within their jurisdiction.

Moore looks like everyone's idea of an FBI agent: clean-cut, Dick Tracy jaw, close-clipped black hair, muscular physique. His Dick Tracy jaw stiffened. "Cross is on his way. He's bringing the FBI."

I sighed audibly as we reached the bottom of the staircase. The downstairs was being overrun with local law enforcement, and I worried about evidence being destroyed. "We've done all we can. That idiot Rakes ordered me to wait. I'll stay but only because I want to be here when Cross arrives."

I'd spent my entire career watching local and federal law-enforcement agencies fight over jurisdiction. I'd seen investigations bungled because one group with-held information from the other. Knowing that, why did it always surprise me when the boys refused to share the toys?

In Sam's formal living room, I stationed myself at a window that overlooked the street. A SWAT team in full turnout gear squatted behind police vehicles, the house their target. Up and down the street, curtains twitched, and I hoped no one got trigger-happy, because Glocks had a way of practically firing themselves.

I watched and waited. Traffic at this hour peaked, and it could take Ed Cross as long as thirty minutes to arrive. Rain began to fall in steady torrents. It dripped from bare branches in icy streams and pelted the back of the woman who ran hunched forward, head bent, from a black van to the shelter of the stoop. Her tan trench coat was not fastened, swirling around her white clini-cian's jacket. A police officer rushed to meet her. The noise of their voices and footsteps carried as they moved through the hall and climbed the stairs.

Where was Jesse Taylor? I worried he was being hassled. The young cop stood guard in the doorway, but I swept past him, and although he looked unhappy about it, he was smart enough to keep his mouth shut. I walked through downstairs rooms, searching for Taylor.

Dining room, library, the formal living room I'd left behind, all were furnished with fine antiques that bore the imprint of Emily Claiborne's tasteful touch. A mere twelve hours ago, these rooms had housed a celebration. Now they were as dreary and depressing as the cloudy day outside and the national mourning that lay ahead.

I pushed through swinging doors into the kitchen.

Jesse Taylor leaned on his elbows at the kitchen table. Beside him, a sympathetic homicide detective was trying to calm him. I took in the details of the kitchen. Coffee was fresh and fragrant in the brewer. The lemony froth of beaten eggs filled a chipped blue bowl on the counter. From the table, two sets of eyes looked up at me. Jesse's chocolate-brown eyes dripped tears that clung to his lashes. "He's dead, isn't he, General Kelly?"

"I'm afraid so, Jesse." I patted his shoulder.

"I knew it. I knew it the minute I saw him."

"Tell me what happened," I said kindly.

The detective stood up. "General Kelly, it sure is an honor to meet you, ma'am. I'm Detective Lewis. Anything I can do to help, you just say the word."

My hand disappeared between his two broad ones.

"Thank you, Detective. Please sit down. I just want Jesse to tell me what he saw."

"I was getting to that, ma'am. He's pretty upset."

Jesse blurted, "I found him, General Kelly." Tears rolled down his cheeks, and he made no attempt to wipe them. "Usually, the senator is stirring when I get here in the morning. He comes down while I'm frying his eggs and sausage. Looks at the morning papers. We talk, you know. Always asks about my wife, the kids, just the nicest uncle you'd ever want to know.

"When he didn't come down at his usual time, I thought he must be sick. The senator is always on time. I went up to check on him. Found him just sitting there in his favorite chair, kinda like he was napping, you know." He lifted his eyes to mine, pleading with me not to make him say it.

I put my hand on his shoulder again, encouraging him to go on.

"I saw the bullet hole. I knew what it meant, but I

didn't want to admit it. I thought they could save him, so I called nine one one. Then you came. Oh, mercy, why would anyone want to do such a thing to that good man?" He buried his forehead in his palms and squeezed his skull as if trying to wring answers from his brain.

"Excuse me." I fled from the kitchen with my fist wedged tightly against my teeth. A rage was building in my chest. I was going to scream. I was sweaty and jittery and didn't know where to turn, only I had to get out of sight.

Ducking into a tiny powder room tucked under the stairs, I braced myself against the sink. In the mirror, my face was white and my eyes seemed to pop from their sockets. I looked like a madwoman. I had to get a grip on my emotions. "Dear Lord, give me strength."

Someone tapped on the door. "General Kelly, are you in there?" Colby.

"Give me a moment alone," I replied irritably. "Just leave me alone!"

I wet a tissue and dabbed at my temples where my pulse throbbed. Letting cold water gush over my wrists, I began to feel steadier. "All right, Kelly," I told my reflection, "if you let yourself fall apart, you're not going to be of any use to Sam or yourself. Now, get some backbone, girl. There's a job to be done here."

I opened the door and faced my anxious detail. Moore said, "Cross will handle this. Let's get you out of here."

"No. I'm fine. We can't leave. There are things we must do. This case is being bungled. I've got to go back up there and take a good look around before those keystone cops ruin everything."

"Ed Cross said to leave it to him," Moore argued from behind Colby's shoulder.

"I know. I know. That's just what I'd expect him to say. Now, come on you two, stick with me." I started for the stairs.

Colby hung on my arm. "General Kelly, are you sure you want to do this? You've had a shock. Let's go somewhere and sit down."

I shook loose and didn't bother to reply. She meant well. "Come with me."

I was the ice maiden of controlled rage.

Detectives ransacked a Philadelphia highboy. *Stop pawing through his underwear,* I wanted to shout. Sam would be incensed to see those prying hands rifling through his intimate apparel.

Similar to the study next door, the bedroom was neat and orderly, everything in its place. Not at all what you'd expect if two men had struggled here. That puzzled me.

The partially raised window puzzled me as well. I made a mental note to ask Jesse about it. Below curtains that flapped in the wet breeze, a technician crouched, attempting to brush silver-black powder on the sill, but the sill was wet and the powder turned to mud.

The perpetrator had been clever. If that window was his point of entry, by leaving it open when he left, the rain had effectively washed away crime-scene evidence. Even the sopping-wet carpet would not yield usable footprints.

Then I noticed the window screen was missing. Was this a significant clue?

I stepped nearer to the bedside table. The book which Sam had been reading and which his bifocals marked was the Bible.

A uniformed officer blocked the way to the study. I pushed toward him. "Ma'am, you can't go in there."

"Officer, I appreciate you're following your captain's

orders, but I assure you I'm authorized to attend any crime scene."

"Yes, ma'am." The officer, little more than a teenager, moved to let me pass.

At first I saw nothing but the shoulders of detectives. Their hulking presence filled the small room. When the forensic technicians arrived, they'd find extraneous footprints and trace. The scene was being muddied by the detectives themselves. One actually smoked a cigarette, the ashes dropping to the floor. A police photographer rotated around the chair, snapping pictures of Sam's defenseless body from various angles. I felt violated for him.

Off in a corner, the woman in the trench coat leaned against the wall as she scribbled notes on a clipboard chart. Although we'd never met, I recognized her from newspaper photos. Barbara Grant, the District of Columbia's chief medical examiner. I looked around for Lauren Colby and saw her standing at the door with the uniformed cop.

An audible thrill ran through the detectives, and I whirled around to confront them. Captain Rakes lifted a revolver aloft by a yellow pencil inserted in the barrel. My dislike for the man intensified. With dramatic flourish, he dropped the weapon into a transparent evidence bag. A .38 Army Colt Special.

Sam's own weapon?

Unexpectedly, broad shoulders parted, and once again I was face-to-face with my dear, dead friend. I forced myself to study him dispassionately. His closed eyes puzzled me. There were just too many puzzles in this case. In crime-scene photographs I'd viewed in countless courtrooms, victims kept their eyes fixed on their tormentors, the way you'd stare at a cobra about to strike. Why would Sam have closed his eyes?

Rakes moved to my side, his dead eyes meeting mine questioningly. I said, "Ed Cross of the Criminal Division is on his way here. Don't move the body before he arrives." My tone left no room for argument.

Rakes didn't get it. "It's the medical examiner who makes that decision. Let's talk. Taylor found the body, went outside looking for us, saw you, called you inside. What brought you here in the first place?"

"I have no intention of answering your questions. You have no authority in this case."

"You were here late last night, were you not?" His tone was accusing.

"What are you insinuating?"

He shrugged disarmingly. "Not a thing, ma'am. Merely stating a fact."

"Because the senator and I are friends. Other of his friends were here as well."

"You were the last to leave." His tone mocked me. "What time was that?"

"Eleven." How had he managed to put me on the defensive?

"I'd like to have the names of the other guests," Rakes said.

I folded my arms. "I'll provide that information to AAG Cross."

Rakes' smile did not touch his eyes. "You know, General Kelly, you were the last person to see the senator alive."

I couldn't help it. I puffed up. "No, Captain. You're dead wrong. His murderer was the last person to see him alive."

THREE

"Can you fix the time of death?" I asked Dr. Grant.

"I'll be able to determine that after we get him to the morgue. I can hazard a guess. Cadaveric rigidity has already set in the jaws and upper body. There's still flexibility in the lower extremities. Rigor begins with the muscles of mastication and progresses downward."

"Could you translate that, please?"

"I mean death occurred about seven hours ago. I haven't taken the body temperature yet. I didn't want to move him. I have to factor in the coolness of the ambient air."

She consulted her watch. "Don't hold me to it just yet, but I'd say he died between midnight and one A.M."

I nodded. Tears welled in my eyes, and I blinked them back. At one A.M. I'd been sound asleep. My telephone had stopped ringing at midnight and did not ring again until about three A.M. when Vernon Young called. Grant's expression registered understanding. Although we'd never met, I knew her by reputation. Behind thick lenses, her eyes were intelligent and sensitive. She was a large-boned woman who wore the scholarly air of distraction. She was about my age, forty-five. We'd both been students during the self-indulgent Reagan era. I'd wager Grant hadn't had the time for self-indulgence any more than I had.

She'd have been a diligent student with a four-point-oh grade average, the type other students called a nerd.

She wouldn't have noticed, and if she had, she wouldn't have cared. She'd have been absorbed in her textbooks and loving every minute of it. Except for the time spent in the science labs, squinting at deadly viruses on glass slides. She'd have loved that more. I felt I could easily read her because she was a lot like me.

I'd gone to Cornell on a scholarship, then on to New York University Law School. After graduation, two wonderful things happened to me. First, Jack Kelly proposed. Second, I was offered an ADA's position on the Manhattan district attorney's staff. I accepted both and have never regretted either decision. During the next ten years, I was the busiest woman in Manhattan. By night, I paced our small apartment's nursery with colicky babies. By day, I paced courtroom corridors, prosecuting Mafia chieftains. The hard work paid off. I moved up through the ranks at the DA's office. My caseload was horrendous, but I always took time to dash home to read bedtime stories to my children, even if it meant grabbing a cab back to the Manhattan Criminal Court Building late in the evening.

My children were grown now, and my family scattered. I didn't see them nearly as much as I'd like to. I lived, mostly by myself, in a modest rented town house in Georgetown from which I commuted to Federal Triangle each day.

One of the detectives jostled me. Colby glared and chastised him sharply with words I didn't catch. She lifted her jacket lapel with its clip-on transmitter and murmured something to Moore. Coordinating positions. During the past year, I'd become used to being the center of their eternal vigil.

Grant regarded Colby with frank curiosity.

"This is Agent Lauren Colby, one of my security

detail." The two women shook hands crisply. Colby feigned disinterest in our conversation as she intently scrutinized the comings and goings of detectives.

"I'd like to know as much about Senator Claiborne's death as you can tell me," I said.

"There's little I can say with certainty now, General Kelly…"

"Call me Ann, please."

"I'm Barbara. I expect the autopsy will verify just what we assume: death was caused by a gunshot wound to the head."

"Did he die instantly?" What I really wanted to know was if he had suffered.

"Probably death was instantaneous. He wouldn't have suffered." She seemed to read my mind.

He would have known death was imminent, I thought. *He would have known he was staring down the wrong end of the barrel and he was about to be shot.* I intended to ask Barbara Grant about Sam's closed eyes, but something caught my attention that unnerved me.

From where I stood, I had a clear view through the bedroom and into the hall. Two paramedics had reached the top of the stairs with a collapsible stretcher between them.

"They're coming for him." I reached out a hand to the wall to steady myself.

"Yes. I need to get the body to the morgue as quickly as possible."

"You should not move him until agents from the Bureau arrive."

"There's nothing they can do I haven't already done," Grant replied confidently. "There's very little that can be done here, anyway."

"Exactly where are you taking him? I'm very concerned about the improper way this investigation is being handled."

"General Kelly…Ann. Now that he's in my custody, everything will be handled according to protocol. You can rely on that. They'll take him to Bureau headquarters where I am a consultant. The Bureau will be involved in every step of this investigation from now on."

"Then you are aware they should have been in charge from the start. Have you worked with Captain Rakes before?"

"On occasion. Captain Rakes has his own…"

I thought she was going to say *agenda*. Instead, she said, "Excuse me, Ann, I need to supervise the paramedics."

I moved out of the way, back into the upstairs hall, and found a chair outside a guest bedroom and waited. Within minutes, the paramedics returned, the bulging body bag between them on the gurney. I averted my eyes. They started down the stairs.

"Wait!" Barbara Grant shouted over the railing. "Make sure you come back for the chair!"

I made the mistake of turning. Through open doorways, I caught sight of Sam's leather chair and thought I would double over. While the entry wound had been clean, the exit wound had expelled bloody bone and brain fragments.

I cast my eyes about, fixing on any distraction. On pale blue wallpaper, a gallery of family portraits was displayed. In many of the pictures, an attractive teenage boy smiled openly and disarmingly. His grandfather, Sam, appeared in several of the photos with him.

Sam's only grandson, Brian, had lived for eighteen precious years. He'd been a brilliant student and was excited about the prospect of retracing his grandfather's footsteps through West Point and into the army. Sam had confided Brian wanted to be just like his "papa." Brian attended a public high school in Maryland where he was an honors student. Shortly before graduation—Brian was to be the valedictorian—an expelled troublemaker returned to campus brandishing a stolen semiautomatic rifle. It was the noon hour, and many students were eating lunch on the lawns or getting into cars to go to fast-food restaurants. The shooter opened fire indiscriminately on his classmates. Brian managed to sneak up behind him with the intention of wresting the rifle away. Just as he was about to spring, the boy suddenly whirled around and opened fire at close range. The bullets tore through Brian's chest. Brian was one of nine students who lost their young lives that day.

Sam told and retold this tragic story at the Senate hearings on gun control, but the retelling did not lessen the tale's horror. He used it to illustrate our position that we had to get guns out of the hands of children. Weapons were too easily obtained from gun shows and through unscrupulous dealers. Juveniles armed themselves with twenty-twos, thirty-eights, twelve-gauge semiautomatic shotguns, even MAC-10s. Each school year, one million students carried guns into classrooms.

Sam threw his full weight and influence behind the Brady Bill and gun-control legislation. A man who'd been admired by the nation, his support of the five-day waiting period and the assault-weapons ban earned him many enemies, among them the powerful National Rifle Association and sundry crackpot militia groups who called themselves Second Amendment warriors.

In a group picture taken before the tragedies struck the Claiborne family, Sam appeared with his wife,

Emily. Emily was gone now, too, a victim of breast cancer. On either side of the happy couple were Brian and his mother, Dr. Sarah Preston, a neurologist at the National Institutes of Health. Sarah appeared carefree—then. In the months I'd known her, she rarely smiled. Soon she would be getting a call from the robotic Captain Rakes, and I cringed to think of that cold man breaking the news to this already broken woman.

There *was* something I could do for Sam. Warning Colby not to let Grant leave before I could speak with her again, I motioned for Moore to accompany me into an empty guest room. Borrowing Moore's cell phone, I called Dr. Sarah Preston at her laboratory. At first, the neurologist was pleased to hear from me, thinking my call was a social one.

"Sarah, are you alone?" I asked. "Is someone there with you?"

"Yes," she answered cautiously. "Irving, my assistant, is here in the lab with me. Why, Ann? What's wrong?"

"Let me speak with him for just a moment, please."

"What is this about? You're scaring me. It's Daddy, isn't it? Something's happened to Daddy? Tell me at once."

A jumble of thoughts raced through my brain. These past few years had been pure hell for Sarah Preston. Yet she had a right to know. "I'm sorry, Sarah," I said gently. "Your dad's been shot. I'm afraid he's dead."

"Noooo," came her wrenching cry.

"Hello? Sarah? Sarah, are you there?"

A crashing sound indicated the receiver had slipped from her hand. Then a confused male voice spoke in my ear. "Hello?"

"Irving?"

"Yes. What did you do to Sarah?"

"Irving, this is Ann Kelly. I'm a friend of Sarah's. Sarah's father died this morning. You've got to stay with her. Don't leave her alone for any reason and make sure she's sitting down. Call her pastor or her closest friend. Get someone to stay with her. Will you do that?"

"Yes. Wait a minute. Sarah wants to speak to you."

"Ann?" Sarah's voice was distant and hollow.

"Are you all right, Sarah?"

"How did it happen?"

I hesitated.

"Ann? Tell me. I have a right to know."

"He was murdered. The police and the medical examiner are here now."

"Murdered!" Sarah gasped. "The medical examiner? Where are they taking him?"

"To the morgue at the Hoover Building," I replied.

"I have to go to him. I'm leaving now. Will you meet me there?"

"Yes, of course, I'll meet you."

What else could I say? There was nothing Sarah could do at the Hoover Building. She would not be allowed to view the body until after the autopsy. I knew that, and as a medical doctor, Sarah had to know it as well. If it made her feel better to be there, then how could I refuse her? I would meet Sarah and take her to my office and try to get some lunch into her.

"Don't try to drive yourself," I warned.

"No. I'll have Irving drive me."

I dreaded what was to come. It was all I could do to hold myself together. Now I'd have to be strong for someone else.

FOUR

BARBARA GRANT SUPERVISED the wrapping of the leather chair in a large, tent-like plastic bag. Satisfied it was properly sealed, she dispatched the technicians to the Hoover Building. I watched them struggle down the stairs with the heavy chair that was a repository of trace evidence.

Grant started for the stairs but, upon seeing me there, paused. "The lab techs will give it a thorough going-over. The bullet's in there. We'll turn it over to the Firearms Unit and match the bullet to the weapon. The chair will be examined under a high-powered laser beam. That will expose trace like hair and fibers. Leather is excellent for revealing prints."

"When will you have the results of the autopsy?" I asked.

"Prelims, this afternoon."

"Call my office when you have them. I'll alert my secretary to find me wherever I am."

"Will do."

"There's a chance the senator's daughter will show up at your lab. She's threatening to do so," I warned.

"I'm sorry to hear that. Grieving relatives can get very out of control, especially if they think we're hiding something from them. You never know how they'll react."

"I'd appreciate it if you'd handle her delicately. She's been through a lot recently."

"If you can persuade her to wait, that would be best."

"I'll try," I promised.

"Tell her I'll release the body to her just as quickly as I can. Maybe as early as tonight. I can't promise, but I'll try. I'm keenly aware of how families feel about the autopsy procedure."

"Sarah Preston is a medical doctor, and unfortunately that makes her think she can handle just about anything. She's not thinking too clearly right now. I'll take care of her."

"Take care of yourself, too, Ann. You've had a shock."

"Before you leave, Dr. Grant…Barbara, there's something that's been troubling me."

Nervously, she adjusted her glasses. "There's a lot wrong here, I know."

"None of that is your fault." I paused a moment to reflect. "I'm having a problem with the fact Senator Claiborne's eyes were closed. I knew Sam. He was first and foremost a warrior. A hero. Face to face with a murderer, he would not have shut his eyes. He would have stared the man down. Sam had looked death in the eye many times. He would have said, 'Go ahead and shoot. Don't expect me to grovel or beg.'"

"Perhaps he was asleep in his chair when the killer sneaked up on him," Grant suggested.

"Wearing his uniform over his pajamas? Besides, we know he'd already been to bed."

"Hmm. Well, if, as you say, he would have challenged his killer, then perhaps he did *not* close his eyes. Perhaps the killer closed them for him…postmortem."

"That's just what I've been thinking. But why? Do you have any theories?"

Grant took a moment to consider. "The killer might be the religious type. I mean, we know he's evil, but maybe he's caught up in religious ritual. Perhaps he felt compelled to perform an act of piety for the dead." She lifted open palms, their emptiness illustrating her lack of the facts. "I'm afraid I'm just guessing."

I stared over Barbara Grant's shoulder at the photograph of the forever-young face of Sam's grandson, Brian. "Then it is possible he left prints, isn't it? On Sam's eyelids?" For the first time, I felt hopeful.

Grant's eyes sought mine, weighing my suggestion.

I forged on. "You *can* lift fingerprints off human skin. I know you can. I've seen the evidence in my cases."

"Well, yes." She hesitated. "It has been done. Only rarely. Don't go getting your hopes up. First of all, we don't even know the killer touched his skin. The technicians will dust the entire house, but most of the prints they'll find will belong to the senator and the other prints you'd expect to find, his daughter's, the houseman's."

"Mine," I said. "All those cops roaming around here today."

"Yours. Theirs. Yes, we'll check his skin for prints. It's standard procedure in homicides. Orthotolidine under an alternate light source will cause fingerprints to jump out. If they exist."

"Good. That's what I wanted to hear," I said. "See what you can find. Because as neat as everything is here, I think the perp manipulated the scene. He's cleaned up everything, and my hunch is there'll be few fingerprints found."

"You may be right. The chair and the senator's clothing may yield some clues."

Fierce, angry voices rose from the downstairs entry hall. *Uh-oh,* I thought, *the marines have landed.* I leaned over the balustrade to witness the spectacle. Captain Karl Rakes said something I couldn't make out in clipped, chilly tones. Edgar Cross, DOJ's rough-and-tumble assistant attorney general of the Criminal Division, boomed a threat. "I'll have your badge for this, Rakes!"

Rakes maintained his cool front. The man was an enigma to me. He headed for the door, seemed to have second thoughts, turned on his heel to retrace his steps, and mumbled something to Ed. Ed turned crimson.

The damage done, Rakes trotted out. *Arrogant bastard,* I thought.

I made my way down to the first floor. Ed executed a little salute with two fingers to his sparse hairline. He looked as if he had just declared war. "Thanks for getting us over here. I'm gonna hang that guy's ass in a sling!"

For the first time that day, I smiled. If anyone could accomplish that feat, it was Edgar Cross.

BACK IN THE CAR, I called my administrative assistant from my mobile phone. Sybil Parker runs my office, and I didn't know what I'd do without her. She was responsible for my schedule and the office operations and had guided me through DOJ's bureaucratic labyrinth since early last spring when I assumed the AG's post.

Next year Sybil would reach retirement age, and I shuddered to think of the confusion I'd face when she left. Fresh from high school and her blue-collar rearing, she came to work for the Department of Justice as a clerk-typist and remained at DOJ for all of her working life. I just hoped I'd have her energy and moxy when I was sixty-four. Recently she'd been making noises about how bored she'd be when she retired, how she'd have time on her hands with nothing to do. Every chance I got, I made my pitch, trying to persuade her to stay on to see me through my term.

"The Judiciary Committee's called twice, General Kelly. Is something wrong?"

"I'll explain when I get to the office. In the meantime, please call the committee liaison and tell her it's impossible for me to meet with them this morning. Extend my apologies and explain it's unavoidable."

They'll all know why soon enough, I thought. "Clear my calendar for the rest of the day. I'm on my way in and I'll be there in about twenty minutes."

"Bill Cavanaugh called twice. He says it's urgent he speak to you at once." Her voice held a question.

William Cavanaugh is the director of the FBI, the largest and most powerful of the thirty-two agencies I oversaw. "Call Bill and tell him I'll be there in a matter of minutes. I'll call him first thing. Right now, I've got a more important call to make."

When we'd left Sam's house, I'd been struck by the absence of reporters. I had expected to see journalists and cameramen pushing against police barricades. Somehow, they'd not yet got wind of the murder. It wouldn't be long before they'd be camped outside Sam's house. My office would be under siege.

The ambulance had already left when I climbed into my car. Rakes was gone, too, leaving the salvaging of the investigation to the competent Edgar Cross. Yet, not even Ed was capable of restoring a compromised crime scene.

I closed my eyes and leaned my head against the headrest while taking deep breaths. My temples were pounding, and the small of my back was tied in knots.

I wanted to pitch a fit but couldn't afford the luxury of hysterics.

Instead, I asked, "How's the traffic, Carlos?"

"It's moving, AG, is all I can say for it."

We were on M Street in Georgetown, cruising toward Rock Creek where we'd pick up Pennsylvania Avenue.

I lifted the receiver of my secure mobile phone. It was equipped with an encryption device. The number I dialed was similarly encrypted.

"This is Ann Kelly. I have to speak to him at once."

After a brief pause, President Jefferson Monroe came on the line "Ann? What's up?"

"Something terrible has happened, Mr. President. I wanted to be the one to tell you. Prepare yourself for a shock. Sam Claiborne is dead."

"Jesus!" Silence. "You're sure about this?"

"Yes, sir, I saw his body with my own eyes. He was murdered. Someone entered his bedroom and shot him during the night."

Monroe's silence meant he was thinking. His was a deliberative style.

"Mr. President?"

"Hold on a second, will you, Ann?"

I heard the buzz of his voice as he spoke to someone in the room. No doubt Chief of Staff Adam Kohn-Darby was nearby. Adam was never far from his side.

"Has anyone been apprehended?" he asked.

"No, sir."

"Where are you now?"

"In my car. Still in Georgetown. I just left the senator's house."

In the background I heard the hyper voices of television newscasters. The media had the story.

"The reporters have got it, Ann. I'm going to transfer

you to Jill so she can work you in. I want you in here ASAP." Abruptly, he disconnected.

The phone was picked up at another extension by the president's scheduling assistant. "He's got a tight schedule, General Kelly. So what else is new?"

I didn't share what was new with her. She'd hear the bad news soon enough.

"Can you be here at two fifteen? We'll squeeze you in after the Israeli ambassador."

"I'll be there."

As abruptly as the president, she hung up.

Again I tried to rest my head on the back of the seat. My agents were silent and watchful, knowing full well when to remain silent. I didn't have the luxury of reacting like an ordinary citizen. I had to maintain a tight rein on my emotions. My staff would take their cue from me. It was up to me to set the tone.

I reminded myself I was in charge; I was the one for whom "the buck stops here." I had no supervisor to advise me. I was the one expected to come up with the answers.

Over the next few days—maybe weeks—I'd be asked all manner of impertinent questions by the media about Sam Claiborne's death and my discovery of the body. I'd be required to give press conferences. I'd have to brief the Judiciary Committee, as well as DOJ staffers.

I reminded myself I was no ordinary citizen—not anymore. I could not afford to give in to grief. I couldn't let down my guard until I was alone. I had to build a wall around my most private feelings.

These restrictions came with the territory.

Since March of last year, I had lived and worked in a glass house; someone was always watching and judging. If we were to apprehend Sam's killer, only a cool head would prevail—my cool head.

I can do this, I told myself. *I'm up to it. I'll make you a promise, Sam,* I vowed. *I'm going to find him. I'm going to see that he's punished. Then, after that's done, I'll let myself cry.*

Until we caught this bastard, I was going to be as tough as Sam would be if he were after my killer.

FIVE

CARLOS MANEUVERED MY CAR onto a slip of concrete identified as RESERVED ONE. We were in DOJ's underground garage. Overhead, seven stories of limestone
soared. The neoclassical-revival structure was listed
on the National Register of Historic Places. Renamed
the Robert F. Kennedy Department of Justice Building in 2001, we were located at 950 Pennsylvania Avenue NW, on a trapezoidal lot just south of the J. Edgar
Hoover Building.

Similar to other structures of the Federal Triangle,
the Justice Building had been a WPA project authorized
by President Herbert Hoover in the early thirties. Once
upon a time, the area was the site of seedy taverns and
brothels, called, ironically, "Murder Bay."

The architects of the Justice Building had wished
to make a statement. Visitors were to be impressed
by its majesty, its orderliness—and perhaps just a little bit cowed. It was to be a material representation
of the stability and harmony of the Constitution itself.
Twenty-foot-high aluminum doors dwarfed those who
passed through them. Four-story, massive Doric columns adorned the facade; they rose from the third floor
to the pediments along the roofline. On good days, I
could get a little sentimental about this place where I
officiated. On bad days like today, I had no time for
sentiment; this was just an office building where the
hard stuff got done.

My heels clicked over pavement as I stepped into a private elevator with Agents Colby and Moore at my side. Inserting my key card, I got the elevator moving. It rose slowly and smoothly and made no stops. The doors did not open on the lobby where huge New Deal murals depicting muscular laborers lend a wash of color to the vast, dusky marbled space. No matter how high the Dow Jones Industrial Average might climb on Wall Street, inside this place, it was always the Great Depression era.

As the doors slid open onto the fifth floor, the first thing I saw was the attorney general's seal. How humbled I had felt the first time I saw that beautiful blue-and-gold emblem affixed to the wall outside my office. The escutcheon portrayed a rising eagle with outstretched wings, its right talon clutching an olive branch, its left a sheaf of arrow. Beneath, printed in a semicircle was the Latin motto *Qui Pro Domina Justitia Sequitur,* which translated as "who prosecutes on behalf of justice."

My assistant, Sybil, was on her feet at once, trotting along beside me as I rushed into my private office. My detail branched off, heading for the office where they hung out until Sybil notified them I was once again on the move.

Dropping my briefcase, I fired off a salute to Robert Kennedy's portrait. It was a habit of mine, and this morning's ritual was automatic. Kennedy's likeness hung above my fireplace mantel. The youngest attorney general was casually dressed in a navy blazer, his hands thrust deep into khaki trouser pockets as he strolled the Hyannis Port beach. A stiff wind ruffled his blond hair.

On my first day here, a porter brought the portrait to me and merely asked where I wanted it hung. He'd rescued it from the dark oblivion of a basement storage room where it had been banished by my predecessor. The porter had no doubt I'd want it restored to a place of prominence. He couldn't have been more correct.

I accepted the mug of coffee Sybil offered and handed her my cell phone. "There are photos on this phone. Plug them into the computer and set up a secure file for them. They are shocking, so be forewarned."

Sybil gave me a severe look but took the phone, thrust it into her skirt pocket, and did not ask a question.

She lowered herself into the chair opposite mine, her normally stalwart expression intensified as she prepared herself for what I had to say.

"Bad news travels fast, General Kelly."

Thus, I filled her in on my firsthand knowledge of Samuel Claiborne's murder. We reviewed what we'd be up against for the next few days—the calls from the media, the president, and the country demanding answers, staff briefings—and how she should handle the phone calls and my schedule.

She regarded me over readers. "This is a real tragedy, Ann."

"Yes, it is," I agreed solemnly.

She rose quickly from her chair. Sybil is a heavy woman but light on her feet. Like Lauren Colby, she favors sensible flat shoes, which she wears with mid-calf wool skirts and cardigan sweaters. Her salt-and-pepper hair is clipped short. Her only adornments were a faux-pearl chain attached to her eyeglasses and a plain gold wedding band.

She handed me a computer-printed summary of my phone messages and assured me all my appointments had been canceled or reassigned to my deputy. "I'll get Cavanaugh for you." She left me to contemplate the tall stack of papers on my desk. I scooped them up and set them on the chair Sybil had just vacated. *Later,* I promised.

Bill Cavanaugh was an acquaintance of more years than I wished to count. We'd first met in New York University's law student's dining hall, a pleasant room with a vivid checkerboard floor in a Georgian-style building that overlooked historic Washington Square.

By the mid-eighties, female law students were no longer a rarity at the prestigious law school. Even so, we were still a minority, so those of us who were fortunate enough to gain admission were the focus of a lot of male attention. The male law students I studied with were, for the most part, a randy bunch.

With all due modesty, I have to admit I was quite pretty in those days with my bright auburn hair, my girlish fresh skin, my big blue eyes. Today my hair is dusty with gray. My eyes are still deep blue but I spot a new worry line each time I look in the mirror. My figure is starting to sag in important places. Only my skin has held up.

My husband, Jack, tells me I am beautiful. He loves me and is not objective. Besides, he hasn't seen me since Christmas. He hasn't seen how the pressures of this job have carved new crevices in my face.

In our law-school days, Bill Cavanaugh was much too dedicated to his studies to concern himself with coeds. The first thing that struck me about him was his intensity. Even his "Black Irish" looks—coal-black hair, white skin, piercing blue eyes—were intense. Flirtatious repartee had no place in Bill's style.

The subject that consumed his every waking minute was the newly passed Racketeer Influenced and Corrupt Organizations Act and its impact on breaking up

Mafia alliances. He'd argued its ramifications to anyone who'd listen, grasping its full potential as an aid to prosecution long before any of the rest of us caught on. Sharing park benches and sandwiches in Washington Square Park under ancient poplar trees, we debated how law enforcement could use the racketeering act to cut a swath through *omertà,* the Mafia's code of silence.

Bill was an older student and very ambitious. He'd already obtained his *Juris Doctor* from Fordham University and was pursuing the LL.M., a master's in criminal law, when we met. After NYU, he joined the Federal Bureau of Investigation as an agent, got assigned to the Organized Crimes Unit, and found his niche drafting persuasive memos on the usefulness of RICO.

Our paths crossed again in the nineties. Bill was then head of the Organized Crime Unit. I had been promoted to executive assistant district attorney for New York City. Our careers seemed to parallel in the early years of the millennium as well. I'd been appointed U.S. attorney. Bill became a federal judge.

Now we were reunited in the nation's capital. After years of directors who were little more than White House political flunkies, the Bureau, under William E. Cavanaugh, had finally assumed the high moral tone to which the taxpayers were entitled.

"Good morning, Ann," he greeted me over the phone.

"How's your family, Bill?" I asked.

"Everyone is well, thank you." His formal good manners were not affected. He had never shed his parochial-school and altar-boy demeanor.

"I'll get right to the point. We've got a real problem on our hands. The investigation of Senator Claiborne's murder was compromised the moment that idiot Rakes failed to notify us. I know you were close friends with the senator, so let me extended my condolences. His passing is a great loss for all of us. He was truly a great man."

"Yes, he was. I don't know what we'll do without him."

Quickly, before I broke down, I changed the subject. "I had Brad Moore phone Ed Cross from Sam's house. The M.E. told me she had called Cross, too."

"Cross filled me in. The medical examiner works as a consultant for us, so no problem there. We're okay as far as the autopsy is concerned. She had the good sense to have the chair delivered here instead of letting the locals get their hands on it."

"I called Metro's police commissioner from my car," I said. "It was a frustrating conversation. He was predictably uncooperative. I did get him to agree to look into the matter. However, I'm not counting on much from him. He's a political appointee. He'll do whatever it takes to cover his backside."

Bill was a stickler for the letter of the law. "The district committees in the House and Senate oversee local affairs. The only powers the mayor and the commissioner enjoy are those granted to them by Congress. It's called Home Rule Charter, for God's sake, and they are all aware of how things work. Or they should be aware. You'd think those idiots would get it by now."

I let Bill vent.

"Forgive me, Ann, I'm preaching to the choir. Rakes has no excuse. He knows the homicide of a U.S. senator has got to be investigated by my agency. What on earth was the man thinking? Was he deliberately trying to sabotage this investigation? If so, why? Or is he just plain stupid as well as arrogant?"

"I don't know what makes him tick, Bill. He had the

nerve to try to throw his weight around with me. He's overconfident for starters. Has a self-inflated ego. Add to that cold and unresponsive."

I went on. "You say the investigation was compromised. I'm aware of that. I saw that firsthand. Are you referring to a specific problem I'm not aware of?"

"Afraid so. The murder weapon hasn't been turned over. Cross is screaming for it, but some detectives took it back to Metro PD."

"Rakes took it. I saw him bag it with my own eyes. Go around him."

"We're doing just that. We're getting an injunction. How's all this going to look? Claiborne is...was loved by millions. He was a damn good man, a national treasure.

"Now, what's going to come across to the folks back home is it's Beltway politics as usual. The feds and the locals bickering over jurisdiction instead of catching the killer."

"I don't want any public bickering," I told Bill. "That means putting a lid on Cross. He has a bad case of verbal hip-shooting."

"I've already cautioned him."

"Well, make sure he's discreet. If he can't be, assign someone else. I'm meeting with the president at two fifteen. Have Cross call me right away. I've got to have something positive to give Jeff."

"Tell him the truth. Tell him we've got a mess on our hands. Level with him. You don't have to coddle him. I've worked with him a lot longer than you have. He's as tough as steel and as sharp as a razor."

SIX

"Daddy was the only family I had left," Sarah Preston sobbed.

"I know how you must feel."

"When my mother died, I felt like such an orphan. Now I really am one. No matter how old we are, we still need our parents. Someone we can always go home to, where we'll feel welcome."

Her comment touched a nerve. "I felt like an orphan when my mother died, too. I was fourteen. Old enough she'd started to become a friend. One minute she was there. The next she was gone. Killed by a drunk driver who was going the wrong way on Interstate Forty."

Sarah reached for my hand. "Here I am feeling sorry for myself. At least I had my mom when I was growing up. I had my dad for forty-one years."

Suddenly I was seeing Sam's bedroom, seeing the book on his bedside table, his bifocals. "Was it Sam's habit to read the Bible before he fell asleep?"

Sarah stopped walking. We were in a lower-level corridor in the Hoover Building. Colby and Moore had stayed behind. I didn't need their protection in this fortress. "Not that I can remember. He prefers his military histories. The Civil War, World War II. His favorite is Herodotus' *Histories,* especially the battle of Thermopylae. He reads and rereads it. The book is falling apart."

Giving her head a shake, she eyed me speculatively.

"You must have a reason for asking about his reading habits. What is it? What did you see?"

I leveled with her. "There was a Bible on his bedside table, open, his bifocals marking the place. I assumed he'd been reading it before he fell asleep."

She shook her head. "I don't know. I suppose he could have."

I didn't like what I was thinking. I was getting a glimpse into the killer's mind, a good look at evil. I remembered Sam's closed eyelids and Grant's comment the shooter might have closed them as an act of piety. I remembered the neatness of the murder scene, how Sam looked as if he'd been dressed up and set out for public viewing. The killer had manipulated the crime scene, arranged things as if for a stage set. Sam's uniform was a costume. Then it dawned on me. The killer himself placed that Bible on Sam's bedside table. The marked pages were marked by him. I had to get my hands on that Bible.

Therefore, my first impression had been correct. Sam wouldn't have submitted easily. There *had* been a struggle in those rooms. After killing Sam, the killer had arranged the upset furniture and lamps and returned every object to its proper place.

I also suspected he'd worn gloves. That, or he'd wiped off everything he'd touched. Still, it was virtually impossible to remember everything one touched, and fingerprints turned up in unexpected places. *Like eyelids?* I wondered. The scene had been dusted by the Metro Crime Scene Unit and then again by FBI agents. Prints were going to turn up somewhere; I'd stake my career on it. Then we'd have him. I had to get a message to Ed Cross to have him pick up that Bible at once. I couldn't leave Sarah.

She'd insisted on coming to the morgue. She was putting up a brave front. She wanted to be here because this was where her dad was. My conscience wouldn't permit me to let her come alone. She hadn't seen him dead. I had. I suspected she was in shock.

Irving had driven her to my office. She'd marched in, dry-eyed and stoic. When I put my arms around her, she'd dissolved into tears. Sybil and I had helped her to the sofa in my small sitting room. Sybil had brought tea and made soothing noises while I had ducked back into my office to take important calls.

The pager on my waistband vibrated and my hand flew to it. *Now what?* I wondered. Who was tracking me down already when I'd only been gone from my office for five minutes? I lifted the pager and read the number on the face. There were house phones on the walls, and I found the nearest and tapped in an extension.

It was the security officer in the lobby. "There's a Miss Molly Preston here, and she says she's come to take Dr. Sarah Preston home."

"Thank You, Lord, for answering prayers," I whispered.

"Molly's here, Sarah. She wants to take care of you. Why don't you go with her? You'll just have to wait around here for hours. Dr. Grant will call you the moment she can release him."

Sarah wavered, pathetically torn.

I pressed her. "There are arrangements for you to make, and Molly can help. Probably someone from the Pentagon is trying to reach you. They'll give him a military funeral at Arlington, you know. He will receive full honors." I smiled my encouragement.

"All right, if you think I should go." She seemed to withdraw into herself. All the fight had gone out of her.

We walked back to the lobby together. The moment she saw Molly Preston, she threw herself into her sister-in-law's arms. I watched them leave the building, clinging to each other.

THE FBI LABORATORY was established in 1932 as a single-room facility, outfitted with one microscope and scant equipment. Seventy-eight years later, it had grown into the multiple sections and units law enforcement had come to rely on: the Firearms and Toolmarks Unit, the Explosives Unit, the labs that performed analyses from serology to gamma-ray spectrometry. Until 1975, these facilities were housed in my building, the Department of Justice headquarters.

Stark beige walls and charcoal doors lined the corridors. Behind those doors, seventy-five hundred agents and support staff labored. I retraced my steps to the Forensic Pathology Section, asking the receptionist to inform Dr. Grant I was outside. Recognizing me, the clerk became flustered but reached for the telephone at once.

I paced the small area, too agitated to relax. The autopsy suite and its support laboratories were necessarily located here so the causes of death in cases under federal investigation could be determined. The complex cases—instances where corpses had been rendered unidentifiable by the ravages of fire, water, and time—were referred to the Forensic Science Research and Training Center in Quantico, Virginia. There, a team of forensic anthropologists employed unusual, and often macabre, methods to ascertain identities. *Are they close to identifying the victim of the Charleston church fire?* I wondered.

I remembered Dr. Grant was a leading authority on

the identification of skeletal remains. In fact, she had authored textbooks on the subject, which were currently in use at the training center.

She came through the door. "Welcome to my world." Her lively smile belied the morbid nature of the tasks she performed here.

"I was in the building, and I hoped you might have some news for me."

She removed her glasses and polished them with a corner of her white clinician's coat as she seemed to be deliberating. "We're just about to scan the chair. Come and watch. I think you'll find this interesting."

I hesitated. "I don't think I can face that chair again."

"How stupid of me. I should have explained." She repositioned her glasses. "The, uh…samples…have already been collected and delivered to other labs for analysis. It's the first thing we did."

She was handling me delicately, and I appreciated that.

"With the exception of the bullet hole, the chair looks like any ordinary chair." A pause. "That is, to the unaided eye. If you think you'll find this offensive, just say so. I'll understand."

I considered. I thought I could trust her not to subject me to an experience I couldn't handle. "You know, I've used videotapes of laser-light examinations in court. I think an actual demonstration would be fascinating. If we find a clue on the chair, I'll be glad I was there when we discovered it. I'm anxious to find any bit of evidence that will lead us to this monster."

"Come with me, then."

SEVEN

GRANT LED ME down a hallway and into a laboratory. "A bit of evidence is the operative word." She held the door for me as technicians looked up curiously from microscopes and laminar-flow hoods. Cold air penetrated the sleeves of my wool jacket. Colorful sweaters peeked from under technicians' lab coats. A radio played unobtrusively from a bookshelf—golden oldies. The liquids in numerous decanters, test tubes, and petri dishes gave off a medicinal odor reminiscent of the scent I'd detected earlier on Grant's person: formalin.

As we walked, Grant explained the procedure I was about to see. "The word LASER is an acronym. It stands for Light Amplification by Stimulated Emission of Radiation. In layman's terms, it is a high-powered, non-pulsating light that permits us to see latent prints and trace evidence otherwise invisible to the naked eye."

She pushed open a heavy door that led into an adjoining suite where figures in lab jackets were lifting a plastic tent from Sam's blue leather chair.

"The chair has been fumed," she explained. "We peel packets of Super Glue open and set them next to containers of warm water under a plastic tent. The fumes are released and coat the chair with a white sticky substance."

She had been correct about the chair seeming inoffensive. The only reminder of the murder was the black hole in the chair back.

Grant introduced me to scientists from other sections of the FBI Laboratory. I shook hands with special agents from the Latent Fingerprint Section, or LFPS, from the Firearms Unit, with a serologist, and with an assistant medical examiner. They seemed pleased to see me.

"It's an honor to have you here, General Kelly," a young Asian woman named Eileen said. "Usually the top brass are not interested in how we reach our conclusions."

A male tech named Drew operated a computer terminal. As he tapped the keyboard, the large monitor lit up and claimed our attention. Drew manipulated the keyboard, booting up a program.

Grant indicated a large piece of equipment on a stainless-steel wheel-based table. "The laser light apparatus. Ours is a sophisticated model called an Argon Ion Laser. Incorporates a video camera and will transmit images onto the computer monitor. The light enhances minuscule particles. The computer magnifies and projects those images onto the monitor and at the same time creates a permanent file."

The firearms expert said, "I've already extracted the bullet, General Kelly. We'll subject it to numerous tests in the Firearms Unit to determine the type of weapon that discharged it and the distance from which it was fired. As soon as we have the suspect weapon in our possession, we'll be able to confirm if it in fact fired the bullet."

If we ever find that gun, I thought. One of the techs handed me a pair of orange-tinted plastic goggles. I watched how the others had fit them snugly over their eyes. I adjusted them to my head securely so no stray radiant energy could hit my eyes from any angle.

"Would someone get the lights, please?" Grant requested.

Immediately, the room was pitched into darkness. The computer monitor cast an eerie blue light.

"Eileen will operate the laser's wand. Everyone ready? Okay, Eileen, let's do it."

There was an air of excitement and anticipation as Eileen hit switches on electronic equipment attached to the Argon. She held a wand in her hand that radiated a blue light, which bounced over the floor like a cobalt coin.

Inch by inch, she swept the wand over the chair. Its icy-blue beam enhanced what looked like a layer of cobwebs.

I watched intently. "This is impressive."

Grant told me, "The Argon reveals evidence we'd never find without it. What you're seeing are hairs and fibers."

Whose hairs? Fibers from what?

Grant continued, "Eileen, let's have a better look." To me she said softly, "You don't have to worry about seeing blood splatter. Blood doesn't fluoresce, and that's what we're doing here, enhancing particles that fluoresce."

Eileen flipped switches and immediately the section of the leather being illuminated glowed a brilliant purple. Strands of hair and lint sparkled like fine neon-lit threads.

"What's your power level?" Grant asked.

"Five-thirty nanometers," Eileen replied.

"Okay. Let's get them," Grant said.

In the flowing air that vented the laser equipment, the tiny particles waved like underwater hydras. Eileen was assisted by two technicians, the blunt tips of their forceps moving in and out of the spotlight's range as they extracted the glowing strands, one by one. It was too dark to see what became of the trace, but I assumed the technicians deposited the particles into evidence envelopes. The forceps moved rhythmically in and out of the light's beam.

Slowly, Eileen swept the circle of light downward as the moving tweezers denuded patch after patch. They worked with team-like precision, the light inching downward as the particles rhythmically disappeared into evidence bags.

"Is that lint?" I referred to the coarse, curled fibers that were being plucked.

"By their wave and tensile strength, I'd say they are wool. I suspect they will match the wool from Senator Claiborne's uniform."

A particularly brilliant bit of thread was being extracted.

Grant was at my side. "That looks like cotton lint, maybe from a dust cloth. It glows so brightly because it absorbs the light. It doesn't have the tensile strength of wool fiber. See how easily it shreds in the pincers."

"Every particle will be removed from this chair?" I asked.

"Every particle from every inch," a voice out of the darkness assured me.

The light progressed to the chair's wings.

"There you have hair. Human hair," another disembodied voice said. "By its curl and wiry quality, I'd say it is African-American hair."

Sam's hair, I thought.

"Stop! What's that?" I pointed to a dark oval smudge.

"You're very good, General," Eileen commented.

On the computer monitor, a white arrow cursor scrolled down the vividly colored screen.

My eyes were fixed on that blurred smudge. Was it what I hoped it would be? In the darkness I heard only the soft sounds of breathing and the humming of equipment. A rush of cool air from an overhead vent brushed the back of my neck uncomfortably, causing my hair to stand on end.

"It's not very clear," Grant said. "Let's spray."

Eileen produced a spray bottle containing a red liquid and squirted a shot onto the leather. We waited as the pungent-smelling chemical dried.

The fingerprint expert explained, "Rhodamine Six G enhances the presence of inherent latent print fluorescence. Most of the prints will be easily identifiable as belonging to the senator or members of his household. We might get lucky and find one the perp left behind."

Grant said to Eileen, "Let's try another wavelength."

Eileen snapped a switch and instantly the chair was bathed in a fiery orange glow. The smudge glistened an iridescent blood red.

"That's better." Grant explained for my benefit, "The smudge is being electromagnetically charged because it's absorbing radiation from the laser. That's what gives it that iridescent quality."

"This is a nice clear image," the fingerprint expert said. "I'll take pictures, one-to-one, for comparison. The computer will provide another permanent record."

At the computer, Drew's hand guided the mouse, and an image corresponding to what we were seeing under the light was magnified and projected onto the screen. Next to me, I felt Grant stiffen with intense concentration. The screen commanded our full attention as the print outline was duplicated. We were looking at a crescent-shaped pattern about two and a half millimeters in diameter, vividly red on the blue screen. The crescent contained a series of tented arches under which a broad line curved vertically.

"It's a fingerprint, isn't it?" I guessed. "What's wrong with it?"

In the gloomy light, I saw the white shoulders of the fingerprint expert approach the monitor. He stood to one side of the screen and traced the crescent shape on the glass with the tip of a pen.

"Yes," he said, "it's a partial. From its size and shape, I'd say we are looking at the ridge of a man's thumbprint." The pen tip tapped the screen over the broad wavy line. "We've got a problem."

"I can see that, but what is it?" I asked anxiously. Were we to find the killer's print only to have it unusable?

"It's some type of scarring, General Kelly. It's unusual and I'm not able to tell you any more than that at this time."

"Scarring? You mean someone intentionally mutilated his fingertips in order to disguise his prints?"

"That, or some sort of accident."

"This type of print is not associated with anyone in Senator Claiborne's household?" I asked.

"No one we know of at this point. It's still early in the investigation."

"I want a full report on your findings. Keep me informed at every step of your progress," I said urgently. "I'm due to brief the president at two fifteen. If you have anything to report by then, call Sybil Parker in my office. She'll locate me wherever I am. Keep up the good work, all of you. I'm immensely impressed."

I thanked Barbara Grant for allowing me to observe. "I've stayed long enough. I really must get back to my office."

"I'll walk you out." She steered me toward the exit.

Behind us, activity in the room returned to normal. Voices murmured as specialists resumed their visual dissection of Sam's blue leather wing chair.

We slipped off our goggles. After the dim interior, the overhead lights were blinding.

"What about DNA?" I was desperately grabbing at straws. "Can't we find some evidence that will give us a DNA sample?"

"If the perp left behind just one strand of hair with a follicle. That's all it takes. We've made tremendous strides in DNA identification."

Her pleasure irritated me. "What good does that do us now? What is the status of the autopsy, anyway? I really don't understand why you're out here making a fuss over a chair when you should be attending to the senator's body."

Grant reared back in a defensive posture. Unfairly, I was making her the target of my repressed frustrations. In some foolish way, I thought if she was with Sam at all times, she could protect him—from what, I wasn't sure. From stares? From callous remarks spoken by mortuary orderlies?

The bright lights and the discovery of a problematic fingerprint fueled a headache, and so, too, did the realization Grant had been having a good time in there. They all had been having a good time, playing with their toys, while my friend laid cold and dead on a stainless-steel table somewhere in Grant's surreal world.

Her reply was clipped and precise. "Presently, the body is exactly where protocol requires it to be, in the radiology suite. The X-ray technicians do not need me to tell them how to film bones. The first thing I did upon his arrival was record body temperature. I can fix time of death at between midnight and one A.M."

"I want you to call me as soon as you've completed the autopsy."

"If you remember, General Kelly, I promised you prelims by this afternoon. It has always been my intention to call you immediately." Her tone was guarded but angry.

Was it any wonder I had few friends?

EIGHT

CLOUDS WREATHED THE Washington Monument. A light drizzle washed Pennsylvania Avenue and dripped from silky blossoms and bud-swollen limbs. Typically in April, the Capital is overrun with garden clubs. They form long lines for tours of the White House gardens. Today the streets were mostly deserted, with tourists preferring shelter in the dry galleries of the Smithsonian Institute.

Carlos exited onto E Street and looped around the White House to the northwest gate. Psychopaths had fired rounds of ammunition over the fence one time too many, resulting in the closure of Pennsylvania Avenue to vehicular traffic between the White House and Lafayette Park.

We drove through a security checkpoint, and Carlos deposited me at the north portico. I left him and my agents in the car and nodded to the marine who held the door for me. No fewer than five officers of the Uniformed Division of the Secret Service greeted me by name as I strolled the short distance to the Oval Office.

Despite the armed-camp atmosphere, the thrill of sailing undeterred through the West Wing of the White House still gave me a buzz. Although I knew that once inside the Oval Office I'd be subjected to intense grilling from the chief, I was proud to be an insider here. It was a dream come true for me.

The president worked in shirtsleeves at his desk,

white cuffs rolled back, expression intent, briskly slashing through a document with bold red strokes. *His speech?* I wondered.

"Have a seat, Ann," he invited. "I'll just be a minute."

I slipped into the chair in front of his desk and took the opportunity to admire the antiques in the room. I am an inveterate collector of antique furniture and paintings, and those on display in the White House are the finest I'd seen outside of a museum. Our New York apartment was furnished with the treasures I'd lugged home from Sotheby's auctions.

Named "The Resolute," the President's desk was constructed from timbers of the HMS *Resolute*. Wrecked by a storm off the American coast, the English ship was rescued by our navy and towed back home to England. In 1880, as it was being dismantled, Queen Victoria directed that a desk be made from its timber and presented to President Rutherford B. Hayes with the gratitude of the English people. The desk remained an obscure antique until the White House photographer captured little John Kennedy crawling through its hidden panel while his bemused father feigned attention to affairs of state.

The president assembled the pages, scribbled a few notes, then buzzed for a secretary, who appeared instantly and silently to take the pages from his hand. Leaving us, she pulled the door quietly shut.

Jefferson Monroe studied my face as if he might read my secrets. This was a habit of his and disconcerting to those of us who reported directly to him. "I've got a press conference in an hour, and I still don't know what I'm going to say. I'd like you to stay for it."

"Yes, Mr. President. I'll give you all the help I can."

Monroe seemed restless, leaned back in his chair, lifted his arms, and smoothed the hair on the back of his head. "I know you will, Ann." The armpits of his starched white shirt were damp. "I hope I never have a day like this again."

"It's a tragic day, Mr. President." My hands lay quietly folded in my lap, body language I'd learned in Sunday School classes at my father's church.

Outwardly I was composed. Inwardly I was seething. Except for a shoulder bag, I had brought nothing—not a briefcase nor a file—to this meeting. The few facts I knew about Sam's murder were committed to memory.

The president continued to complain. "They're not satisfied with Jane's news releases." He referred to Jane Middleton, his press secretary. I had heard she'd been badgered by bureau chiefs into scheduling a televised presidential news conference.

We all knew it was necessary. Until the commander in chief stood before the cameras and addressed the nation with the words, "Yes, a United States senator has been murdered in his own home," there would be shocked disbelief.

"It's something I've got to do." He shrugged. "Tell me everything you've done and everything you know. What you saw this morning and what has happened since. I haven't had time to focus on this tragedy. I've been squirreled up here with the Israeli ambassador since lunch."

He shook his head and muttered to himself, "Carter thought he had this Mid East thing licked some twenty-odd years ago, and here I am putting out the same brush fires."

I said, "I was briefed by the medical examiner and Assistant Attorney General Edgar Cross only moments ago."

Ed and I had finally made contact. I instructed him

to retrieve the Bible from Sam's bedside table, to turn it over to the Fingerprint Division after noting the passage that was marked by Sam's bifocals. That scripture, I suspected, would be relevant.

"Glad Cross is on the job. He's prickly, but he gets things done."

"Yes, sir. According to the medical examiner, death was instantaneous as the result of a massive brain hemorrhage caused by a thirty-eight-caliber solid-point bullet. The bullet passed through the skull, doing minor damage to bone." My tone could have been computer generated for all the emotion in it. I had reminded myself to hang tough before I'd entered the room.

"So I can tell them he died instantly, he did not suffer? Those vultures will show no mercy; they'll ask all the grisly questions, especially that jackass from Fox, the bloodsucker. So if I can say he didn't suffer, that'll help."

"He did not suffer, Mr. President."

The President nodded. "Continue."

I lifted my chin. "Time of death is estimated at approximately midnight to one A.M. this morning. That was maybe a couple of hours after I left his house. You knew I was there?"

"Yes. Someone told me—don't remember who. A birthday party?"

"Yes, sir. I think I should tell you I was probably the last person to see him alive, in case someone from the press makes an issue of it."

"Why would they do that? Who knows about this?"

"Captain Rakes of Metro P.D. Bill Cavanaugh. Ed Cross."

"The media won't hear it from them. Maybe this

is something we ought to keep to ourselves for the time being."

"Very good, sir. Sam celebrated his sixtieth birthday at a party last night. About a dozen close friends."

"I heard something about that," Monroe said.

"I was the last to leave. The others began leaving at about nine thirty. Sam sent his houseman to his quarters right after dinner, and there was no one else in the house. Sam and I had brandy in the library and chatted for a while. I left at around eleven."

"And the houseman? What's his name? Are his quarters part of the house?"

"His name is Jesse Taylor. He lives in an apartment over a detached garage at the rear of the property. In fact, I happened to look up the driveway as I was walking to my car and saw his lights were out."

There had been thick cloud cover last night. The garage and the apartment over it had been almost invisible in the shadows and the pools of inky darkness that shrouded the backyard. In about an hour, the storm had struck violently.

I experienced a slight shiver as I considered the eeriness of what I was about to say. "The shooter may have been hiding in the backyard, watching me as I left the house. He'd have seen the downstairs lights go off, then the upstairs bedroom lights come on. Then darkness when Sam went to sleep. There's a big oak tree in the backyard. We found evidence—scraped bark— someone climbed that tree recently, and a window was partially open."

"He didn't have a burglar alarm?" Monroe's tone conveyed his disapproval.

"There's an alarm system in the house. According to Taylor, Sam was a fresh-air fiend—a habit he'd picked up in the military—and would not have an alarm on his bedroom window. He sleeps with it open."

"On a night like last night?" the president asked incredulously.

I shrugged. "I suppose he thought it was unnecessary to set an alarm on a second-floor window."

"That indicates someone had been watching the house over a period of time to learn Claiborne's routine."

"That seems likely, sir," I agreed. "If he'd been scoping the house, he'd have known which room was Sam's bedroom from the light patterns. He'd have seen the window was raised at night."

I shifted in my chair. "Cross has got a team out there now, examining the grounds and the tree for physical evidence. With this rain, the evidence, if there was any, would have washed away."

I paused for a second, watching the president tent his fingertips and lean back in his chair.

"Fingerprints from inside the house are being matched with those you'd expect to find."

"Taylor didn't hear gunshots?" Monroe asked.

"No, sir."

"Does this Taylor check out?"

"Yes, sir. He had security clearance before he went to work for the senator. Besides, he's a relative. I think a great-nephew. He loves Sam." I corrected myself. "Loved," I mumbled.

"He didn't hear anything even though he's right there on the property?"

"He says he's a sound sleeper. His wife and children were visiting her mother."

"What about a silencer? Maybe the shooter used a silencer?"

"Not with a .38 revolver. Doesn't work. There was only one shot fired, and with the storm, no doubt the single gunshot was mistaken for thunder. That is, if anyone in the neighborhood heard it."

Monroe nodded thoughtfully.

"Here's the scenario Cross and I have put together, Mr. President. Sam was asleep when the shooter entered his room. The shooter carried a weapon and used it to force Sam to get up and dress in his military uniform. Then…"

"What?" Monroe exploded. His fist banged the desk's surface. "You're telling me we've got some kind of nutcase on our hands, someone who gets off on dressing up a distinguished war hero in his uniform? Then shooting him?"

He bounded out of his chair and began to pace furiously, circling the office. I turned to follow him with my eyes. "Shall I go on?"

The president grunted. "Yes, tell me the worst of it. I've got to know."

"It has not been confirmed, but we believe Sam was killed with his own weapon, his army pistol, which is normally kept in his bedside-table drawer. He was shot at close range."

The president stopped, rubbing his temples with both hands. "This is making me sick."

"Yes, sir. Me, too," I allowed myself to comment.

"How did you happen to be the one to find him?" He was anticipating the press corps' question.

"I was scheduled to meet with the Senate Judiciary Committee this morning. I offered to pick Sam up and drive him downtown. Technically, it was Jesse Taylor who found the body."

The president nodded. "How could this happen?" I

didn't think he really expected an answer. "Sam was a trained military officer. He knew how to handle himself. Wouldn't he have put up a fight?" He shook his head in disbelief.

"You're forgetting he's older now, sir. Coming out of a deep sleep, he'd be groggy. He wouldn't be wearing his glasses; his vision would be foggy. There'd be no time for him to go for his weapon. Anyway, the intruder must have had his own gun trained on him."

"You said you think the murder weapon was Sam's. Can't ballistics make a positive ID?"

"The Bureau hasn't been able to take possession of the weapon yet, sir. Metro P.D. is dragging their feet about turning it over." I sighed. There was no way I could fully brief the president without telling him about the intransigent Captain Rakes.

"Dragging their feet? What's going on, Ann? What's Metro P.D. got to do with this?"

"We've run into a stone wall, Mr. President. Its name is Captain Karl Rakes."

NINE

THE PRESIDENT LOWERED his weight onto the corner of his desk and stared down into my face. I swallowed hard, dreading I had to be the one to give the president so much bad news and that I, his Number One law-enforcement officer, was involved. "I'm afraid the investigation has been compromised, sir."

His eyes flashed, but he seemed to check his temper quickly. "Okay. Okay. Let's assess the damage. Tell me exactly what happened."

"Metro P.D. arrived right after I got there. Jesse Taylor had called nine one one. A nine-one-one call goes to a dispatcher, who would have sent an ambulance, but also would automatically inform Metro P.D. Captain Karl Rakes was in charge. He failed to notify the Bureau as he is required to do."

"Those guys know better than that. What's wrong with that idiot?"

"I have no idea what makes Captain Rakes tick, but I called Commissioner Gates, who assured me Rakes has been suspended pending an investigation of his actions."

"Damned straight," he commented. "For all the good that will do. The damage is already done."

"You know how they are, Mr. President. They're all little empire builders. The smaller the empire, the more petty its emperor. Gates isn't going to do much; he's the mayor's appointee. There's no love lost between District government and Congress. In fact, they're gleeful when they can make one another look bad."

"That man's history." Monroe got up and looped around the office once more, stopping before a window to stare out into the barren Rose Garden. Rose bushes were bare stalks under bleak skies. On the South Lawn, *Marine One* waited in readiness.

The Oval Office was smaller than one expected. It was as cozy as a study in a grand, private residence, warm with soft cream walls and soft gold carpeting.

The hominess was deceptive. In reality, the president lived and labored in a secure bunker. Windows wore four-inch-thick bulletproof shields that distorted the view of the Washington Monument. Seismic sensors buried under flower gardens and lush green lawns detected the lightest of footsteps. From the rooftops, Redeye antiaircraft missiles aimed into White House airspace.

Over all were the watchful eyes of Big Brother, law-enforcement's newest, most sophisticated spy satellite— so solidly omnipresent it was as if God Himself was looking down and saying to man, "There is no place to hide."

Yet, by far, the most intensely secret and secure room in the White House lay directly under the American-eagle-embellished carpet. The Situation Room served as a presidential command post in times of national emergency. A signal board linked the commander in chief to Homeland Security, the Pentagon, the State Department, the CIA, and military and intelligence installations around the globe.

The president turned, and for one fleeting moment I saw his mask had slipped. "How could this happen?" His voice was robbed of its usual vitality.

"It's not good," I murmured.

His eyes implored me to give him encouraging news, to hand him a way out. We were alone, and he trusted me enough to let down his guard.

As much as I wanted to help, I had but little hope to offer. "We were able to get a partial print that might belong to the shooter off Sam's leather chair. The fingertip is badly scarred. We're comparing it to prints on file right now. The M.E. described the scar as hypertrophic, which suggests it's the result of an untreated burn. Chances are his other fingers may be burned and scarred as well."

"Good. Then we'll find him." Monroe's voice held resolve.

"It's going to be hard to trace. If his prints are on file with IAFIS, the chances are they date from an earlier period, before the mutilation."

Monroe raised an eyebrow. "Do you think the mutilation was deliberate?"

"Could be an accident."

"A fire?"

"Or a gun accident."

"What do you mean?"

"It happens. Say a shooter is unloading a semi-automatic and he's racking the slide but the cartridge is stuck. So he slips his hand down the slide to help it along. The cartridge breaks free, leaves the support of the chamber, bangs into the ejector, and sparks fly. Gunpowder ignites and the case explodes, resulting in cuts and burns to the shooter's hand and fingers. This would be consistent with the scar pattern on the latent we found on the chair. It's not an uncommon accident among gun enthusiasts."

He groaned. "I've had it up to here with the gun nuts.

They're showing up at town-hall meetings with pistols strapped to their hips and ankles. There's nothing we can do. All legal, if they're in one of those states that permits the carrying of unconcealed weapons.

"Jeez," he groaned again. "This is not what the founders had in mind. Those guys are not protecting anyone. They are inhibiting free speech through intimidation.

"OK, any other bad news? Tell me the worst. I don't want to be hit with any surprises from the press corps."

"Actually, it's not all bad, sir. Cross spent productive time this morning with a federal judge, obtaining an injunction against Metro P.D." I checked my watch. "He should be taking possession of the weapon and other evidence right about now."

"Good. Good." Monroe returned to his seat and sat bolt upright, shaking his head from side to side. "Jesus. I don't get it. Why would anyone want to shoot Sam Claiborne? Everybody loved him."

"Not everybody. In the last few years, he's made powerful enemies," I reminded him.

"You're referring to his stand on gun-control legislation. Do you think it's them, those NRA nuts and their paramilitary crackpots? Are they behind this?"

I wanted to say I didn't know, but it was better not to admit that to the president. One had better have the answers when briefing him. "We've got them under surveillance."

"God, those guys are better armed than our police forces."

"Our police forces fear them, sir. We've got up-to-the-minute data on them. I'll review all that. This is more than another case for me, Mr. President. This is personal."

"Okay. Right. I know you two were friends."

"Sam was a good friend of my father, sir."

"Yes. How is the Right Reverend?"

"Fine, Jeff. His installation takes place over the Easter holiday."

"This weekend?"

"Yes. In New York."

"Give him a hug for me."

"Will do, Jeff."

Silence followed and filled the Oval Office. "Let me try this out on you, Ann. You say the killer has burns on his hands. Here my administration is being dragged down by these frequent church arsons and you're telling me Senator Claiborne's killer has burn scars on his fingertips. Is it too much of a stretch to suspect there's a connection? Could this guy be our arsonist?"

"That has occurred to me, too, Mr. President. We have no evidence at this point to believe Sam's murder and the church arsons are related."

I wished it were as simple as that. Catch one bad guy, solve multiple crimes.

Monroe said, "We haven't ruled out there are *not* any useful prints, have we?"

"No, sir. We're working on that right now."

"Well, keep the pressure on. Push them. This is a top-priority case, and I want the Bureau on top of it. Nothing else is more important. If you've got to assign every goddamn agent you've got, then do it. Bring in private consultants if you need them."

"No one at DOJ will rest until we've apprehended Sam's killer. You have my word on that, sir."

"Okay, let's talk about the church arsons for a minute. After last night's fire, the subject is sure to come up. What progress are you making?"

"Do you want me to field those questions?" I volunteered.

"I might. I'll take it as far as I can. I want you on the podium with me in case I have to turn the mike over to you."

At the top of the attorney general's job description was Item Number One: Make the Chief Look Good.

I said, "I've got two hundred field agents on the job from the ATF and the Bureau. They're sifting ashes, seeking any evidence we've got a racist conspiracy on our hands. I'm in constant communication with the head of the task force. He's feeding me details on this latest fire in Charleston."

"We've got to put a stop to these arsons. The vice president met with a delegation from the National Council of Churches this morning. They're demanding more federal intervention. Their position is there's a conspiracy of ideas fed by racial hatred, and that's creating a climate of tolerance for the church arsons. An atmosphere of terrorism."

I said, "We are beginning to suspect some of these arsons are the product of a domestic terrorism plot."

Monroe studied me intently. "What do you base that suspicion on?"

"Many have similar M.O.s." I then realized an equal argument could be made that with hate radio, and the proliferation of how-to manuals on the Internet, the arsons could be the work of copycats. "Our agents are very good, Mr. President. Give us a little time and we'll find the link."

"Time is something I'm short of. I've got the Southern governors, the National Council of Churches, and prominent black leaders leaning on me. Who do you suspect?"

I hedged. "We've got any number of suspects under

surveillance. There's no shortage of hate groups in America."

How had my predecessors ever handled this job? Here I was just barely a year into this jungle and already I was facing a brand of domestic terrorism that was unleashed by the president's race. Right-wing militias that had virtually disappeared during the past eight years were now making a virulent resurgence ever since our first black president had taken office.

"Well, I've got no choice, Ann. I've got to tell the press about the body in the fire. It's better coming from me than someone leaking it to the *Post*. Demonstrates we're in control."

We are not *in control,* I realized.

"Have you been able to ID the corpse?" he asked.

"A team transported the remains by helicopter to the Forensic Medicine section at Quantico early this morning. So far, all we know is the corpse is male and middle-aged. They're looking at military dental records, prison dental records, and searching the universal databases. If he was carrying identification cards on him, they were burned in the fire, along with his clothing." And skin and tissue.

"They've x-rayed his bones and might be able to identify him through fractures and other anomalies of bone structure."

Monroe grunted.

"If the dental search yields nothing, the forensic experts have got a three-dimensional computer program that will re-create a face based on dimensions and peculiarities of the skull. Dental comparisons are still faster and a lot less complex. South Carolina agents are searching missing-persons records."

"Could he be the arsonist? Maybe got trapped in his own fire?"

"We haven't ruled out that possibility, sir." I paused but had no choice but to articulate the worst possible scenario. "As I said, we cannot rule out domestic terrorism."

The president exhibited no emotional response. He seemed subdued and resigned. "We've been thinking along those lines ourselves." I wondered what else White House advisors had counseled.

He got up from his chair and came around the desk to stand near me. His eyes bore into mine, and I felt the intensity of his gaze and the full force of his power.

"Ann, it's important to me these two cases get resolved quickly. We're finally coming out of this nasty recession. We've won some battles and we've lost some battles, but mostly we've won. My administration has accomplished too much to let these problems drag us down. I'm appealing to you to help me out here. Turn your other stuff over to your deputy. I want you out there in the field, personally involved in these investigations. Maintain a high profile. Get out from behind your desk. Call news conferences. Better yet, go on down there to Charleston and throw your weight around. Offer a reward. That'll bring 'em out of the woodwork."

I must have looked astonished for his tone softened. "Just do what I'm asking, Ann. Our polls show you're popular. You're new and still in the honeymoon period. Use it. People like the way you handle yourself. They trust you. Get out there and mingle. Go on local TV and offer rewards. Make it easy for an informant to approach you. Fix this thing for me, and I'll be eternally grateful."

I was momentarily speechless.

A light tap on the door spared me from answering. Press Secretary Jane Middleton and Chief of Staff Adam Kohn-Darby stepped inside.

"They're waiting for you, Mr. President."

The makeup lady entered and accompanied the president into his private study.

Jane Middleton looked me over. "The president wants you at his side on the podium. You'd better go fix your face."

I regarded her immaculate, professionally made-up, coiffed persona. I excused myself and went down the hall to a powder room.

"What just happened in there?" I asked the haggard woman who gazed piteously at me from the mirror. What had been put to me as a personal request was in fact a direct order from the commander in chief. Lead the investigations, he had instructed. Not from behind a desk. Get out in the field.

I knew where the president was coming from. I knew we could expect public outrage over Sam's murder.

No laggard himself, Monroe had recently toured burned churches in the South. "When these attacks are motivated by hate, they're an affront to our basic commitment to religious liberty and racial tolerance," he'd told the citizens of Greeleyville, South Carolina.

The vice president had said, "Those cowards could burn the building down, but they couldn't burn the faith out."

Returning to Washington, the president had encouraged Sam Claiborne to introduce legislation to increase prison terms for convicted church arsonists and to fund a National Church Arson Task Force, made up of specially trained agents from the Bureau and the Treasury Department's Bureau of Alcohol, Tobacco and Firearms. In a rare display of bipartisanship, Congress passed the Church Arson Prevention Act. DOJ got four-point-six million dollars in grant money to beef up security around targeted churches.

In the White House powder room, I combed my hair and applied blush to my pale cheeks as I weighed what the president was asking of me. *I'm a prosecutor. I'm not an investigator,* I told myself. Yet how could I refuse the president's direct order—for although couched in terms of a request, that is what it had been—that I snoop around at fire scenes and interrogate informers? A touch of lipstick brightened my face. I straightened my blouse, buttoned my jacket, and squared my shoulders.

We marched as a unit behind the president into the White House Press Briefing Room. I took my place at the president's side and listened, expressionless, as he extended condolences to Senator Claiborne's family. When he announced to the press and all of America that Attorney General Ann Kelly was going to conduct a hands-on investigation of Senator Claiborne's murder and the church arsons, I wanted to bolt off the podium.

TEN

THE SKY HAD GIVEN UP its futile attempt to resemble day, fading into eerie pinkness with clouds churning low over the rain-washed Capital. During the hours I'd spent inside the White House, the jet stream had changed course with exotic warm winds blowing across the Potomac from points south. The air smelled faintly brackish as it does when it blows off the Potomac.

I got into my car and we drove through the White House gates. The rain had stopped and sightseers jostled one another on the sidewalk outside the ornate wrought-iron fence. Then, catching sight of my car, they galloped toward us, a herd of wild horses whom I realized too late were not tourists but reporters. They surrounded my Cadillac with single-minded purpose. Camera lights drilled blindingly into the windows but could not penetrate the black shield.

"Don't stop!" I called to Carlos.

"Keep going! They'll move," Brad Moore shouted.

Unmindful of their own safety, reporters pressed against my car.

"Do you have any leads, General Kelly?" someone shouted.

"What are you going to do next?"

"General Kelly! Over here… Who died in the fire?"

As we pulled away, I heard the final question, which made my blood boil. "Is it true you were alone with Senator Claiborne last night? What was the nature of your relationship?"

BILL CAVANAUGH AND Ed Cross were waiting in my conference room. Sybil had arranged for sandwiches to be
sent up from the basement cafeteria as it was the dinner
hour. Bill and Ed were dining off paper plates when I
settled into my chair. The room smelled of dill pickles
and mustard.

Sybil hovered, wanting to help. Aware of the toll this
day had cost me, she did what she could, removing my
sandwich from its paper wrapper and popping open
a can of Diet Coke. I was glad she was in my corner.

"There's a list of messages a mile high on your desk,"
she said from the doorway. "Would you like me to stay,
General Kelly?"

I scarcely heard. *Who is responsible for the leak?* I
asked myself, hearing the smutty accusation over and
over: *"What was the nature of your relationship?"* This
was going to get uglier.

"General Kelly?"

"Yes?" I shook off my demons.

"There's no problem with my working late if you'd
like me to stay."

"No thanks, Sybil. You go on home now."

"Return your children's calls first," she instructed.
Cathy and Tom had seen me on television, obviously.

"And the bishop. He called, too."

At sixty-four, Sybil had no problem telling anyone
what to do. Age empowered some individuals, dimin-
ished others. On days like today, it was all I could do
not to put my head on her motherly shoulder and weep.

I had not eaten all day, yet I had no appetite. These
days I seemed to exist on coffee and snatches of food
on the run. Today was one of the worst days of my life
and food seemed irrelevant. Noting the agony of frustration on Bill's face, I suspected things were going to
get a lot rougher.

"There's been a big foul-up at Metro P.D." I knew I was in for another round of bad news.

"The Property Room can't find the weapon."

I spread my hands. "So, where is it?"

"That's what I'd like to know. Lost or stolen. My bet's stolen."

"I saw Rakes put the gun into an evidence bag with my own eyes. How could this happen?"

"We don't know how it happened," Ed interjected.

Edgar Cross, a big, beefy man, had already scarfed down two sandwiches. He nudged his paper plate to the center of the table, smeared a paper napkin across his lips, rolled it into a ball, and slam-dunked it into the plate. The corners of his mouth twitched in what passed for an Ed Cross smile.

Ed had thinning dark brown hair and small brown eyes. Deep folds ran from the sides of his nose to a series of chins. My overall impression of him was that somehow a large bear had stumbled out of the wilderness and into DOJ headquarters.

He said, "I got a special agent in charge, name of Jackson, heading up a team to work exclusively on the Claiborne case and report directly to me."

He leaned massive forearms on the table. "The revolver—a .38 Army Colt Special—and its serial number were vouchered in at Metro P.D.'s Property Room, but when my guys went to take possession, it was nowhere to be found. They're all scurrying around like mice over there, looking for the missing ordnance."

"What do you think is going on here?" I asked. "Could this be nothing more than a bureaucratic snafu, or do you think someone is deliberately removing evidence?"

"Jackson says the Property Room supervisor was

sincerely baffled. I've got confidence in Jackson's ability to read a man. The revolver had been signed in, and no one had signed it out. It should have been there. I'm thinking someone with access to the room lifted it."

"And the motive?" I asked.

"A cover-up would be my bet. Someone covering someone else's ass. That'd be my best guess."

Tampering with evidence? I rubbed my aching temples. "I've got another problem. Someone leaked to the press I was the last person to see the senator alive. The press is having a field day with that tidbit. They were waiting for me when I left the White House."

I looked directly at Ed. "Only three people knew that: Bill, Captain Rakes, and you."

"Well, don't look at me," he said. "You know I make a point of never talking to them scumbags."

This was true. Ed avoided the press. Bill was above suspicion.

"So it's Rakes. But why?"

"Professional jealousy," Bill replied.

The room was quiet as I swallowed chunks of a dry sandwich later I would probably not remember eating.

"The president has directed me to assume a hands-on role in the Claiborne murder investigation and the church arsons."

"We heard," Bill said. "I told you he was smart. Now he's on record as shifting the burden to Justice."

"Some news conference," Ed commented.

"'Maintain a high profile' were his exact words. I've got my marching orders, now you've got yours: find that revolver. What about Rakes; have you questioned him?"

"For hours! They should call that guy 'Stonewall' Rakes. He insists he turned the revolver over to Property but there's a cosmic black hole in the Property

Room with evidence falling through it all the time. The Property Room people say 'no way.' I don't know how those friggin' people get anything done over there."

Ed was doing a slow burn. It didn't help that stress and fatigue were causing me to take the offensive with him. Only Bill Cavanaugh appeared to remain unruffled.

"Okay," I said. "Let's move on. I suppose someone is talking to Senator Claiborne's friends who were at his home last night."

Ed replied, "Agents have set up appointments and are conducting interviews today and over the next few days. Just between us, I don't think they'll turn up anything. Can you picture the senate chaplain climbing through Claiborne's window to off him? Still, they're all suspects until they provide alibis, even the senators and the congresswoman. Personally, I don't see it."

"Halle Burden, the senator's aide, is completely devoted to him," I added. "Anything back yet from IAFIS on the partial print we lifted from the senator's chair?"

"It's only been a few hours," Ed replied defensively. "Could take as long as twenty-four. You know how many prints they got on file?"

"No, I don't know the exact number. I'm sure you're going to tell me."

"A bunch," he said with a smirk.

My frayed nerves couldn't take much more. The Bureau's assistant deputy director of CID was not one of my favorite people. He was frequently insensitive and tended to put his heavy feet down on the politically incorrect side of most issues. I'd had conversations about my disappointment in him with Bill in the past, but Bill always defended Ed, telling me Ed was outstanding at his job. Somewhere along his rise from agent to ADD, he'd acquired the manners and speech of a dolt. Originally, it had been intended to disarm suspects, but now he was stuck with it.

Bill had said, "When push comes to shove, Ed is your man." I was still waiting to be convinced this was indeed the case, and patiently trying to give him a chance. Today I had no patience to spare.

My frustration level mounting, I gazed wearily at Depression-era murals that soared from the walnut paneling to the vaulted ceiling. On other occasions, *Justice Granted* has had a calming effect on me, for the painting depicts a robed, benevolent judge dispensing justice to the downtrodden. The second mural was dispiriting, and I avoided it when I could. *Justice Denied* was portrayed by none other than the Grim Reaper.

There were instances when, no matter how committed I believed myself to be nor how hard I worked, justice was simply out of reach, and this mural was a constant reminder of my failure. *I won't fail now,* I promised myself. *I owe it to Sam to succeed.*

I focused on Ed. "Did you pick up the Bible from Sam's bedside table?"

"Done. That was pretty smart thinking." He sounded as if he was surprised I was capable of deductive reasoning. While Ed had to prove himself to me, I tended to forget I was on trial with him, too. He'd served through four attorneys general. "No prints, not even the senator's as you'd expect. The perp wiped it clean. Forensics is giving it a thorough going-over. The bifocals, too. Looking for anything with DNA."

"Did you note the passage it had been opened to as I directed?"

"Two passages were marked." Ed consulted a notebook. "Proverbs 25:5 and Micah 3:1–3."

"We need a Bible." I knew exactly where I could put my hands on one. "Be right back."

I hurried down empty fifth-floor passages. Inside shadowy offices, unattended computer monitors glowed. Most of my staff were gone for the night; only a few diehards remained at their stations. Telephones rang in the background, then stopped abruptly as voice mail intercepted.

I swept through my office and into the adjoining sitting room where earlier Sybil and I had comforted a distraught Sarah Preston. Had that been only this morning? Sorting through my keys, I unlocked the door to what visitors might suppose was a closet. A steep staircase ascended before me. I climbed to a private hideaway some architectural genius had had the foresight to install. Tucked into a small space directly over my office was a cozy room where I could retreat—to rest if I ever got the chance— or catch some shut-eye in times of national crisis. The suite was equipped with a private bathroom and a closet where articles of my clothing hung. There was a daybed, a bureau, and a window air conditioner. I found the Bible on a bookcase, shelved among bound reports. With it in hand, I retraced my steps to the conference room.

Locating the first passage at issue, I read aloud from Proverbs:

"Take away the wicked from before the king, and his throne shall be established in righteousness."

I thumbed through the tissue-thin pages to the Book of Micah and read aloud.

"I said, 'Hear, I pray you, O heads of Jacob, and ye princes of the house of Israel: Is it not for you to know judgment? Who hate the good, and love the evil; who pluck off their skin from off them, and their flesh from off their bones; who also eat the flesh of my people, and flay their skin from off them; and they break their bones, and chop them in pieces, as for the pot, and as flesh within the caldron.'"

My instinct that we stood on the perimeter of something very evil intensified.

Ed remarked, "Those guys didn't mince words, did they? So what does all this fire-and-brimstone stuff have to do with us?"

"These verses refer to corruption in government," Bill said.

"You mean he's telling us he's a revolutionary?" Ed asked.

"Exactly. Those passages were selected by someone with strong anti-government views." Bill leaned back and clasped his hands behind his head, his crisp white shirtsleeves gleaming under the ceiling lights. "So, he's putting us on notice and he's making no secret about his motive. Why make a martyr of Sam Claiborne? Or is Claiborne only the first?"

"Please. Don't even suggest that." The thought was too terrible to contemplate.

Bill asked Ed, "Exactly how were the passages marked?"

"Two purple silk ribbons marked the pages. The verses were underlined with ink, purple ink. The Bible is over at forensics, then the chemists will take a look at the ink. It's a stretch, but something may come of it."

I tried to shake off the feeling we were deliberately being permitted to glimpse the surface of something widespread and ugly. An anti-government killing spree led me again to thoughts of domestic terrorism, which further led me to contemplate the multiple church arsons.

"Okay, let's get it out on the table. We're all thinking the same thing."

"Domestic terrorism." Ed sneered.

"It's what we're all thinking. Who are we watching?"

Ed said, "Every state in the Union has got its white supremacist groups and its skinheads. Add to that, in the South there's a Klan cell organized at every wide place in the road. Our field offices keep a sharp eye on all those birds. We're watching a Viper Militia out in Arizona.

"In Texas we've got the Republic of Texas Militia under surveillance. Those are the nutcases that claim Texas' statehood was never ratified and the rest of the nation should just let them go their own way, secede, and form their own little wacko nation. Hell, the way the Mexican cartels have overrun Texas, plus all the bank robbers and crazy mass murderers they got down there, I say good riddance."

I sighed noisily. "That is not an appropriate observation for a person in your position, Director Cross. I certainly hope you never express those sentiments in public."

"These walls got ears? 'Course I don't." My criticism seemed to roll off his back. "Then there's the big Mothers, the Montana Freemen. We haven't heard the last of those white knights."

Bill observed, "We've got surveillance set up in every state. We've got undercover agents infiltrating their groups. Something's going to break."

"The president advised me to offer rewards for information leading to an arrest in the Charleston church arson. What's your opinion on that?"

"What do I think?" Ed snorted. "I think some of those turkeys would turn in their old grannies for a buck. The cell-phone towers will come crashing to the ground with all the punks calling to snitch on each other."

Bill said, "The boss calls the shots. I'd say try a quarter million for starters. You can always up the ante. Trouble is, those militia groups are all so paranoid, word doesn't leak to outsiders. If the arsons are the result of a conspiracy, then we're looking at a group that is organized across state lines. It'd take another messiah to organize all those self-appointed Masters of the Universe and keep them in line. If that happened, then watch out." He shook his head sadly. "Truth is, we don't know what, or who, we're up against."

"Who's bankrolling them?" I was new to the subject of domestic militias, with a lot to learn.

"Ho, ho." Ed wasn't laughing. "You'd be surprised how many upstanding citizens are closet racists."

"Did you ever hear David Duke speak?" Bill asked.

"Just sound bites," I replied.

"What makes the guy so scary is he believes all that rubbish he spouts, about European-Americans becoming a repressed minority. If he was stupid, it wouldn't be so frightening. He's not."

I changed the subject. "What about my trip to Charleston tomorrow? Is everything lined up?"

Bill replied, "You'll be met by a specialist from Arson Services, name of Douglas Wimbish. He's the best in the Bureau. He'll take you to see what's left of the Mt. Zion Baptist Church and explain anything about the fire you want to know. Are you attending the service?"

Bill referred to a special prayer service that was scheduled for the next day in Charleston. The service had been originally conceived as a demonstration to comfort and support the parishioners of burned-out Mt. Zion Baptist Church.

"Lamar Chisholm is going to speak. He's going to turn it into a political rally." Chisholm was a prominent black leader with political aspirations. "So, no, I think I'll stay away."

"You're smart," Ed said. "It'll be a media circus."

"The president suggested I appear on local Charleston TV, and that's not a bad idea. Public Affairs is setting it up."

Bill shot his spotless white cuff and checked his watch. "Ann, I've really got to get back to my office. I've got calls to return, and I'd like to get home at a decent hour, tuck my boys in for a change."

"I've got calls to return." I stood and shook hands with both men. "Thanks for everything you're doing. Keep me informed on all aspects of both cases—good or bad."

ELEVEN

MY DAUGHTER CATHY'S cell phone rolled over to voice mail. A recorded voice informed me the number was either switched off or out of the service area. I knew it was not out of my service area because I often reached her on her cell phone. She'd switched her cell phone off, and I couldn't help wondering why as she knew I'd be returning her call.

Next I tried her dorm number. The phone rang twelve times before a female student picked up. Then I held on and waited for almost ten minutes while the young woman went to look for my daughter.

Cathleen Kelly was following in my footsteps and Jack's. At eighteen I'd left my Southern home to attend Cornell University on a full scholarship. I studied pre-law. Cathy had been awarded a partial scholarship, and like Jack, journalism was her declared major. She was only seventeen but because of her outstanding academic performance had been granted early admission to the freshman class. We were very proud of her.

Finally her dorm mate spoke into the phone. "I'm sorry, Mrs. Kelly. I can't find her. She must have gone out to eat. I'll tell her you called."

"Please do. Thank you for looking for her."

There wasn't a moment I wasn't worrying about Tom and Cathy. Would one of my enemies seek revenge on my children?

Tom was studying in his room at NC State. He answered his cell phone on the first ring.

"You looked great, Mom. The guys were all excited to see you."

"And you? Were you excited?"

"Yeah, you know I was. How many guys get to see their mom up on the podium with the president?" He paused. "Mom, I'm sorry about Senator Claiborne. He was a good friend to our family."

"Yes. He was a great friend. An extraordinary man. Are things okay there?" I was prompted by the sadness in my son's voice.

"Sure. Fine," he replied too quickly. "We've got midterms tomorrow. Then I'll be home on Friday. Let's do something special this time, okay? Just you and me."

Something *was* wrong. "You haven't forgotten Grandpa is spending Easter with us, have you? His ordination is on Sunday at Easter services. You and I will squeeze in some private time on Saturday afternoon. Good luck on your tests. Good night, Tom. I love you."

"Me, too, Mom."

Tom had always been the steady one. At nineteen he was an engineering student at NC State in Raleigh where my father, about to be ordained as Bishop Timothy Maguire, would preside over the Episcopal Diocese of North Carolina. I grew up in Wilmington in my father's parish. I made a promise to myself I wouldn't let anything interfere with my Saturday date with my son.

Then I called my father and, after a long chat with that remarkable man, felt immensely reassured and optimistic. My father was an upbeat, positive person who always said just the right words of encouragement to me.

Despite our comforting conversation, sleep wouldn't

come that night. I lay in bed reviewing the day. A rewind button in my brain kept replaying the reel where I got my first look at Sam's murdered body.

I replayed the scene in the morgue, the brilliant laser light sweeping over Sam's chair. Relived my excitement when I thought we'd discovered the perp's fingerprint.

Then there was my regret at my inexcusably rude treatment of Dr. Barbara Grant. I went through life trying to make up to people for the way I ran roughshod over their feelings. Grant was someone I admired, which made me feel all the more repentant. Why was it each night when I should be sleeping I was reviewing my day and finding myself wanting?

I didn't realize I'd drifted off until the telephone woke me. When it rang after midnight, I answered with my pulse racing. I wished I could just turn the blamed thing off as normal folks did, but the few people who had access to my private number must be able to reach me. My deputy and assistant directors, the president, the FBI, my family, all must have access to me, even during the night.

I mumbled a hello. The voice that said my name sent thrills of pleasure along my spine.

"Jack? Oh, Jack, it's so good to hear your voice." I was coming fully awake and feeling connected for the first time in weeks. I sat up in bed and rearranged the pillows. "Where are you?"

"I'm at Bagram Airfield. Being patched through over the IFOR satellite. I'm sorry to disturb your sleep, sweetheart, but if I want to use their phone, I've got to do it at their convenience." As we had learned from experience, cell phones were often useless in Afghanistan.

I breathed a sigh of relief, knowing he was at least safe at Bagram. When he was out with the troops, imbedded with them as they patrolled…or worse… Well, I wouldn't think of that right now.

I glanced at the glowing red digits of my bedside clock in the darkness of my warm, comfortable room. Twelve thirty A.M. That meant it was about nine A.M. in Afghanistan.

"Hearing your voice is a better tonic than sleep any day." I smiled. "You should know that."

"Yeah, I do." I was sure we were both recalling reunions when staying awake, talking, and making love were more important than sleep.

"Thank God you're not in Kabul."

"That was last week," he reminded me gently.

"You were there?" I panicked.

"Yes. There is so much unrest over the elections."

"Those goddamn cretins were attacking foreign journalists in the streets!" My fears were mounting. "Were you hurt?"

"No. I was one of the lucky ones. Don't you ever forget I'm lucky, babe. My good luck started the day I met you. I got some exciting shots of the air strikes at Kunduz. Did you catch them in *Newsweek?*"

"No, not yet," I admitted guiltily. "You know I will. Sybil is one of your most ardent fans. She keeps a scrapbook for me, and I'll look at them soon, I promise. I'm just thankful you're safe. Oh, Jack, I miss you so much."

The tears I'd held in check all day rolled down my cheeks. I cried for Sam; I cried because I was lonely and missed my family; I cried for the dangerous world we lived in. I wanted my family all together again, like we used to be. I started to plead with him to come home, to snatch my happiness while it was there to grab. That wouldn't be fair, and I swallowed my plea. Jack's work was as important to him as mine was to me.

"You know I miss you, too, sweetheart. And the kids. How are they?"

"They're fine. They'll be home for spring break this weekend." Home for the Kelly family was the apartment we'd owned in New York City since the children were babies. "Daddy's already there attending the bishops' conference. He's staying at our apartment. He'll be formally installed at Easter Sunday mass."

I wiped away tears as we chatted comfortably in the dark, just as we used to before we were separated, when he was no further away than the next pillow.

"Ordinarily he'd be installed in his own diocese," I explained, "but the presiding bishop decided to hold a special ceremony at St. Bartholomew's this year. They're all in New York for this convention, so it makes sense. It's great for me and Cathy because we don't have to fly to Raleigh. Tom's eager for a few days in New York. I'm happy that, at last, Daddy's contributions to the Church are being recognized and rewarded."

"I'm glad for him, too, Ann. Congratulate him for me and give him my best. I can't talk too long, babe. There are others waiting for this phone. I saw you on television last night; that's what I called to tell you."

The president's news conference had been telecast at three P.M. which would have been about eleven thirty the night before in Afghanistan.

"Our reception of international news is usually spotty at best, but last night the signal was strong. There was my beautiful wife on the screen, standing next to the president. You looked like an angel. I dreamt about you…about us. Really, Ann, I'm so sorry about Sam's death. How are you holding up?"

Leave it to my wonderful husband to worry about me when he was struggling to stay alive in a war zone. Improvised explosive devices, at which the Taliban were so expert, exploded around his convoys daily, and I prayed none were inscribed with his name.

"I'm fine. I'm going to catch that bastard."

"I heard what the president said, that you're going to take an active role in the investigation. I want you to be careful, sweetheart. You're in as much danger there as I am over here."

"Ah, but you don't have sharpshooter Lauren Colby at your side." I hoped to divert his attention. If he was worrying about me, he might get careless about his own safety.

"Ann, I've got to go. They're tapping me on the shoulder. I love you, sweetheart."

"I love you, Jack."

OUR LOVE WAS REAL. Our marriage and our children were real. Then so were the arsonists and serial killers who walked among us. I had to protect my loved ones from them. I was not able to protect Sam. I would catch the guy who did this and make him pay.

Now I was fully awake and for once hungry. I slipped into my robe and slippers and quietly made my way down the stairs and into the kitchen of my silent, empty house. I recalled there was a casserole in the refrigerator, some spicy Cuban concoction old Mrs. Perez, Carlos' mother, had dropped off because she thought

I was too thin—"skeenny" as she said. I zapped it in the microwave and poured a glass of light white wine.

I lifted my glass to the empty chair opposite me. "Here's to us, Jack."

TWELVE

THE NEXT MORNING, Maundy Thursday, I flew to Charleston on a DOJ jet. Agents Lauren Colby and Brad Moore accompanied me. A PR team had been dispatched to Charleston at daybreak to finalize arrangements with talk-show host Dana Love and to establish ground rules for my television appearance.

Leaving Washington, I was relieved to flee half-staff flags that fluttered in gentle breezes and newspaper headlines that screamed AG LAST TO SEE CLAIBORNE ALIVE. It was sensationalist journalism at its worst. The columnist, if he'd bothered to check his sources, would have learned I hadn't been alone with Sam on Tuesday night for more than a few minutes. Those few precious minutes harbored nothing unseemly.

Ironically, we were favored with the first pretty day of spring, the kind of day that made you feel exhilarated just to be alive. I was keenly aware that one of America's favorite sons was not here to enjoy the fine weather. If he had been, if this nightmare had never happened, I'd be getting a call about mid-morning from him, inviting me to an *alfresco* lunch on the Capitol Building's terrace.

After weeks of rain, the air was crystal clear and promised fine weather up and down the Atlantic seaboard. We drove to Andrews Air Force Base where the Department of Justice based its fleet of jets, turbo-props, and helicopters.

On board, I employed my laptop computer to compose notes on what I'd say to my Charleston audience. My tone had to be just right. I had to reach the viewers, to connect with them. To convince them the burning of a poor black church was a threat to everyone's religious freedom.

A steward brought me breakfast on a tray. "The captain said to tell you he'll be flying along the coast. He wants to avoid the congested airspace over Raleigh International."

Warm sun toasted my left shoulder through the portside cabin window. I gave up on work, yielding to the pleasure of my bird's-eye view.

Chesapeake Bay stretched far to the east, glittering with a trillion dazzling sunbeams that flashed from the water like leaping golden fish. Pleasure crafts with colorful sails dotted the bay as the silhouettes of freighters and shrimp boats trolled the horizon.

The earth was bathed in a golden wash so intense it cleansed. On a day like today, how could any heart contemplate malice? How could a human mind be so perverted it spent such a day plotting the cold-blooded murder of a beloved war hero? Or planning the destruction of an impoverished community's house of worship?

Yet he walked among us like any other mortal, no doubt unremarkable looking, someone's brother, father, son. He drove the beltway, got frustrated with heavy traffic, ate when he was hungry, slept when he was tired. Cried when he hurt.

North Carolina's barrier islands linked along the coast like a bracelet of chunky pearls. Nags Head and Ocracoke. Cape Hatteras where the famed Hatteras

Light had been moved inland, far from the encroaching tide. I closed my laptop computer and prepared to deplane.

We touched down at Charleston Air Force Base shortly before nine A.M. A frontal high had pushed into the area during the night, bringing southerly winds with temperatures that were predicted to peak in the high eighties.

On the airfield, Vernon Young and Douglas Wimbish waited for me alongside a shiny black limousine. They had led a team of federal investigators to the scene of the Mt. Zion Baptist Church fire in the early hours of Wednesday morning. It had been Vernon who'd awakened me at four A.M. yesterday to tell me another church had been sacrificed to flames and bigotry and its burning embers had yielded the body of a human.

Dr. Vernon Young headed the National Church Arson Task Force for the Civil Rights Division. He held a doctorate in political science and had come to DOJ from the faculty of Howard University. A carryover from the former administration, he was an able and devoted administrator whom I had no reason to replace.

Maturity had mellowed him. Innately dignified and self-possessed, he gave the impression things came easily for him, yet I knew that was not the case. His speech was graceful and low-key. At weekly staff meetings, he was articulate and confident. Never guilty of shooting from the hip or the lip. His reports were concise and thoroughly grounded in research. I had learned to rely on him.

"Ann, I'm glad you came. It's good for morale to have you here. A real shot in the arm. Believe you me, these people need a morale boost." He clasped my outstretched hand in his own warm ones.

Perhaps the president is right, I couldn't help but think. Perhaps my presence and the prestige of my office would help to expedite this investigation.

"Meet Doug Wimbish," Vernon introduced.

Wimbish was the specialist for the FBI's Arson and Bombing Investigative Services whom Bill Cavanaugh held in high esteem. He stepped forward to shake hands. Both men wore short-sleeved shirts in deference to the warm weather and the relaxed Southern style. Wimbish's forearms were bronzed and muscular. His days were spent out of doors, picking over the rubble at fire scenes. Round spectacles and a receding widow's peak gave his face an owlish appearance.

Massed around waiting patrol cars were South Carolina state troopers in black-and-gray uniforms. They would escort our motorcade into the city. I settled into the back of a limo that smelled of new leather with Vernon and Wimbish for company. My security detail climbed into a Chevy Suburban with Bureau agents from the Charleston field office.

"The special agent in charge for South Carolina is driving in from Columbia," Young informed me.

Airmen on the field saluted as we caravanned slowly by. We rolled out past the guard post and through open gates. Electrified fencing kept saboteurs out and prevented abundant white-tailed deer at neighboring Francis Marion National Forest from wandering onto the runways. Palmettoes and longleaf pines grew densely right up to the airfield.

Our motorcade detoured around emerald-green golf courses intersected with marshy swamps. To the east lay Ft. Moultrie, Sullivan's Island, and the Isle of Palms resort. Even with the windows closed, I could smell the briny ocean nearby.

"What can you tell me about the fire?" I addressed Wimbish, who sat facing me. He reached over his shoulder to close the privacy shield that separated us from the driver.

"Same M.O. as most other fires we've investigated this year," he replied soberly.

"How is it similar?" I felt my suspicions were about to be confirmed by fact.

"The same accelerant, that is, kerosene, was used in this fire, as it was used to start the most recent arsons in Orangeburg and Lumberton, and earlier fires in Georgia."

I leaned forward. "How are you able to determine the type of accelerant used?"

Wimbish warmed to the subject of his expertise. "A gas chromatographer classifies the product with regard to distillation range, such as gasoline or kerosene."

"Can the gas chromatographer identify a specific brand of kerosene?" I thought we might be able to trace the brand to a local distributor.

"Unfortunately, no. That is beyond its capability. However, I can tell you kerosene is a highly volatile accelerant, more volatile than gasoline or paint solvents. It was spilled inside the sanctuary, which indicates someone either broke into the church or else had access to the church. If there was a break-in, evidence was destroyed by the fire. That's why arsonists are so hard to catch."

"Had access? You mean someone with a key, like a church officer or a janitor?"

"Yes, that's what I mean, General Kelly, but I don't believe this was an inside job."

"Oh? Why not?"

"Because typically when insurance fraud is committed, valuable property is first removed from the building. This congregation owned little of value. The building was underinsured. It doesn't appear to be a case of insurance fraud. Our questioning, thus far, has turned up no one with a revenge motive, nor do I think it will. These are simple people and most are elderly."

"What about a pyromaniac?" There was always that possibility, and that might account for the body in the fire.

"Accelerant was spilled outside along the foundation as well as inside. The fire was ignited from outside, so whoever dropped the match—we are assuming a match or a cigarette lighter provided the spark because we've found no trace of fused chemical masses or electronic devices—was not inside. The area around the body, and the body itself, had been thoroughly drenched with kerosene. There were deep burn trails in the area around the body and significant charring on the sections of the hardwood floor that were salvageable. We know the body was deliberately left inside the church."

"How do you know that?"

Vernon Young interjected, "Because the man was already dead when the fire was set around him. I spoke with a member of the forensic medical team at Quantico early this morning. Death was caused by a twenty-two-caliber bullet to the head."

"A twenty-two? The trademark of a gangland assassination?" A twenty-two doesn't have the velocity to penetrate the thickness of the skull twice. Once inside, it boomerangs, ricocheting off hard bone, causing incredible damage to the brain. Because of the mess it makes, it's the assassination method of choice among the mobs because it sends a loud, clear message to their enemies.

"Surely you don't think these church arsons are the work of organized crime?" I asked skeptically.

Outside my window, green trees flew past while a motorcycle trooper kept pace with our car.

"Not in the usual sense," Vernon replied. "Organized crime, that is, the Mafia, is not into church arsons. Churches are simply not the focus of their scope. Besides, most are Catholics and they have too much respect for churches.

"With the exception of the few fires we know for a fact were caused by accident or by a lone perpetrator, these multiple fires in unrelated areas do indicate arson by an organized group. At this point, we don't know which group, and no one has come forward to claim credit as happens in the cases of political protest—animal-rights groups destroying research labs, that sort of thing."

Wimbish leaned forward to make his point. "Ann, there are just too many similarities in the signature patterns for me to conclude these fires are unconnected and coincidental. This is the work of one coordinated group."

"Explain what you mean about signature patterns," I said.

Wimbish elaborated. "There's the dousing of the accelerant on the church floors. The accelerant is always kerosene. There's been no evidence of candle plants or Molotov cocktails as the ignition product. There's the telltale manner in which the accelerant is always spilled around the altar. It is as though someone is conducting seminars on how to set a church on fire."

"Have you checked the Internet to be sure someone isn't doing exactly that?" All manner of evil was broadcast over the Internet these days, most of it protected by the First Amendment.

"In fact we are," Vernon replied. "A team of computer specialists is surfing the Net looking for a recipe that would result in the type of arsons we're seeing."

I said, "I feel so badly for the congregations who've lost their churches. Obviously, they've denied themselves necessities over the years in order to build and maintain their churches. I know what my father's churches mean to their congregations. They are the center of the universe for the elderly and the widowed and the sick. As for the children, ah, often the church provides the nurturing they aren't getting at home. I hope God has a special punishment for these villains who are desecrating His houses."

"I know *we* do," Vernon replied simply.

OUR MOTORCADE HEADED southeast, down the middle of the peninsula between the Cooper and Ashley rivers. With pastel beauty, Old Charleston jutted into the harbor like an exotic Caribbean port. Historic residences along the Battery turned their pretty pink-and-green facades seaward. Along cobblestone streets, spiky palmetto fronds waved in soft winds, and white church spires pierced blue skies. Missing was one of the city's lesser steeples.

I was delivered to Concord Street and the television studio where *Good Morning Charleston* was telecast live Monday through Friday at ten A.M.

Studio lights shone with the heat of miniature suns, and camera lenses zoomed in for close-up shots of my face, which had been painted and powdered by the makeup artist. The intense lights tended to wash one out. My hair had been brushed and sprayed in place, and someone had added a pair of gold earrings.

Dana Love introduced me to her studio audience. Applause greeted me as I stepped onto the set. Love told them how honored she was to have me, that she had interviewed governors and senators but never the attorney general of the United States. Dana Love was in her late twenties, groomed to anchorwoman perfection with her tailored suit, short haircut, and makeup as vivid as my own. I was to learn she was brazenly ambitious.

Not bothering to refer to my notes, I spoke to the people of Charleston from my heart. "It's my job to stop these church arsons, to apprehend those responsible. Also I want you to know that as a bishop's daughter, the practice of burning houses of worship is particularly heinous to me. If we permit the arsonists to get away with burning our black churches and our synagogues, what's to stop them from setting fire to all the churches in America? Each and every church is precious.

"I'd like to talk to anyone who has any information about the fires. I'll guarantee you confidentiality and protection. We're offering a quarter of a million dollars for information leading to the arsonist's arrest. On your screen you will see an eight-hundred number that's been set up to take your calls. If you have information, I'd like to talk to you."

I paused to take a deep breath. *So far, so good,* I thought. Then Dana Love hit me with a double whammy. Ground rules had been established by my advance PR team, but they apparently meant nothing to her. She had promised not to discuss the Claiborne murder case so we could concentrate on the fires. It seemed Ms. Love had little interest in the burning of a poor black church when there was the murder investigation of a powerful senator to be probed.

"Do you have any suspects in Senator Claiborne's murder?" she asked.

I couldn't help myself—I narrowed my eyes and

glared at her. How dare she put me on the spot that way? "I wouldn't want to compromise the investigation by commenting on it at this stage. Suffice it to say the FBI is conducting a full investigation."

I turned away from her and looked directly into the red eye of the camera. "My concern this morning, and the reason I am here, is to address the arson and murder that occurred yesterday morning in your beautiful city."

Love leaned forward intently. "General Kelly, tell me exactly what the Justice Department is doing to solve Senator Claiborne's murder."

"Dana," I said in exasperation, "it's premature to discuss that now. Let's get back..."

Love interrupted, her voice lowered by an octave as if she and I shared a confidence. "General Kelly, reliable sources say you left Senator Claiborne's house at almost midnight the night he was shot. I don't mean to be impertinent, but just what was the nature of your relationship with the senator?"

Like hell you don't mean to be impertinent, I wanted to shout. Her smirk was fleeting, but it didn't escape my notice. I felt my cheeks flame with anger. *That does it!* I thought and mentally stripped off the kid gloves. *If that's how you want to play it, be prepared* was my attitude. No holds barred.

My smile was cruel. My words were clipped. I leaned toward her. "Dana, the nature of my relationship with Senator Claiborne is none of your business. Since you've seen fit to raise this topic in front of thousands of viewers, I won't leave it hanging so you can imply and hint and spread your dirty innuendo there was something unseemly going on between Sam Claiborne and myself."

Then I leaned back in my chair as she was momentarily silenced. "Senator Claiborne was a friend of my family, in particular of my father, who will be ordained on Sunday as bishop of the Diocese of North Carolina. My relationship with the senator was based on friendship and mutual respect, something you seem to know little about. It was entirely aboveboard. It can be scrutinized by anybody, for there's nothing to hide. There was nothing inappropriate or dirty or backstreet about it. I've got a husband I'm madly in love with, and I've never been unfaithful to him. Is that answer clear enough for you to understand, Ms. Love?"

Love stammered. "Yes, but…but, don't you owe your present position to Senator Claiborne's backing?"

"Well, it's true Senator Claiborne was a strong ally during my confirmation proceedings. Then so were many others. For example, one of the senators from your own home state. Are you going to question Senator Graham's motives as well?"

Love stammered again. "No, no…of course not. It's just…"

I continued, "Samuel Claiborne was a dear friend. His death is a deep, personal loss for me—and my husband. For the entire nation." I looked squarely into the camera.

I felt tense and uncomfortable, but I'd regained my composure. Tension caused my lower back to knot, and the hot lights made me perspire. A throbbing in my temples warned of an approaching headache. I looked directly into the red eye of the camera and consciously relaxed my facial muscles.

"Now, let's get back to the real reason I flew to Charleston this morning."

"But, General Kelly…" Love said.

"Quiet," I said firmly as if I were scolding one of

my children, not caring that her face grew red. I forged ahead, speaking directly to the television audience. "Most crimes would never be solved if it weren't for the cooperation of ordinary, law-abiding citizens like yourselves. Maybe you overheard something or saw something that struck you as odd, something you think is not important. Don't hesitate to call us about it, because to a trained investigator, your information might provide just the break we're looking for. Please, if you have any information about the arson, no matter how trivial it may seem, call the eight-hundred number on your screen or your local FBI office."

Love gave the camera a tight smile as she broke for a commercial. She literally ran off the set, not having the grace to apologize or thank me for selecting her show for my appearance. I'd boosted her ratings immensely. The network big shots were watching. She'd blown what little chance she had to catch a big dog's eye. The important issue had been resolved; I had made my point. I'd gotten my message out, and in the final analysis, that was all that mattered to me.

THIRTEEN

"IT WENT UP like a tinderbox." Mattie Long was an elderly lady with deeply creased skin and sorrowful eyes that spilled tears as she recounted the burning of her church. Mrs. Long was a remarkable ninety-six. The congregation of Mt. Zion Baptist Church called her "Church Mama." Every Mother's Day for the past eighty-four years, since she was twelve, she'd marched up to the pulpit and recited a poem to the mothers of the congregation. This Mother's Day there would be no pulpit to receive her.

We were conducting interviews in the community north of the Ashley River Bridge, served by burned-out Mt. Zion. Mrs. Long had opened her tiny bungalow to investigators, the overflow spilling out onto the porch and into her bountiful garden where reporters trampled flowers. She and I shared her small living room with Reverend Zeke Bell and Dr. Vernon Young. The room, barely twelve-foot square, was dominated by a television set over which hung a portrait of Jesus' agony in the Garden of Gethsemane.

"Did it take the firefighters long to arrive?" I asked.

"No, ma'am. They come quick. The winds blowed somethin' fierce that night and they couldn't save Mt. Zion. God bless 'em for tryin'. Place was so old, wood so dried out, it went all to blazes like that." She made a feeble attempt to snap arthritic fingers. "They turned them big hoses on the fire, but it was jes too late."

"So you watched the church burn to the ground, Mrs. Long?" I asked.

"Oh, yes, ma'am, I surely did. That was the sorriest night of my sorry old life. It's jes down the block, that way." She pointed to the front corner of her home. "The sirens woke me. I rousted my great-nephew—he could sleep through a hurricane, that one—and we went out in our nightclothes. Everyone was in the street, standin' and gawkin' like they was hypnotized or somethin'. 'Spect I did, too." She grimaced.

"Did you see any strangers in the area? Anyone who didn't belong?" Pyromaniacs were known to linger to admire their handiwork.

"No, ma'am." She hung her head. "The police done asked me the same thin', and I had to say 'no, sir, didn't see no strangers.' I surely do wish I seen 'em so we could ketch them devils."

It was hot in the little bungalow, and Mrs. Long, a gracious hostess, had provided lemonade. I looked around for a place to set my glass, but every available surface was covered with crocheted doilies and bric-a-brac.

Zeke Bell, age seventy and pastor of Mt. Zion, leaned forward. "Ever since these church burnin's started up, I've been sittin' up with my church. Sit with it 'til midnight most nights. Folks can't be up all the time, and the devil moves when you think he ought to be asleep."

"Amen to that," Mattie Long said.

Who is the devil? I asked myself. *Is he a solitary devil or a member of a coven of devils?*

Vernon Young inclined his head. "Has anyone in your congregation been reported missing, Reverend Bell?"

"That fire wasn't started by a member of my church!" Bell declared flatly.

"I didn't mean to imply it was, sir," Vernon said kindly.

"That dead man wasn't one of ours, either. I've been to see every member of my little flock, and they're all accounted for. That is the first thing I done when I heard the president tell about the body y'all done found here."

I said, "Dr. Young will leave you his card, Reverend Bell. I want you to call him, day or night, if you think of anything else. You, too, Mrs. Long. Be sure to tell your nephew. Young people hear things on the street. Solving these church burnings is my top priority."

Mattie Long wrung her hands. "Lordy, Lordy, I thought the whole block would be set afire. Flames leapin' across the church roof this way and that. I feared for my home."

I covered her thin hand with my own. "I'm glad you didn't lose that, too, Mrs. Long."

In the Isaiah African Methodist Episcopal Church on Calhoun Street, television crews were setting up for the prayer service that would be televised locally; the prayer service that was turning into a media event, highlights of which would appear on the six-thirty national news. I had decided not to attend the service. Dr. Young would represent DOJ. I would not steal the limelight from Reverend Jay Johnson. Let him lead the congregation and offer solace without the distraction of having the attorney general in the front pew. These were his people. He had worked at the side of Reverend Martin Luther King, Jr. He had earned his place in the limelight.

FOURTEEN

UP CLOSE, the Mt. Zion Baptist Church looked like a bomb had been dropped on it.

"Looks like a war zone," Agent Brad Moore shouted in my ear. FBI and ATF agents milled noisily around us, their shovels scraping rubble.

"It is a war zone," I said.

Moore fixed me with a quizzical look.

"A different kind of war."

I wondered if I had hit upon the answer. Were Southern black churches the first target in a campaign of deadly warfare by an army of white supremacists? This was the tenth church to burn in South Carolina since I'd taken office. That averaged almost one church in this state destroyed every month.

The National Church Arson Task Force team had a uniform of sorts. Navy tee-shirts and navy pants with ATF or FBI stenciled in large letters on their backs. Silver shields were clipped to navy caps. The crew's hands were protected inside blue latex gloves with extra gloves dangling from their back pockets. Their weaponry in this war was rakes, shovels, and cameras.

The agents worked behind broad, yellow fire-scene tape. It was draped from blackened tree to blackened bush to blackened tree and enclosed the church perimeter. Bold black lettering warned FIRE LINE—DO NOT CROSS.

The temperature had reached its predicted high. The

sun was shining; puffy white clouds chased merrily across the sky, and breezes off the river flirted with hats. If it was not for the scorched skeleton of the church in front of us, you could almost believe we had gathered on the banks of the Ashley River for a softball game or a church picnic.

Community residents had set up folding lawn chairs nearby and were sipping soft drinks from coolers. Small children, who knew no better, played tag. One old man stroked his dog—an ancient white-muzzled golden retriever—obsessively as if not to comfort it but himself.

I strolled through the crowd and introduced myself. The reception I got was warm. I asked the same question of everyone. Had they seen or heard anything out of the ordinary? I came up with no leads. These hard-working people went to bed early and got up early to go to menial jobs in hotels and hospitals with shift starts at five and six o'clock.

Everyone wanted to talk to me; everyone wanted to tell me how scary it was to have an arsonist strike so close to home. "What if he burns us out next?" one woman asked. They begged me to do something to stop the fires, and I told them that was exactly what I intended to do.

A bubble of excitement rose from the Task Force. Had they found something of significance? I moved in close for a better look. Agents Colby and Moore were just as curious. From waterlogged ashes, Doug Wimbish extracted some object. It was about sixteen inches long, thin, and cylindrical.

"Oh, my God, it's a bone," one of the spectators cried.

"They've found another body," someone else said.

Is there a second victim? I wondered.

Gingerly, Wimbish deposited the item in a clear plastic bag.

"A bone?" I asked him.

He was hunched down on the ground and tipped his head up to look at me. "No, ma'am. It's a candlestick."

I bent for a better look. The object was charred and twisted from the fire's high temperatures, but I saw it was indeed a silver candlestick.

"I think we can definitely rule out arson for profit, General Kelly."

I looked around for a place to sit while assessing the situation. Spotting an abandoned lawn chair, I crossed the field to it, moving away from the stench of wet ashes and clouds of soot. I carried a paper cup of iced tea and sank into the chair.

Two blackened brick chimneys stood like pillars of some ancient temple ruin. I wondered how anyone could have detected a human corpse in all that rubble, then recalled a soldier of the K-9 unit had made the discovery within hours after the blaze had been put out. The dogs were equipped with special heatproof boots. It was crucial they be let in immediately to search for signs of life. I wondered who the dead man was, why he'd been shot, and why someone hated him so much they'd fed his body to a fire.

I envisioned the blaze as Mattie Long had described it: vandal flames pillaging the small church, leaping over the roof, plundering the altar and pews and crayon drawings taped up in Sunday School rooms. I saw fiery maggots feasting on flesh.

Wimbish was right. This was not a case of arson for profit. This was a hate crime. Only last week an African-

American Pentecostal church in Macon, Georgia, had been set ablaze.

"Thirty-five," I said out loud. Thirty-five churches had burned since I took office. I reviewed the statistics. Fifteen churches had burned to the ground—nothing left but foundations. Twelve were gutted but might be restored if the congregations could raise the funds. Many of the poor churches were underinsured, if they carried any insurance at all. Only seven of the fires had been ruled accidental. The others were set intentionally.

In only ten percent of the cases had suspects been arrested. The other ninety percent of the investigations were classified as "active," DOJ's term for unsolved. Our inquiries were ongoing. There was no shortage of suspects, only a shortage of hard evidence to take to court.

Someone touched my shoulder and I jumped. I looked up to see a state trooper leaning over me.

"Sorry if I startled you, ma'am." He had a soft Southern drawl. He tapped an index finger to the brim of his Mountie hat in a deferential salute. Under the hat's brim, his face was long, lean, and clean shaven. Sunglasses wrapped around his eyes mirrored my own image.

"No problem, Officer. What can I do for you?"

"I'm Officer Hightower, General Kelly, and I've got an informant in my car who insists on speaking to no one but you."

He pointed to a black-and-gray state car parked some sixty feet away at the edge of the field on the side of the dirt-and-gravel road.

"Tell me about him." I got to my feet. "How'd he surface?" None of the agents monitoring the eight-hundred number had contacted me.

"It's a lady, ma'am. She called the state police number,

and as I patrol the area near her residence, the dispatcher radioed me. I went to her home and questioned her. She claims she's got proof her husband is the arsonist, and she wants to tell you about him."

"Then I'm anxious to speak to her. Let's go." This could be the lucky break we needed. I hurried off ahead of the trooper, crossing the field, my heels sinking into soft grass. A cloud of tiny white flies mushroomed up out of the weeds, and I stopped to fan them away from my face.

"Everyone's talking about your television appearance and the reward." Trooper Hightower took my elbow lightly.

I shook him off. "It's okay, Officer. I'm fine."

He apologized. "Sorry, ma'am, no offense intended. It's just this grass is hard walking for a lady in high heels."

I felt guilty. I'd lived in the North for so long I'd forgotten about Southern chivalry.

"Do you know the informant?" I wanted her to be a credible witness. I wanted her to have information that would help us crack this case.

"I know some of her kin. They're reputable people."

Sunlight winked blindingly off the windshield of his car. I approached the driver's side. A metal grid divided the front seat from the back, its network concealing the woman who was about to give me my first lead.

Officer Hightower steered me toward the rear door, his hand guiding me by the elbow. I accepted his help.

He opened the door. The backseat was deep, covered in heavy tan Naugahyde, and empty. There was no woman. "Where has she gone?" I turned to Hightower.

His expression puzzled me, for his smile was mocking. "Got you now, little lady," he sneered and pushed me hard toward the car's interior.

My reaction was swift and instinctive. I lunged for the door frame, got a good grip, and resisted. "Help!" I screamed. The dirt road was soft and powdery, and my heels sank into it.

"No! Let me go!" I was struggling, thrashing out of his grasp, my hands locked on the door frame, my feet rooted in the dirt.

I heard him chuckle. "You're mine." His head was so close I could smell his aftershave and feel his hot breath on my neck.

"No one can see you." His long arms blocked me on both sides. He was playing with me, like a cat toys with a mouse. He was twice my size. One good shove and I was inside that car. He was enjoying the risk he was taking.

I gulped air then jammed my right elbow back, up, and under his rib cage, into his diaphragm. His breath left his lungs in a raspy wheeze.

"Help me!" I screamed.

"General!" Colby ran toward us. "Let her go or I'll shoot!"

I tried to squirm out of Hightower's grasp, but he locked his left forearm under my chin and swung me around. I was in front of him, and Colby wouldn't dare shoot even though her Glock was pointed directly at us.

Hightower's right hand plunged to the holster on his hip for his own weapon. I felt the barrel press against my temple. He shouted to Colby, "Stay back or I'll shoot her. I swear to God I will."

His arm under my chin had my head twisted back painfully. In whirling me around, he had pulled my feet free of the dirt. I had the use of my hands. I lifted one foot and kicked back, stabbing his shin with my high heel. At the same time, I attacked his belly with my elbow.

His grip on my neck slackened. "You and me ain't finished, little lady," his raspy voice whispered in my ear. Then he gave me a shove, and I went sprawling on the ground.

Colby raced toward me and threw her body over mine. "Cover your ears," she shouted. Bracing herself on one elbow, she fired repeatedly at Hightower's fleeing car as I cowered under her, palms pressed against my ears.

FIFTEEN

THE GROUND AROUND US shook with thundering footfalls.

"Stay down!" Colby shouted.

I lay cramped under her, eyeball to eyeball with a blade of grass. After what seemed like an eternity, she lifted up and then I did as well, now able to get a look at what was happening. Hightower's stolen state trooper's car was a receding glint of steel, flying down the dirt road. Trailing behind him like a swarm of mad hornets were other state police cars, the Bureau's black sedans, and Charleston P.D.'s blue-and-white cruisers. Blue lights flashed and sirens screamed, and I watched as they all disappeared in a cloud of dust.

Moore was kneeling beside me. "You okay, General?"

"I'm fine." I tried to control my shaking.

He helped me to my feet, and I brushed the dust off my clothing. Leading me to a lawn chair, Moore tried unsuccessfully to shoo away the Mt. Zion parishioners who offered me water and assistance.

A man of about thirty-five, dressed in a dark gray suit and a subdued tie, approached, and from the way Moore waved him forward, I knew he'd been vetted. "This is Guy Johnson, the SAC out of Columbia."

The young man's face was alive with excitement. "That was a close call, General Kelly. What happened?"

I wasn't ready to confess to anyone, let alone a stranger, how foolish I'd been. "Let's get out of here."

I lifted my shoulder bag and jacket off the lawn chair, made a swipe at the dust on my skirt, and hobbled across the grass. I'd lost the heel of one of my shoes.

Moore supported one of my elbows and Guy Johnson the other. For my part, we couldn't reach the car fast enough. The driver ran to fling the door open and I let myself fall inside. Dropping heavily into the backseat, dust wafted up from under my backside. The new-leather scent was overcome by the stench of wet ashes, hot air, and the dusty sweat of my body. My arms and legs trembled. Colby positioned herself directly across from me and eyed me with concern. She retrieved a bottle of water from somewhere and handed it to me.

Guy Johnson got in beside me. "We need to talk."

"It's time we made tracks," Colby said. "Back to the plane."

Guy disagreed. "General Kelly, we really ought to stop at the field office. File a report while this is all fresh in your mind. You ought to look at photographs before you forget what that guy looks like, maybe ID him."

Moore lost his temper. "Don't you get it, man? She was almost kidnapped back there. We're responsible for her. She can look at your pictures some other time."

"Well, you didn't do a very good job of protecting her, did you?" Guy retorted.

Neither Moore nor Colby uttered a word in their defense.

"You're right," Colby said.

No one deserved the blame but me. "It was my fault. I wandered off."

Moore turned his face to the window, blinked, then looked back at me. "I shouldn't have let you. It's my job to protect you, to know where you are at all times, and I let you down. I got so caught up in what Wimbish was unearthing, I let myself get distracted." Pause. "I'm sorry, General Kelly. If you want to replace me, I'll understand."

"No one's going to replace anybody. I want you to get over that mindset right now. You two are a good team. I need you both." I reached over and patted his knee. "Driver, head into town." I turned to Guy. "Yes, I'll look at your rogues gallery."

Colby was contrite. "I saw you with him. I shouldn't have trusted his trooper's uniform. The state troopers were all around the site. I was fooled. I'm sorry, General, I didn't do a good job for you. I didn't suspect a thing."

"Anyone can get hold of a trooper's uniform," I said. "I know better."

"Not state cars," Moore said. "I won't let you blame yourself. The fault is mine and Colby's. From now on, no one gets near you without proper ID."

"Starting with me." Guy dug in his breast jacket pocket and produced a small leather folder with a shiny shield on the cover. Opening it, he showed me his ID.

"I already saw it, General Kelly," Moore said.

I looked from the SAC to his picture. "You look like a lawyer."

Guy returned his ID to his coat pocket. "Guilty as charged. I've got a law degree from Tulane. Joined the Bureau right out of school. I never did practice law. Ever since I was a little shaver, I wanted to be a G-man. Guess I'm one of the lucky ones to get my wish."

Outside my window, small bungalows flew by. Two small children shared a tire swing in a dirt front yard. They stared, then waved, their tiny faces all smiles. *These people deserve to live in peace,* I thought. *They should be able to sleep through the night without hate-*

filled radicals coming into their neighborhood and burning down their churches. The faces I'd looked into this afternoon were filled with pain and confusion. I knew that when I lay my head down tonight, I'd see those faces again.

"I'm like you, Guy. This is what I've always wanted to do. No more talk about placing blame. It's over and behind us." I knew it wasn't over for me. "We've got a job to do, and we're going to do it. So on to the field office. I want to catch that guy." I sighed and leaned my head back. "Just let me close my eyes for a minute."

What I'd told Guy was true. As a young student, I'd dreamed of one day achieving a position like mine, but women didn't get to be attorneys general in the seventies and eighties. In those days the post was handed to old men. I hadn't known exactly what I was aiming for in those days, but I did know I wanted to…needed to… fix things, set society on course, maybe not eliminate evil, but control it.

SIXTEEN

"OKAY, GUY, let's get down to the nitty-gritty. You can speak freely in front of my agents."

"AAG Cross telephoned me and told me to meet you here and bring you up to speed. Of course, I'd have come, anyway. The AG in my backyard and all."

"I'm glad you came," I said.

"I was late because I had an impromptu meeting with our undercover agent, Bud Starr. We've been watching one of our more troublesome paramilitary groups, and Starr's trying to infiltrate their group."

"Are these the people responsible for the fires?" I asked.

"That's what Starr's trying to find out. This group is well-organized and very secretive, but he thinks he's earning their trust. He's learned enough to know they've got someone tough and ruthless heading up the group. His followers just about worship him, even though they fear him. They call him 'The Commander.'"

"The Commander," I repeated reflectively. "Maybe a former military officer?"

"We don't know who he is. Not yet. Or where his base of operations is located. It's somewhere here in the Southeast. Starr's had good luck in the past. If anyone can come through for us, he can. The militia calls itself POSSE."

"Posse? As in the old militia group from the sixties?" I asked. "Aren't they defunct?"

"I believe you're referring to Posse Comitatus. Yes, they disbanded decades ago."

"I've read the reports on them," I said. "They were paranoid like all the rest of those mavericks. Claimed the government was interfering in their lives."

"I've made a point of looking them up. They were organized by a former member of the pro-Nazi Silver Shirts. Posse wouldn't acknowledge any federal authority over their lives. They set up their own common-law courts. Passed bad checks. Lots of harassment of anyone who stood in their way. Authority was vested in the local sheriff, who was usually one of their own."

"They refused to pay income taxes," I added. "Claimed the Sixteenth Amendment had never been ratified."

Lauren Colby snorted.

Guy said, "They believed any government official who was at cross purposes with their movement should be hanged in the public square. They did, too, hanging federal officials if they could get their hands on them, shooting federal marshals."

The mood in the car grew solemn. I stared out the windshield as we inched south on Lockwood Boulevard. The bridge shaded the boulevard, clanging noisily with traffic.

Staring out the window, I couldn't help but wonder aloud, "Is that what they wanted with me today? To take me prisoner and hang me in their public square? It's no secret I'm an enemy of those militias."

"The truth?" Guy asked.

"Of course the truth."

"Now we're assuming the phony state trooper was a member of Posse or a similar militia. Those guys see themselves as white knights standing up for an oppressed society—the white man as the minority. Truthfully, they'd love nothing more than to get their hands on the attorney general. Almost as good as the president."

Lauren Colby gave Guy a look of intense resentment but remained silent.

I, too, remained thoughtful for a moment. "So this new Posse is no different from the old regime? Espousing the old ideologies?"

"Yes, ma'am. The difference is they're better financed and better armed. Some of the older members are former Posse Comitatus members. Plus, as you know, with a black man in the White House, the militias are making a resurgence, crawling out from under the rocks where they've been hiding and waiting. They are gaining strength and supporters today in the same places the old Posse was strong."

I evaluated what he was saying.

Guy faced me squarely. "Like the original Posse, they're placing frivolous liens on the property of public officials. Naturally, the liens are scams and have no legal teeth to them. In these days of numerous foreclosures, this can create a God-awful mess. They're more a nuisance than anything else. For the people who've had the sale of their property tied up, it's more than harassment; it's cost them money."

"The Republic of Texas Separatists and the Montana Freemen engage in those quasi-legal activities," I said.

Guy Johnson's laugh was a mirthless bark. "We call them 'ROT.' The Republic of Texas, R-O-T."

"Tell me about the militia groups in South Carolina."

"We've got active Freemen groups. Then there's always the Klan, the neo-Nazis, the skinheads. For the most part, the members are semi-literate, uneducated farmers, garage mechanics, a lot of unemployed men with time on their hands and bitterness in their hearts. They blame blacks and women for getting the jobs they feel are rightfully theirs. The organizers know just how to play those good old boys like a bow plays a fiddle. Know how to appeal to their base instincts, how to keep them stirred up."

"The man who accosted me did not seem uneducated. He was well-spoken."

"That fact will help us identify him," Guy said.

We approached the sprawling Medical University of South Carolina complex and wound around it to President Street and the FBI's resident agency. The driver pulled into a parking space, but we remained in the car, preferring to finish our conversation in private. The air conditioner blasted cool air as outside my window a red-hot setting sun sizzled on the Ashley River.

Guy said, "By the way, the new POSSE is an acronym. Well, loosely. The kind of thing you'd expect from those guys. It stands for Protectors of Second-Amendment Security."

"Aha. So they're riding that high horse, the Second Amendment. That just means they're armed to the teeth." I reflected for a moment. "We were all surprised when the Supreme Court agreed to revisit that issue. If they get their way, members of law enforcement will be sitting ducks with every pothead taking aim at police officers. Do me a favor, will you, Guy, and call Ed Cross for me and tell him about my attempted kidnapping."

"Be glad to." He paused and cleared his throat. "General Kelly, I think it would be a good idea if you let me assign some of my agents to your security detail while you're here."

"I hate to admit it, and I hate to take your agents off other assignments, but under the circumstances, I think you're right."

"I'll set it in motion right away. You know, if we can ID that fake state trooper, we might be able to figure out his motive from his background."

"That is a hope," I replied.

I spent the next two hours fruitlessly poring over the photographs of known criminals. Someone brought me coffee, and I fortified my brain with caffeine. I scrutinized each long-jawed face, picturing it with mirrored sunglasses and a Mountie hat, but couldn't recognize my assailant. What we needed was a computer artist, but none was employed by the Charleston resident agency, and there was not time to have one flown in. I'd arrange to meet an artist at the Hoover Building as quickly as possible.

Charleston agents returned to headquarters frustrated and empty-handed. The perp had gotten away. The state car had been found abandoned on a secondary road, at a place where the assailant had either left his own car or was picked up by an accomplice. He had fled, and as we had no description of his getaway vehicle, the search for him was temporarily suspended. Technicians were dispatched to tow the state car in and give it a thorough going-over by employing the latest forensic technology. Soil and vegetation samples might provide a clue as to where the perp came from. The car had been stolen from a state highway-maintenance yard, we learned.

The situation was spiraling out of control, becoming more and more dangerous, escalating from arson to murder to my attempted abduction. I was nervous and much too tired to make the flight home. What I wanted most was a hot bath, a bed, and a few hours to contemplate these latest developments.

SEVENTEEN

AT NINE P.M. I checked into the Melrose House Hotel on Meeting Street while South Carolina Bureau agents studied everyone who came and went through the lobby. The night manager, a dapper little man named Willis, seemed in awe of my entourage and chattered nervously. He informed me the best suite in the house had become unexpectedly available, and he wanted to make a present of it to me. My staying there would be good for business.

I was alarmed. "No one must know I'm here."

"Well, yes, of course," he acquiesced. "How fortuitous. The entire seventh floor is unoccupied tonight. We were expecting the editors and crew of *Southern Living Magazine* here to cover the Azalea Festival. With the heavy rains and the cold spring we've had, the azaleas are in pretty dismal shape. They canceled just a few hours ago." He spread his palms and shrugged his shoulders as if to say "I'm stuck with empty rooms. Take the suite off my hands."

"You're very kind, but I can't possibly accept your offer."

He bobbed his head knowingly. "Yes, yes, I understand. You must not only avoid impropriety, you must avoid the appearance of impropriety." He grinned at his own brilliance.

"I'll take it." I surprised us both. Tonight I longed for pampering and creature comforts. His saying the entire

floor was unoccupied clinched the deal. I was lucky to
be alive, or at least not bound and gagged in the trunk
of that fake trooper's car. I handed him my American
Express card. "You must charge me your regular rate."
Life is too short not to indulge oneself occasionally.
When the bill came, I'd apply the government's per
diem to the charges and pay the balance myself.

"I'll need two adjoining rooms for my agents."

"Yes, General Kelly," he replied crisply, "I do have
such an accommodation. Two rooms, one on either side,
both with connecting doors to your suite. They are single rooms, and I'm bound to accept the government
rate for them. No question about that. I'm sure you'll
be comfortable. I'm having flowers and fruit sent up to
the suite right now. How about a nice bottle of wine? We
stock a good selection. Please allow me the pleasure of
at least doing that for you. White or red?"

I hesitated.

"All my other important guests accept," he said en-
couragingly.

"Okay. Thanks. Keep it simple. Beringer's Zinfandel,
if you have that." There was no rule against accepting
a ten-dollar bottle of wine.

A uniformed bellman carried my garment bag and
overnight case to the seventh floor. I'm always packed
and ready to go. My job requires frequent travel; I average three speaking engagements a week. I carry a
change of outfit and underwear, nightgown and robe,
toiletries, and a flashlight. A SIG Arms Compact P-239.
I've never had to use the SIG in my travels, but the
flashlight has come in plenty handy.

The suite was tasteful and comfortable, and I could
hardly wait for everyone to leave so I could get out of
my clothes. Furniture was eighteenth-century reproduc-

tion; colors were burgundy and teal. A Chippendale sofa
was placed with its back to the door, creating a cozy
seating arrangement on one side. Behind it, traffic could
flow unimpeded into the bedroom and bathroom. The
sofa was handsomely upholstered in burgundy stripes.
A soft mohair throw in muted burgundy tones invited
me to take a nap.

I crossed to the center of the room as the bellman
demonstrated a remote-control console built into an
end table. Buttons operated the TV, lamps, and drapery
track. One could control the room's equipment without
leaving the comfort of the sofa. He moved into the bedroom to hang my garment bag in the closet. I tapped on
the connecting door to tell Agent Moore I'd be turning in soon.

"Leave your side of the door unlocked, General,"
he advised.

After this afternoon's near miss, I knew he was right
and did as he instructed.

The bellman said good-night and left. With the door
double-locked behind me, I walked to the windows and
surveyed the city.

Charleston's main thoroughfare, Meeting Street,
stretched below. The hotel was in walking distance of
the harbor, yet from this angle the bay was not visible.
I could see the Circular Congregation Church and the
Gibbes Museum of Art. The unexpected pleasantness of
the night had brought young people out, and their mood
appeared festive. Tomorrow was Good Friday, the start
of the Easter holiday, and I imagined many of the revelers were college students on break. They reminded me
of my children, and I experienced a pang of nostalgia.

My own mood was anything but festive. My left
eye twitched annoyingly as I dialed room service and

ordered comfort foods: a cheese omelet, hot buttered croissants, and a pot of hot chocolate.

One moment more and he would have taken me. I'd made it so easy for him. I'd let down my guard and been really careless. I knew better.

During my years as a prosecutor in New York, my life had been threatened many times. I lived in fear for my safety and the safety of my family. It was at that time Jack and I decided to send the children to boarding schools. It was then, too, I learned to shoot a handgun and to shoot it well, pumping bullets through cardboard bad men with circles for hearts.

While I waited for room service, I unpacked my travel bag and peeled off my dusty clothes. They stank of smoke, and I sealed them in a plastic bag. I pulled on an old robe, worn soft and frayed. It's my old friend, left over from the days when my children were young. It ties me to them and comforts me when I'm away from home. I'll never throw it away. I look at it and remember Sunday mornings and little faces, French toast and Canadian bacon, and the *New York Times* spread all over the breakfast table.

The sight of the SIG lying on the bed brought me back to the present. I picked it up and inserted a fifteen-round magazine. I racked the slide, and a bullet rolled smoothly into the chamber. Then I released the automatic firing-pin lock and tucked the weapon into my robe pocket.

A light tap at the door preceded a voice that called, "Room service." Moore heard the knock right away. Swiftly he opened our connecting doors. "I'll take care of this."

Leaving the connecting door ajar, he went back through his own room to open his door to the hallway and admit the waiter. With the door ajar, I observed a young man wheel the cart into Moore's room. Taking in Moore's shoulder holster, he surveyed the room anxiously.

"Is it true the attorney general is here?" he asked. "Are you expecting trouble?"

Moore did not reply but instead instructed the man to leave the cart, tipped him, and saw him quickly out the door. If someone could pose as a state trooper, why not a waiter?

After he left, Moore brought me my tray and bid me good-night. I dined in robe and slippers on comfort foods while lounging on the sofa. The wine was crisp and cold, and after two glasses, my eye stopped twitching. I was too tired to watch TV or catch up on the latest news in Charleston. I'd get a full briefing in the morning, and if any emergency occurred, the news would reach me fast.

I carried my wineglass into the bathroom where I filled the tub and emptied complimentary bath oil that smelled like gardenias under the bubbling tap. Wineglass on the tub edge, SIG close at hand on the lowered lid of the toilet, I sank gratefully into the warm water. I practiced reaching for the SIG as particles of imaginary soot floated around me. If I heard so much as a pin drop, I'd be out of the tub in a bound, the powerful little nine millimeter in my hand, ready to give as good as I got.

The bathroom was old-fashioned, a throwback to the days when life was lived on a grand scale and an army of servants labored to keep everything immaculate. White floor tiles were tiny octagons; the tub was large enough for two. A porcelain sink bowl rested on a delicate fluted column, and unsightly plumbing was hidden from view inside the wall. Fixtures were polished brass with white porcelain detailing. The towels were white, too, and I pulled a blanket-sized towel from the rod.

Despite my serene and secure surroundings, I could not relax. I reassured myself Moore was on the other side of one door and Colby on the other. There were two FBI agents watching the lobby. Yet I was too wrought up for sleep.

Wrapped in my cozy robe, I wandered back into the sitting room, the SIG in one hand, the wineglass in the other. Catching sight of myself in a mirror over a credenza, I cringed at the woman who could have been a character out of a Joan Crawford movie.

I sank onto the sofa and was on the verge of laughing or crying, I didn't know which, when the control panel caught my attention. I played with the buttons— opening and closing blackout drapes, turning the TV on and off, dimming lights—as if I were in a trance. My thoughts returned to the afternoon's events.

Who was the man who tried to push me into the back of a stolen state car? Had he selected me in particular to be his target or would he have settled for any one of us, Vernon or Wimbish or Guy Johnson? He had a lure ready for me, and I swallowed it, hook, line, and sinker.

After my conversation with Guy about the paramilitary groups, I began to wonder if the president was right. Were we the victims of an anti-government conspiracy? Did that conspiracy include the murder of Sam Claiborne? Was I its newest target?

I analyzed what I knew about the victims. On the one hand, there was Sam, a senator and war hero. Polls showed he was still immensely popular with the public, still trusted by them. He shared one characteristic in common with the congregations of the church arsons, his African-American heritage. Other than that, they had nothing in common I could see. The body in the fire, what was its race? For the time being, that question was a mystery.

Sam had made enemies of the NRA and the paramilitary groups when he introduced bills to strengthen the Hate Crimes laws. How did that relate to his role as a general? There had to be a connection, otherwise why bother to dress him in his officer's uniform? All along, I'd felt whoever murdered Sam was controlling other events, setting a scene, directing his own perverse dramas.

The first ten Amendments to the Constitution were written in 1791 by the conventions of a number of states as their condition for adopting the Constitution. The Second Amendment consists of one simple sentence that over the centuries has befuddled the best legal minds.

A well-regulated Militia, being necessary to the security of a free State, the right of the people to keep and bear Arms, shall not be infringed.

Considering that at the time of the Second Amendment's creation America had just gained its freedom from England, I tended to think the intention was the individual states were free to maintain militias, that is, their National Guards, and their state and local police forces. The paramilitaries interpreted it to mean the ordinary citizen could arm himself for a war and should be allowed to own military weaponry equal to the legitimate armed forces.

The framers of the Amendments could not have imagined that in the late twentieth century their words would be used to protect pornographers and pedophiles and to arm insurrectionists in their war against a duly-elected government.

I piled dirty dishes on the tray and carried it to the credenza. The woman who looked back at me from the mirror appeared older than her forty-five years. I brushed my hair back from my face with my hands. Something had to be done about the way I looked before Jack came home.

Ordinarily, I would have set my tray of dishes out into the hall for housekeeping to pick up, but I couldn't risk opening the door for even a second. I verified the metal security device was clamped shut. "Snug as a bug," I mused aloud to myself.

Attempting to get cozy in my little armed-camp, I brought pillows in from the bed and piled them on the sofa. Then I stretched out. For the time being, I had everything I needed: a half-bottle of cool wine, my trusty SIG within reach on the coffee table, and the efficient remote control at my fingertips. For the time being, no one could get to me.

The chirping of my cell phone was a jarring note. I slipped the phone from my robe pocket and checked the incoming number. Oh, no. Ed Cross' booming voice. "Ann, I want you to get your butt back up here pronto. I don't know what's going on down there, but you're in danger. Come home. We can take care of you here."

I was so taken aback I was speechless. "Who do you think you're talking to? Don't you ever address me in that tone again."

Silence. "Sorry. Sometimes I come on too strong. I'm just worried about you. Damned worried."

I softened. "Apology accepted. Now, let me assure you I'm perfectly safe. I'm locked in a suite at the Melrose House Hotel. My detail is in rooms on either side of me. I'll be fine here until morning. I've got to get some sleep. Then I'll have an armed escort to the airfield. I'll be back in Washington before noon."

"Well, you should have come straight home."

"Ed, I'm dead tired. I've been running on four hours of sleep a night. I'm worn out. I've got to get some rest."

"Yeah, I see. Johnson told me all about how that guy tried to abduct you."

"I asked him to call you. I want you to do all you can from your end to find out who he is. You've got a general description. We think he might be associated with one of the militias down here."

"Will do. You watch your back from now on."

"Aye-aye, sir." I felt like I should be saluting. Then I snapped my phone shut.

Pulling the soft mohair blanket over my legs, I flipped on the eleven-o'clock news. I couldn't avoid seeing how I'd fared in my news broadcast. There I was on the screen, larger than life, tense and glowering. Alongside airbrushed Dana Love, I came across as angry. What the hell, with the way she'd double-crossed me, I had been angry. Then the sound of my own voice mesmerized me, and I was compelled to listen uncritically. I spoke authoritatively and convincingly. If I were a local resident with knowledge of the arsons, I'd trust me enough to make that call. I might look frazzled around the edges, but I had done a credible job.

Suddenly, I was too tired to move. I tapped buttons, and the television screen went blank, the lights dimmed, then vanished, and the room was thrown into soothing darkness. I pulled the soft blanket up under my chin and curled on my side, molded a pillow to fit my neck, and pressed my back comfortably into the sofa's curve.

I don't know how long I'd been asleep when an intrusive noise woke me.

EIGHTEEN

I OPENED MY EYES. The room was dark with faint light coming from the bedroom. I heard noises, a grinding sound like metal scraping against metal. Then a muffled thud. The sounds seemed to be coming from the bathroom beyond the bedroom, and I thought I must be disoriented. *Someone is pushing a squeaky service cart in the hall, that's all,* I told myself, but I couldn't close my eyes again. The hair on my arms bristled.

Faint light shone through from the bedroom where blackout draperies were not closed. Illumination from city lights spilled through blinds and sheers. I saw a shadow move inside the bedroom. Someone had entered my suite! I felt the vibration of his footsteps as he crept over the carpet.

I pressed deeper into the sofa and watched as he stood silhouetted in the bedroom doorway. He was listening. He could see I was not in the bed, and he was wondering if the suite was unoccupied and he'd broken into the wrong rooms. How had he gotten in? There was a window in the bathroom, but we were on the seventh floor.

He couldn't see me. The back of the sofa blocked me from his view. I could see his outline. I stretched out my hand and groped over the coffee table. My fingertips traced objects, and I took care not to knock over the wine bottle or wineglass. Cold steel met my fingertips. I lifted the SIG without making a sound. Rolling smoothly off the sofa, I assumed a crouched firing position. "Freeze! Don't move or I'll shoot."

From the bedroom doorway came a startled cry, then a whirl of air and the vibration of footfalls. I heard him fumble at the door, undoing all the locks I had so carefully fastened. His back was to me, and he was an easy target. I'd never shoot a fleeing intruder in the back, and he was counting on that. A flash of light hit my eyes as the door flew open, and he fled into the hallway.

In an instant, Brad Moore and Lauren Colby were throwing open their connecting doors and hitting light switches. "General?" they called.

I lifted my head from behind the couch. "He ran into the hall," I shouted excitedly. "Get him!"

"You stay with her. I'll go after him." Moore, in undershorts and a tee-shirt, plunged into the hall, arms extended, Glock steady in both hands.

I sat on the couch, pulling my robe tight around me, my arms hugging my chest.

Colby was crossing the room toward me when we heard a gunshot, followed by two shots fired in rapid succession.

"Brad's in trouble." She dashed out into the hall with me at her heels. Her weapon was drawn, supported by both hands, and she was prepared to fire. I withdrew my SIG from my pocket.

The empty hall with its papered walls above wainscots, lighted sconces, and patterned carpeting looked deceptively normal. Further along, the next door led to Colby's room. Beyond that, a red Exit sign glowed over the fire-stairs door. Colby sidled along with her back to the wall.

"Stay inside," she said in a loud whisper.

I hovered in the doorway to my room and watched. For the first time, I noticed she was wearing pajamas.

Moore burst through the door from the stairwell. "Call an ambulance. He's down. Call! I've gotta get my pants."

He drew me back into my room with Colby following. With the door secured behind us, he dashed into his own room. Colby hurried to the phone.

"Wait." My hand steadied the receiver. "Speak only to the night manager. We've got to keep this quiet. Put me on when you reach him."

Moore returned, fastening his pants, a crumpled shirt tucked under his arm. He was speaking into a small radio, communicating with the agents in the lobby, who no doubt heard gunfire and were on their way up.

"What happened?" I asked him. No sound came from the hall. I reminded myself the floor was unoccupied except for us.

"I was chasing him down the stairs when he turned and fired at me." Moore pulled on his shirt.

That explained the first shot we'd heard.

"I returned his fire and wounded him. He's not dead. I wasn't trying to kill the guy, only to stop him. I think I punctured a lung, but he took a nasty fall, and he's unconscious. I just told the other agents to find him and hold him."

"General." Colby waved the receiver at me.

I said to Moore, "Go call Guy Johnson. Get him on the phone. I'll be right there."

"Willis, this is Ann Kelly," I said to the night manager. "We've had an intruder up here, and my agent wounded him. He's on the fire stairs, between the sixth and seventh floors." I looked to Moore for confirmation. He nodded.

"Now, listen very carefully, and we'll talk about that later," I said firmly, for the night manager had started to apologize, then to jabber about bad publicity. "There will be no publicity. We're calling an ambulance. By the time the paramedics get here, they and the hospital will know to say they've got a heart-attack patient. That is what you're to say also to any guests in the lobby and to your employees. Do you understand? In the meantime, don't let anyone into that stairwell except our agents."

The night manager and I reached an agreement, and I hoped he'd live up to his end. Someone had blabbed I was here. The waiter knew. My intruder knew as well.

I hurried into Moore's room to speak to Guy Johnson, who waited on the phone. I told him what he had to do and realized I was committing my first cover-up.

"I want you to come over here and come alone. Bring a fingerprint kit."

Back in my suite, Colby was checking the bathroom. Lights blinked on in the bedroom and bath. "Well, I see how he got in."

"Go wait for the ambulance," I told Moore.

I joined Colby in the bathroom. "Don't touch anything."

"There," she pointed, but it wasn't necessary. The opening was at least three feet high. "It must lead through the walls."

I had seen it earlier when I was taking my bath. "It's a plumber's chase." Colby eyed me curiously.

The small door in the wall that housed the plumbing had been pushed open from the inside, accounting for the squeak of metal I'd heard.

"The plumbing runs from the basement to the roof through this shaft." I knelt down and peered into the dark interior. "All the pipes and valves are hidden behind the walls. These little doors were installed so a plumber could have access to make repairs. Let me get my flashlight. I'll show you."

I retrieved my flashlight from the bedroom and shone it down the shaft while Colby and I knelt and peered into the darkness. "See those rungs that climb the wall. They let the plumber climb down deeper into the shaft when he needs to. He only has to go down about halfway between floors to reach the trouble spot. I can't imagine anyone climbing those rungs all the way from the basement. He could have gotten into the shaft on another floor."

Colby regarded me with awe. "How do you know all this stuff?" She shook her head. "You amaze me."

I smiled. "I've studied antiques, and when you read about antique furniture, you can't help picking up details about the construction of old buildings."

The warbling of sirens rose from the street below. Moving together to the sitting room windows, we looked down. Under throbbing red lights, paramedics carried an empty stretcher across the sidewalk and into the hotel. I saw Brad Moore trotting along beside them, yelling instructions, while the night manager wrung his hands.

"I'm just going next door to get my robe," Colby said.

She returned, and in a matter of minutes, the paramedics were leaving by the front entrance, rolling my intruder on the stretcher between them. One jumped into the rear with his patient; the other slammed the doors shut, then dashed to the cab. The ambulance pulled out into traffic, lights flashing, siren warbling.

There was a light knock on the door. Moore had returned, bringing Guy Johnson. Quietly and efficiently, my door was dusted and prints were lifted. The same was done to the bathroom's half-door.

"I think we all need a drink." I opened the bar. I selected a miniature bottle of Tanqueray, wishing it were iced. There were cans of Coke and soft drinks in the refrigerator. Colby brought extra glasses from her room.

"Can we trust the night manager?" Guy asked.

"I don't think he'll talk now, but someone leaked I was here, and I think he just couldn't keep the news to himself. But now? Well, this is different. A shooting in his hotel. He doesn't want the publicity. It would be bad for business if guests found out there'd been a break-in and a shooting. He's got the hotel's reputation to think of, and maybe his own job on the line.

"What did the paramedics say, Brad? Will he live?"

Moore sipped whiskey, and I approved. The shooting had visibly shaken him. "One flesh wound and one punctured lung. He'll live. They're worried about his head injury. He got that when he fell. He's comatose."

"Guy, you go to… Where did they take him?"

"MUSC's knife and gun club." He giggled. "The medical center. Trauma unit."

Moore was worse off than I'd realized. "You okay, buddy?"

His eyes met mine. "I've been an agent for eight years, General Kelly. Would you believe this is the first time I ever shot someone?"

"The first time is rough." Colby patted his arm.

Guy Johnson lifted the phone. "I'm assigning an agent to guard the wounded man. We've got to talk to him the minute he wakes up."

I asked, "What did he look like, Brad? I never really saw him."

"Little, scrawny guy. Wearing a hotel-maintenance

uniform. The night manager took one look at his face and said he wasn't one of theirs."

"Amazing. Now I know it *is* me they're after. They were resourceful enough to find out where I was staying, down to the exact room number, to penetrate hotel security, and to know enough about the hotel's layout to find a way into my suite. Let's hope our intruder comes out of his coma soon. And talks."

NINETEEN

IN THE MORNING, Guy Johnson brought unsettling news. None of us had slept well enough or long enough. I, who had longed for a full eight hours of rest, was scraping by on four again. I shuddered at the prospect of more bad news heaped upon the events of yesterday and last night.

"I had a disturbing call from State Assemblyman Daniel Rosen's office this morning," Guy reported. "Rosen is missing. He hasn't been seen since Wednesday morning when he left his house for the airport. He was on his way to Washington to participate in a gay-rights rally."

"Rosen is gay?" I asked.

"Openly gay and openly Jewish. Makes him a target for a lot of hate groups."

"Now he's missing. So we've got a missing state representative and an unidentified corpse." Fingers of fear played my spine.

Guy went on, "His staff here in Charleston thought he was in Washington, but he never showed up, and his friends called his office here."

He nodded solemnly. "Rosen's aide was able to give me the name of his dentist here in Charleston without involving his family. No need to alarm them, maybe needlessly. Full-mouth x-rays of the corpse are being hand delivered from Quantico. Rosen's dentist should have them now."

On the drive to the airport, Guy took the call from

the local field office. "It's confirmed." Guy disconnected. "The victim in the fire was State Assemblyman Daniel Rosen."

Vernon Young was seated in the back of the limo
with Guy and me. Agents Colby and Moore shared the
front seat with the driver. We were departing Charleston, a convoy of black limos and boxy SUVs headed for
Charleston Air Force Base and the DOJ jet that waited
to fly Vernon and me to Andrews.

"OK, Guy," I said on the tarmac at the airfield. "You
know who you should be looking at. The neo-Nazis, the
KKK, the neo-Confederates. Your contact will be Ed
Cross. Keep him apprised of all developments."

"Aye-aye, Chief." He grinned. I grinned back but by
noon that day I found myself in tears.

CLOUDS ROLLED IN and a large shadow spread its black
stain over the land. Why was gloomy weather always
typical of Good Friday? Far up the hill behind me towered the majestic Custis-Lee Mansion, former home of
Mary Custis and Robert E. Lee, original owners of the
estate that became Arlington National Cemetery during the Civil War. The George Washington Memorial
Parkway and Lady Bird Johnson Park spread below
along the banks of the Potomac. Off to my right, I could
barely make out the distinctive shape of the Pentagon.
I caught glimpses of the Washington Monument and
the bridge over which Carlos Perez had driven Vernon
and me, and my security detail. Vernon stood erectly
on my right. Mrs. Young on his right had linked arms
with him. She had met us at the grave site.

Several hours after leaving Charleston, I was one of
an assemblage who braved winds on a hill in Arlington National Cemetery, having come to pay our last

respects to one of our own. Among the two hundred thousand souls laid to rest in these hills were presidents, the Unknowns, and the astronauts killed in an Apollo launch-pad fire. Now, on Good Friday afternoon, these hills were about to embrace another war hero, General Samuel Louis Claiborne.

Is Sam's killer here now? I wondered. One by one, I studied the faces of the others, who, with me, were the last to see Sam alive: Senator Miles Norton, Congresswoman Elaine Groves, Senate Chaplain Mike McKee. Sam's campaign manager, Frank Chase. And Halle Burden, Sam's administrative aide.

Beyond the flag-draped coffin, I saw the strained faces of Sarah Preston and her sister-in-law, Molly. President Jefferson Monroe stood close by. As commander in chief, he delivered the eulogy for our dear, departed friend. He spoke of Sam's war record, about his devotion to country and family. Occasionally, he was forced to pause as jets from nearby Reagan National Airport roared overhead. He ended by saying, "We'll miss you, Sam. We'll miss you a lot."

A military band struck up "America, the Beautiful," followed by a solitary bugler playing "Taps," as honor guards folded Old Glory in a precise triangular fashion. The neat bundle was handed to the president, who in turn presented it to Sam's inconsolable daughter. "On behalf of a grateful nation, I pass to you the flag of the Republic."

Tears filled my eyes, and I blinked them back, staring down at the grass because I didn't want to meet other tear-drenched eyes. A sudden command, "Pull!" startled me out of my reverie. Seven rifles fired into the clouds and the air crackled with their report. Three times they volleyed, and my ears rang with their fading echoes. Finally, it was over.

Senators, congressmen, and Pentagon top brass filed among the marble tombstones, hurriedly making their way to cars that would speed them directly to airports. The funeral service had been scheduled for this day and this hour to accommodate their schedules. It was Easter break, and they were anxious to get home. I was, too.

Jeff Monroe paused. "Good job down there in Charleston, Ann." Then he, too, departed, driving with his family to Camp David for a long weekend.

I hugged Sarah and told her again how sorry I was. I asked her to call me if she needed anything. I sincerely hoped she would, but I had my doubts. Right before I left, I rested my hand on the satiny wood of Sam's coffin and made a solemn pledge: "I'm going to find him, Sam, if it's the last thing I do."

I turned to find Halle Burden at my side. Tracks of tears streaked the blush on her cheeks. I pulled her to me in an embrace.

"Halle, this must be devastating for you."

"Oh, God, Ann, what will I do without him? What will we all do?"

"We'll go on," I answered. "Just as he'd wish us to."

"Ann…let's have dinner soon. I need to talk. There's something I need to discuss with you." Halle's face was worried.

I recalled Halle's parents lived in a Connecticut suburb. "Tell you what. I'm flying to New York right now. If you're ready to leave, ride with me."

"Oh, may I? That would be perfect."

Then we two were whisked away in my car back to Andrews Air Force Base.

TWENTY

"WHAT'S ON YOUR MIND, Halle?" I asked after the plane lifted off.

Normally, I would be traveling home aboard a commercial jetliner. Government employees are prohibited from using federal transportation for private use. This misuse of government property had brought down a few of the high and mighty. It was an abuse of power, and the prohibition was right and just. However, in view of the recent threats to my life and safety, Bill Cavanaugh and I agreed it would be foolhardy for me to travel on commercial flights into public airports until the criminals were apprehended.

Halle responded firmly, "What's on my mind is this, Ann. General Claiborne was being threatened."

I turned away from the window to peer at her expectantly. "Threatened? Tell me about it."

Halle had worked for Sam since he was elected to the Senate, and she'd been very close to him.

She didn't answer directly. "I've been offered a position on Senator Puckett's staff. Someone's already clamoring for Sam's office."

I shook my head. "I remember when those guys used to care about how they looked to the world. Ever since Newt, it's like they're all puffed up and wearing brass knuckles."

Halle stared out into the clouds. "I've got the daunting task of clearing out Sam's office. I'm saving his papers. Hopefully, there'll be a memorial library one day. I can't move fast enough for the ghouls who are nipping at my heels."

The steward brought us a light lunch of chicken salad and crackers. I waited throughout the meal for Halle to tell me about the threats. Something was definitely troubling her.

Finally, as we sipped decaffeinated coffee, I prompted her, "Tell me about the threats."

"Sam was receiving threatening letters. I opened his mail. I know. I've seen them. The most recent ones were particularly hateful, full of racial slurs and vitriol. Calling him a traitor. The last one said he'd be dead before he could run for re-election." Halle lowered her eyes to her trembling hands.

"Where are those letters?" I asked softly.

She bit her lower lip. "I've searched everywhere. They're gone. I suspect Sam destroyed them himself, but I'm not sure. He said many times they were worthless garbage, and he didn't want to have them around."

"I wish he hadn't done that." The act of ridding his office of venom was in keeping with his character.

"Did he receive any threatening e-mails?"

"I don't know. He read and answered his personal e-mails himself. I handled the messages to the office."

"This is what I want you to do. Get on the phone right now to someone on the staff. Someone you can trust, someone who has not left D.C. and who has a key to the office. Tell that person to go to the office immediately and remove Sam's computer. They're to take it home, or someplace safe. They're to be careful not to let anyone know what they're doing."

"Good thinking. I knew you were the right person to talk to. I know just who to call. Sonia. She loved the general. He used a laptop. I'll tell her to take hers to the office so she is seen entering with it just in case anyone is interested. I expect the place will be abandoned. Then she's to leave hers there and take his when she leaves."

"Good idea."

Halle made the call as I listened. If there was anything on that computer, even deleted files, I knew just who could trace them. Trace where they had been sent from.

I HADN'T BEEN HOME since Christmas. The town house I rented in Georgetown was a temporary parking place as far as I was concerned. I'd never put down permanent roots there. Home was New York City, no matter where else I might sleep and work. Jack shared my sentiments.

During my Senate confirmation hearings—a proceeding more brutal than the trials of any Mafia hit man I'd prosecuted—I was guilty until proven innocent. Several senators had fixated on the fact I owned a co-op apartment on elegant Beekman Place, and there'd been innuendos about how I'd acquired the funds to buy it. These political opponents of President Monroe were simply using me to get to him. They wouldn't let the matter drop, although I provided copies of the offer to purchase, the settlement statement, and a statement from my credit union displaying a whopping mortgage balance. They seemed not to understand—or rather not to accept—I'd been thoroughly vetted before my nomination. I was squeaky clean—I knew it, and deep in their hearts, they knew it. The rest was window-dressing.

How, they asked, could a family of our means afford a half floor-through apartment on expensive Beekman Place? The implication was I was on the take.

I was about to launch into my fourth explanation when Senator Samuel Claiborne intervened. "I have personally heard Mrs. Kelly answer this question on three separate occasions. She has told us in nineteen ninety-one the real-estate market in New York City was depressed. She has documented the particular apartment she and her husband purchased had been on the market for sixteen months, the price coming down as the owners grew more and more anxious to sell. The Kellys were simply smart enough to get a bargain. So unless you're suggesting these exhaustive documents are forgeries, I urge us to move on to more relevant lines of inquiry."

But had they? For hours on end I'd been questioned about my housekeeper, whom certain senators insisted on calling a nanny—shades of Nannygate on their minds—even though they knew my children were teenagers who lived away from home.

Within thick dossiers on the senators' desks was the sum total of my life reduced to print on paper: my professional records and college transcripts, personal data, the summary of an FBI security check, my financial-disclosure statements, *ad infinitum*.

Included were copies of receipts for the social-security taxes I paid for my housekeeper, Mrs. Hulda Robinson. They had only to look at the documents I'd been forced to supply. Had they, they would have known to the penny the sum my salary as a United States attorney netted me after taxes. They would have known I'd married Jack Kelly, a photojournalist for *Newsweek,* in 1989 and that, unlike many of the loudly professed family-values types among them, we had not divorced nor had we engaged in promiscuous affairs. They would have known we lived at 36 Beekman Place, New York

City, in a seven-room, two-bathroom apartment for which we'd paid $515,000 in 1991 when New York City real-estate prices had hit rock-bottom.

My confirmation hearings had been held during the Thanksgiving season, and outside the Dirksen Senate Office Building, snow flurries turned the skies to chalk. Inside, Room 106 was overheated. Sweat rolled down my back, soaking my white silk blouse and the lining of my best navy suit. I clenched my moist hands in my lap so their shaking would not be captured by news cameramen who huddled at the base of the three-tiered dais. The noise of clattering shutters and buzzing motor drives, the sweltering lights, and my eagerness to pass muster all worked together to make me feel ill.

The president believed in me. The ailing attorney general believed in me. I carried the endorsement of the National Women's Political Caucus, and the representative from my home district had introduced me in glowing terms to the eighteen members of the Senate Judiciary Committee. For me, this nomination was the culmination of years of work that had begun when I was Cathy's age. If I got the post, I would use my position to make the world a better place for her and Tom.

The grilling had gone on for two days. Near the end of day two, I took a head count and saw I had just two inquisitors to go. The next up was Senator Henry Carroll from the Commonwealth of Virginia, a hypocritical, self-righteous man. Senator Carroll had held his position in the U.S. Senate for as long as I'd been out of college—twenty-four years—and that was too long, many believed. Yet he managed to get re-elected term after term, although in the last election the margin had narrowed considerably. His was not a mandate; yet, over the years, he had amassed incredible powers unto himself.

One of my coaches, Bob Trane from the White House legal counsel's office, had warned me Carroll could be off-the-wall. "Don't let down your guard." As if I would. I had cut my teeth on the likes of John Gotti and the Gambinos.

Trane had chuckled as he related the story of a Carroll faux pas that occurred back in the seventies when the senator, then a junior representative, had sat in on the Watergate hearings. "One of the witnesses—I forget which one—had been subjected to hours of questioning without a break. When his turn came, Carroll prefaced his interrogation by congratulating the man on his continence."

"No!" I howled. "Did he really? What an oaf!"

Trane's head and shoulders bobbed. "It gets better. This was on live TV. He looked like a fool."

ON THAT DIFFICULT DAY, Senator Henry Carroll was hunched over a clutch of microphones. Ceiling spots winked off his horn-rimmed, Buddy Holly–style glasses. I could not see his eyes, but I'd looked into them before and knew they were small and mean.

In the Commonwealth of Virginia, the burning of a cross was not a crime, but rather protected by the First Amendment's right to free speech. Senator Carroll was a staunch supporter of that statute.

"Afternoon, Miz Kelly," he drawled.

"Good afternoon, Senator," I responded.

"Now, Miz Kelly, we've had witness after witness parade before this committee, attesting to your fine humanitarianism, ma'am." His honeyed tones dripped venom. "The office to which you aspire is no place for bleeding hearts."

Carroll knew I was not soft on crime. This was mere posturing for his constituents.

"So I'd like to know if these sentimental feelings of yours—and by the way, it's perfectly natural for ladies like yourself to have such tender feelings—are going to deter you from performing your duty. That is, Miz Kelly, do you possess the fortitude to seek and enforce the death penalty for capital crimes, as our former male attorneys general have done so ably?"

Don't rise to the bait, I told myself.

"Let me remind you, ma'am, you are under oath. So tell us, just what are your personal views on the death penalty?"

It was out of line for him to remind me I had sworn to tell the truth. If we were in a court of law, I would have been justified in raising an objection. Courtroom rules of procedure did not apply to Senate hearings, and neither, it seemed, did common rules of civility.

I tried to shrug off his hostility. *It isn't personal,* I told myself, *merely a pose for the folks back home.* My White House handlers had prepped me on the political postures of each of the committee members, the ideologies of their constituents, and which had sold their souls to lobbyists. I had been forewarned.

I took a moment to suppress my anger. In my lap, my hands trembled, and I was not able to control them, but years in the courtroom had taught me how to school my voice so it didn't break when I was nervous.

"Senator Carroll, it is true I'm a compassionate person. My gender has nothing to do with my ideologies. However, I do like to think of myself as a lady, and I thank you for extending me that compliment."

Behind me someone snickered.

"As for my compassion, I save it for the victims, not their killers. Yes, I would like to see more programs aimed at early intervention and prevention. Adopting prevention programs is truly in our own best interest.

"If I might direct you to my record, Senator, you will see that during the years I served as the attorney for southern New York, I sought the death penalty in seventy-three capital cases, and my success rate was a high ninety percent. Hardly the work of a sentimentalist, don't you agree, sir?"

I smiled charmingly.

The senator cleared his throat, preparing to attack again, but I cut him off. "Please, let me finish, sir. You asked for my personal views on the death penalty, and I'd like the opportunity to explain them to you and everyone on this committee."

I paused dramatically and waited until I had their full attention. "The death penalty is a useful tool in deterring crime. While no punishment will ever bring back a life, the death penalty vindicates the suffering the victim's loved ones have been forced to endure. It serves as an example for those who are tempted to kill. Most importantly, the enforcement of the death penalty fosters belief among the citizenry that our justice system is working to protect them. A belief, by the way, that is sorely needed in our time."

I was no longer smiling as I stared into the cameras but grim-faced. There were many who did not share my views on capital punishment. They hadn't walked in my shoes for the eighteen years I'd been a prosecutor. They hadn't seen what I'd seen.

"Finally, let me assure you I will do my best to serve my country, my president, and this Congress."

"That's the least we expect from our attorney general," Carroll snapped. "I'm through, Mr. Chairman," he grumbled. He looked every minute of his seventy-five years as his shoulders slumped and he clumsily whacked at a sheaf of papers, sending them flying onto the floor in disarray.

"The country will get far more than the least from me, sir." I relished the last word.

I had him. His constituency supported the death penalty. Despite his antagonism, it would be political suicide for him not to vote for me. He did.

We touched down on an airfield at a Brooklyn naval base from which the Coast Guard commands the Atlantic area. I was met by two Bureau agents from the New York office. We drove Halle to Grand Central Station, then the agents saw me safely to my apartment door. I barely had my key in the lock when the door burst open and Tom stood grinning at me, arms wide.

"Mom!" he cried.

"I thought you were finished growing." I wrapped my arms around his lean waist. He towered over me. "My little boy." I squeezed him hard.

"Aw, Mom."

Dolly, our nine-pound Shih Tzu, danced excited circles around my feet, her long hair flying, and I reached down to scoop her up in my arms. She licked my chin lovingly, nuzzled my neck, and sighed deeply.

I looked around. "Where's Cathy?"

"Cathy!" Tom screamed, deafening me. "Mom's home."

"Hello, Mrs. Ann," Hulda Robinson called as she hurried from the kitchen to help me with my coat and luggage. Her voice was throaty and rich. I moved into her embrace as Dolly squirmed.

The story of Hulda Robinson reminded me of Moss Hart's comedy *The Man Who Came to Dinner*. Seventeen years ago, a Swedish baby nurse had come for two weeks. Now, almost two decades later, she was still with us. I'd hired her to help me with newborn Cathy while I recuperated. Today, our household revolved around her.

She'd encouraged the children to call her Ronnie. I called her Ronnie, too. She called us Mrs. Ann and Mr. Jack. I'd asked her many times to drop the Mr. and Mrs., but she would not. She was "old-world" in attitude and manners, and I couldn't begin to guess her age. Whatever number I chose, my gut instinct told me she'd be ten years older.

"It's so good to see you, Ronnie. It's so good to be home. Now, where's Cathy?"

Cathy came out of her room, telephone in hand.

"Give me a big hug," I said.

"Just a minute." Into the phone, she said, "Look, I've got to go. My mom's here and I haven't seen her since Christmas. Bye."

I reached out my arms and pulled her close. She was one person who was not taller than I. I stroked hair that was soft and shone like spun copper, hair that felt and looked just as mine had twenty-eight years ago.

"I've missed you," she said sadly, and it almost broke my heart.

"I'm here now, and we have a whole fun weekend ahead of us."

TWENTY-ONE

MY OFFICE CALLED shortly after I arrived home. The president was at Camp David, and Washington was virtually shut down, yet there were people who had to reach me. Sybil brought me up to date on the day's events in my office, which served to remind me I did oversee a department of over 100,000 employees with an annual budget of twenty-one billion dollars. While I had been off playing Nancy Drew, my office was running on automatic pilot.

Ed Cross reached me just as Ronnie was putting dinner on the table with news Captain Karl Rakes of Metro P.D. was still unaccounted for, but a neighbor had volunteered he'd seen Rakes leave his home with luggage on Wednesday evening, the same day Ed had confronted him at the murder scene. As he, Bill Cavanaugh, and I had sat in my conference room speculating on what drove Rakes' hostility, he'd hustled himself right out of town. Where had he gone and why? He was on suspension, pending an inquiry into his conduct of Sam Claiborne's murder investigation, with strict orders not to leave town. So what had caused him to jeopardize his seniority and pension at Metro P.D.? Was he involved in a cover-up of Sam Claiborne's murder by stealing the gun from the Property Room? Or was he himself the victim of threats from the perpetrator and was simply running to save his own skin?

None of it made sense. Not Rakes' behavior at the

crime scene, nor his behavior since. Ed and I speculated about Rakes' role, imagining various scenarios. "We still got nothing on that scarred fingerprint. We're running it through Interpol files now. Something'll come up. It always does if you dig deep enough."

"Thanks. It's after eight. Don't you ever leave your office? Go home." I hung up.

I knew nothing about the CID director's private life, or even if he had a family to go home to.

I WAS AT THE DINNER TABLE with my children when the telephone rang again. I let the answering machine pick up. Ronnie had roasted a chicken, which she served with fresh vegetables and her special endive salad. We were having a real family dinner, something I hadn't had in months, and I gorged myself on my children's presence as it nourished me better than food. Nothing was going to spoil our reunion. Then I heard Vernon Young's familiar voice on the answering machine. I didn't have a choice. I excused myself to take his call in my bedroom.

"Why don't they leave her alone?" Cathy complained as I left the table.

"It's not her fault," Tom argued.

My apprehension mounted. "Yes, Vernon, I'm here."

"Go turn on your TV set. We've got a big fire going right now. I'll wait."

I lifted the remote and clicked the set to CNN. A large fire blazed out of control on my screen.

Vernon said, "It's a synagogue in an Atlanta suburb. Luckily, the place was vacant when the fire was set, but it's Passover and there could've been a full congregation inside."

"We've got to get to the bottom of these fires," I

said. The joy I'd felt at being home with my children was shattered, stolen by the arsonist. "Is this one related to the others?"

"It'll be days before we know if there's a connection. I had files pulled from CRT's database, and I've got the stats right here in front of me. In the past two years, we've had suspicious fires in two hundred and fifty houses of worship in thirteen Southern states. We know some of those fires were the work of individuals working alone, and in fact, many have been solved. Since you've taken office, we've had thirty-six cases of arson with signature patterns so similar that Doug and I have pretty much concluded we're dealing with a master arsonist who is responsible for all thirty-six, and maybe some of the others."

"In how many states?" I asked.

"Five. Virginia, the two Carolinas, Georgia, and eastern Tennessee."

AFTER VERNON AND I said our good-byes, I sat on the foot of my bed and watched orange-and-yellow flames. Firefighters were dark silhouettes against the fire's illumination as they trained water jets on what was left of the Atlanta suburb synagogue. Cameras panned the crowd, and I was stunned to see a familiar face.

I called Vernon's mobile phone number. The telephone rang unanswered, and I finally gave up. Consulting my book again, I tapped in Ed Cross' home phone number. He picked up on the third ring.

Quickly I explained what I'd seen. "Find someone at the site and have them search the crowds. We're looking for a tall man, about six-three, fair coloring, with a long, narrow face. Age about sixty. Get that footage from CNN. They're based in Atlanta and were covering it live, so they'll have it."

"I know how to do my job," Ed said irritably. "Now hang up and let me do it!"

THE DINNER TABLE was empty, my supper cold and congealed. It made no difference for I'd lost my appetite. I didn't wish to lose my children. In the living room, Tom flipped channels desultorily. He'd been subdued all evening and not at all like himself. Cathy's behavior, on the other hand, was predictable; she was nose-deep in a book.

Dolly was the first to hear the key turn in the door. "Grandpa's home." Tom's voice carried throughout the apartment. Dolly ran circles around my father's feet. He scooped her up to get his official kiss. At seventy-two, he doesn't bend easily and took his time in returning her to the floor and straightening his back again.

I walked to him with outstretched arms. "Let's have a hug, Your Eminence."

"'Eminence' is reserved for cardinals. I'm just a simple parish priest."

"Not after Sunday." I smiled. "I'm so happy for you, Daddy." We performed our ritualistic patting of backs. There were no kisses.

We settled into chairs in the living room with Tom giving up the recliner to his grandpa. I stifled a yawn and looked around. My family was gathered together safely. I reminded myself how lucky I was.

Cathy complained, "I feel so cooped up. Can't we go and do something?"

"Hey, that's a good idea," Tom said. "Let's go out and do something exciting."

Exciting! I stared at my nineteen-year-old son.

My family didn't know my life had been threatened only the night before in Charleston. If the enemies who were after me were here in New York, too, I calculated, they wouldn't expect me to leave my apartment at ten thirty. Yet I had to keep my family safe. "I've got two agents down in the lobby. They'll have to go with us," I said apologetically.

"We'll protect you, won't we, Grandpa?" Tom's spirits had lightened in his grandfather's presence.

"That we will, Tommy boy. No one will harm a hair on her head with us around. It *is* Good Friday, and we must be respectful. No painting the town tonight. I'd say a little celebration is in order. I don't get to see my grandchildren nearly enough."

My father was in a frisky mood, and I believed he was more excited than he let on about his promotion in the Church.

"That's sweet, but I can't go out without them. Sorry, guys. Goes with the territory." I tried to make light of their objections. "We're only going to dash around the corner to the Beekman Tower."

Cathy said, "The Beekman Tower is perfect, Mom."

"It's settled, then," Daddy said. "Let's get our coats."

I buzzed the lobby on the intercom and alerted the agents I'd be going out.

The night was warmer than the day had been, an anomaly New York City experienced often. The winds died after the sun set but the sidewalks and buildings retained the heat they'd been soaking up all day. Then there was the steam from the grates. We passed no fewer than eight doormen as we walked south and turned the corner at Mitchell Place just steps to the Beekman Tower Hotel. I'd taken my father's arm, and Cathy walked with Tom, and there was a spirit of frivolity among us. Even the presence of agents didn't subdue our joy at being together. One agent walked ahead of us, the second followed. Doormen smiled and tipped their hats. I wished I could bottle the neighborly essence of New York City and take it to Washington with me, because I surely did miss this.

The Top of the Tower was a glass-enclosed cocktail lounge with spectacular views of the city in four directions. At the grand piano, a man in a tuxedo sang show tunes from *Guys and Dolls*. The *maitre d'*, who knew Jack and me as neighborhood regulars, greeted me warmly as he eyed my two black-suited agents. "Mrs. Kelly, we haven't seen much of you recently. How is Mr. Kelly? Keeping well, I hope."

"He's well, Simon. I'll tell him you asked. This is my father, Timothy Maguire."

"Pleased to meet you, sir." They shook hands formally. "Now, if you'll follow me, I'll see this young lady and gentleman get the best views the city has to offer."

Cathy rolled her eyes, but I was sure she was secretly pleased.

The FBI agents remained at the entrance, watchfully vigilant.

Simon seated us at a table against the south window through which we enjoyed a panorama of the East River and its series of sparkling bridges. We viewed the Chrysler Building's art deco tower, the Empire State Building's spire. Yet far in the distance was the void the twin towers of the World Trade Center used to fill.

"What a wonderful view!" My father was a distinguished-looking man. When he removed his overcoat to reveal his cleric's collar, quite a few heads turned in his direction.

I ordered a bottle of champagne, asking for four champagne flutes. The champagne arrived in a bucket of ice, the waiter uncorked the bottle with a dramatic flourish, and Cathy, Tom, and I drank to Daddy's future as a bishop of the Episcopal Church.

TWENTY-TWO

ON SATURDAY MORNING, a different team of agents greeted me when I got off the elevator in my lobby. Their government car was double-parked at the curb, and we got in.

Dazzling white, blossoming Bradford pear trees marched up the median on First Avenue. A few pedestrians hurried along sidewalks, those with dogs moving at a leisurely pace, and traffic was light. By noon the streets would be teeming. The sun was already high and glowing, blinking off windows and warming the east sides of buildings.

There was a time—twenty years ago when I was an assistant district attorney—I could wander these streets unaccompanied. Powerful criminals didn't think I was important enough to bother with, if they even knew my name. On Saturday afternoons, I could shop at Saks like other working women. Those in the senior positions on the DA's staff got the threats and traveled with bodyguards. I was just another female shopper in casual clothes, safe in my anonymity. As I moved up through the ranks, the luxury of security and anonymity got wrested away from me.

I FLOATED WITH THE CLOUDS, high above the earth. Below, rolling meadows gently wrapped around quaint villages, and church spires pierced the green canopy of trees, reaching for the sky. Suddenly, a flash and a burst of flames and a woman screamed. I awoke with a start, disoriented and heart lurching.

"Mrs. Kelly?" Christina shook my shoulder gently. "Time to wake up now. I'm glad you drifted off." She couldn't know how my heart thumped.

I was at Elizabeth Arden's Red Door, and except for the strange nightmare, I'd been pretending I was just another ordinary woman spending an ordinary Saturday morning having her hair and makeup done. Of course, none of those ordinary women had a female FBI agent guarding her booth. I was tired and it showed on my face. Christina removed all traces of the masque. "Now I'll do your makeup. Is there anything special you'd like me to try?"

"If you could make me look rested, that would be a miracle."

"Oh, that's no problem. You'll be pleased when I'm finished." Maurice, who cut my hair twice a year, experimented with soft bangs that covered my forehead and a natural auburn tint that covered my gray. A stranger looked back at me from the mirror, someone I might pass on Fifth Avenue and admire. Now I could face Jane Middleton or Dana Love and not feel embarrassed about my appearance. If only Jack could see me. I kissed Maurice's cheek.

"Don't wait so long next time," he said. "Congratulations to your father."

"How did you know?"

"It was in the papers." He smiled. "*Ciao,* Madam General."

THE BRONTOSAURUS WAS three stories tall and dominated a first-floor wing of the Museum of Natural History.

Tom and I wandered among dinosaur skeletons, while my security detail trailed us none too discreetly. Tom seemed not in the mood for touring the museum, and I recalled his request for time alone with me.

"You know," I said, "we've haven't been to Rumplemeyer's in ages. How about a double hot-fudge sundae?"

I would have enjoyed the walk down Central Park West, past Columbus Circle, and on to the New York restaurant that appealed to the kid in all of us, but that was not to be. Instead, we were driven by my agents, and one stationed himself inside the front door while his female counterpart remained behind the wheel.

"Don't you get tired of having them wait around?" Tom asked.

"Very tired." I gave our orders to our waitress. "Two double hot-fudge sundaes coming up, hold the whipped cream."

"What's been troubling you, son?" I dipped my spoon into a warm puddle of butter-pecan ice cream.

Tom regarded me with a manner that reminded me of Jack. How grown-up my son had become. "It shows, doesn't it?"

"Yes, it does. Let's talk."

"Okay, here goes. I don't mean to lay a guilt trip on you, Mom, but this is the way things look to me. Dad's over there in Afghanistan where there's a war going on, so he's not safe. Criminals are always threatening you." His eyes darted to the agent. "It's getting to me. I don't want to lose either one of you."

My stomach sank to my knees, and I pushed my ice cream away abruptly. I hated it that Jack's and my choices of careers was taking its toll on our children. At least Tom could express his fears. Cathy muzzled hers.

"Do you think you'd like to talk to someone? Professionally?"

"A shrink?"

"Yes, a shrink. It's not like you think. You don't lie on a couch and talk about your potty training. The therapist is much more involved these days and makes helpful suggestions."

"You ever been to one?" he asked.

"No, but I wish I had when I was your age. Or younger."

"What was your problem?" He effectively diverted attention away from himself, which was typical of my caring son.

"I'm not sure," I replied honestly. "I've buried my grief about losing my mother, and that's not healthy. I want better for you. I don't want you carrying baggage around with you for life because of the choices your parents have made."

"Yeah, I'm willing to talk to someone. Half the guys in my dorm are in therapy. There's no stigma, not like in the old days when you were a kid."

"Thanks a lot. How are other things? Do you mind if I ask you a personal question?"

Tom grinned, again looking so much like his father. "Well, you can ask, but I might not answer."

"Fair enough." I hesitated, then asked, "Any special girl in your life?"

My son seemed unfazed. "Actually, I have met someone, but it's a new friendship, and we don't know how it will go."

He laughed. "Too soon to be doing the 'meet my family' bit."

I looked into my son's eyes. I saw trust and decency there. Tom would do the right thing.

"I don't get to talk to you enough," he complained. "I miss Dad."

I squeezed his hand. "Me, too." Tears misted our eyes. "You know you can call me anytime you need to talk, day or night. Sybil always knows where to find me."

"Okay. I will. I haven't wanted to bother you. I know how busy you are."

"You may not realize it now, but you and your sister are the most important things in my life. And Dad."

"And Grandpa," Tom added.

"And Grandpa," I echoed.

OUTSIDE ON Central Park South, pedestrians strolled leisurely, unhurried because the weather was glorious with spring's promise of summer. A family similar to ours—mother, father, girl, boy—zipped into the park on Rollerblades. This was the kind of family life my son yearned for, yet he'd been born to two workaholics, Jack and Ann Kelly. He wanted fun family outings, and I offered him an afternoon with dark-suited FBI agents who watched us like black crows eyeing carrion.

Oh, Jack, why aren't you here when I need you?

THE QUIET OF my sleeping apartment was shattered by the loud clanging of fire alarms out in the hallway. I jumped awake, my heart drilling a hole through my chest. I was fumbling with my robe when a loud pounding hit my door. My family, their faces puffy and wrinkled with sleep, wandered from their rooms, and Dolly barked furiously from the safety of Tom's arms. "What's going on?" everyone asked.

Through the fisheye I identified the two Bureau agents who were keeping vigil in my lobby. I opened the door. The agent named Frank had to shout to make himself heard above the clanging fire alarm. "There's a fire in the building, and we've got to get you to the lobby." Up and down the hall, my neighbors pulled open doors and peered out.

"Is this one for real?" someone called.

"Oh, that alarm's always going off," another person grumbled.

"Wait there," I told the agent. "Let me get my family."

Clad in robes, my father and Ronnie waited behind me at the front door. Tom slept in sweatpants and a tee-shirt; he clung to frightened Dolly. Cathy, too, was outfitted in sweats, her hair wild. I dashed into my bedroom for my purse and keys and started out of the apartment before I realized I was barefoot. I ran back for my slippers.

The stairwell teemed with irate residents, most in disheveled nightclothes. "Not again," they groaned. Some had taken the time to pull on pants or sweats. There was a lot of grousing, but a few people seemed to be sleepwalking. As my agents herded my family down the stairs, they unpleasantly ordered the others to keep their distance, and we were the recipients of hostile stares. Cathy looked mortified to be singled out for attention. She glared at me. I was unpopular with everyone.

My next-door neighbor, a fiftyish tax accountant, complained, "Probably another false alarm."

"Second time this month," Ronnie added.

The lobby was bustling, garrulous voices caroming off marble walls as we waited for the fire department. "Over here. In this corner." One agent motioned, and the two of them seemed to surround us and cut us off from the others.

Elderly people sat on the lobby's banquettes, and

neighbors formed tight knots with those they knew. Everyone complained to the night doorman, as if it was his fault the alarm system might be faulty. The pets in the lobby saved the day, for as the animals sniffed and frolicked, the conversation became friendlier. My tax-accountant neighbor ventured out into the street where he stood looking up at the building. He returned declaring loudly, "I don't see any smoke or flames."

I didn't smell smoke, either.

"This is so stupid," Cathy said bitterly. "I don't want these people seeing me like this. No one will ever speak to me again."

"Don't worry," I said. "We're all in the same boat."

She simply snorted.

The shrill warbling of sirens grew near, ending abruptly as the fire engine pulled up at the curb. First responders in turn-out gear swarmed the lobby and thudded up the stairs two at a time. They scrambled over the building, searching for the point of origin. Someone shut off the alarm, but its echo rang in my ears.

Finally, weariness overcoming dignity, we slumped down to the floor and reclined there, our backs leaning against the walls. Everyone was irritable and wanted to get back to bed, yet we had no choice but to wait.

At last, the fire captain moved to the center of the lobby. "It's okay, folks, you can go back to your apartments. There's no fire here. It was either a false alarm or you've got a faulty system. We'll be investigating both."

People groaned and boarded the two elevators. As we waited our turn, my next-door neighbor approached me. "You've been away, so you don't know. We've had too many of these. The co-op board's got to get the system fixed."

"Then you don't think it was deliberate?"

He frowned and shook his head. "Why would I think such a thing? This is a secure building. Maybe we got a few oddballs for neighbors, but none of the residents would set off a false alarm." He regarded me with jaundiced eyes, probably believing my career in law enforcement had made me paranoid.

We were able to board an elevator on its third run. The agents escorted us back upstairs. I said good-night to my neighbor and approached my door, key in hand. I stopped suddenly and blinked, thinking I was seeing things.

A large white cross had been spray-painted on my black door. At the base of the cross, swirls of red paint represented leaping flames. I reached out a finger. The paint was still wet. My agent whipped out a phone. "We got an incident here at the AG's. I'm gonna need some backup. Send me some techies."

I get the message loud and clear, I thought to myself. *You want me to know you are nearby. That you can get close to me whenever you want. I get it.*

EASTER SUNDAY MORNING dawned beautifully, a perfect day to walk to church. We drove in a car provided by the Bureau with agents who watched Easter paraders as if they had pipe bombs concealed in their bonnets. On Park Avenue we got out and entered St. Bartholomew's, a breathtaking Basilican church with a domed skylight. We took our places in a roped-off pew.

Four hours' sleep was all I'd been allotted for five nights running. For the second time in forty-eight hours, my door had been dusted for fingerprints, and it seemed to be becoming a routine. Agents from the New York office had searched my apartment and the building, but the graffiti artist was long gone. Two spray-paint cans had been found in a basement garbage can. Whoever handled them had been wearing gloves. When I'd left my apartment only moments earlier, a maintenance man was painting my door a fresh glossy black.

With organ music to soothe my nerves, I meditated. This was my father's day, and I wouldn't permit my job or the past few days' events to impinge on his celebration. I couldn't help thinking Sarah Preston must be sitting quietly in a church somewhere in Maryland, thinking of *her* father and missing him. Tomorrow I'd be officially back on my search for Sam's killer. As my father filed into the altar with the other *ordinandi,* I prayed, asking God to grant me wisdom, courage, and kindness.

The presiding bishop opened the service with "Alleluia. Christ is risen." The congregation responded, "The Lord is risen indeed, Alleluia."

Holding hands, Tom, Cathy, and I watched, listened, and participated as the ordination proceeded through The Presentation, The Examination, and The Consecration. At the Celebration of the Eucharist, we, as the new bishop's family, entered the altar to assist with bringing the bread and wine to the table.

I STOOD IN THE RECEPTION LINE with my father at the celebration that followed the service. Daddy, in his element, shook hands and offered advice. I fairly burst with pride.

Then my cell phone vibrated. Recognizing Bill Cavanaugh's number, I knew I had to take the call. I moved away from the celebration, off to a side hallway, my security detail mere steps behind me.

"Ann, I wanted to alert you personally," Bill began.

"What's happened?" I realized I was gritting my teeth.

"There was a demonstration this morning outside Camp David. A large group of men bearing arms. They said they were exercising their Second Amendment rights."

"Were shots fired?" I asked.

"No. None. They wore weapons in full view. Since the guns were not concealed, they weren't breaking any laws. Still, the message was loud and clear."

"Were there threats against the president?"

"These guys were fairly quiet and orderly. They wanted to make a point, and they made it. It was a form of intimidation. The threats have been made all over the Internet and on talk radio. From those uninformed individuals who call themselves the 'birthers' to the tea baggers. They are outraged a black man occupies the White House, and they won't stop until something happens."

"What was the outcome? Are they still there?"

"The marines had the camp secured. There was never any threat to the president. The governor of Maryland called out the National Guard. The Guard dispersed the demonstrators. Get this, the demonstrators say they will sue. That their civil rights have been violated.

"Anyway, the president asked me to assure you he was fine—no harm done—and he sends his best wishes to you and your father."

SADLY, DADDY'S VISIT ENDED, and we drove to LaGuardia with agents in a government car. Cathy and Tom said their good-byes at the apartment, so it was just Daddy and me in the backseat.

"Wish Jack had been with us today," he said.

"Me, too." I squeezed his hand. "I really miss him."

"How often does he call?" Daddy asked.

"Not often. I never know when he'll be able to call because he has no regular schedule. He's imbedded with the troops and travels with them through small villages and in mountains where there is literally no means of communication, except two-way radio. Jack sends a courier to the airport in Kabul with his rolls of film. Someone flies in from New York to collect them, then flies out on the very next flight," I explained.

"I hope for your sake he comes home soon." He patted my hand.

As I said good-bye, I warned, "Don't tire yourself with all the packing, Daddy. Accept help."

TWENTY-THREE

On Monday I was up before the sun and dressed in a suit and low-heeled pumps. My household slept in the dark apartment. I turned on few lights, for I was gifted with excellent night vision.

In the kitchen, the coffee stopped dripping. I filled a mug and carried it back to my room.

Dolly, whose keen little ears heard my movements and who makes it her business to know precisely where each member of her pack is and what we are doing, left Cathy's room to join me in my bedroom. She watched knowingly as I put on my coat. Her black button eyes and her disapproving sniffs at my shoes told me she knew I was leaving and she didn't think much of it.

I kissed her little head and scratched her chin, her favorite thing. "Good-bye, girl. I'll be back on Thursday. Look after my brood."

I planned to work a short week, to fly back to New York on Wednesday evening, to declare Thursday and Friday vacation days, and spend a long weekend with my children before they returned to school, amusing ourselves in the city with entertainments of their choosing. Those were my plans, but in this job, the best-laid plans most often went awry.

Lauren Colby met me at Andrews, and I was glad to see her.

"What have you done to yourself, General Kelly? You look marvelous."

I smiled. "Oh, I just had my hair done. Did you have a nice Easter weekend?" We hurried across the airfield to the waiting car.

"Super." She looked radiant. "I went camping on the Blue Ridge Parkway with a friend."

Colby was always doing physical things like camping, hiking, rowing. I wondered who her friend was but didn't ask. If she wanted me to know, she'd tell me or bring him by. Or her. I knew little about her personal life. In her security-clearance file, a personal life seemed almost non-existent. Unlike Brad Moore, who gave us a daily report on his kids' development, Colby remained circumspect and seemed to live for work, her physical-fitness regimen, and her classes in the Master's program at Washington University.

I stopped at the office long enough to check in with Sybil and collect my messages. I had not put in a normal business day since Wednesday. My staff was in the process of constructing DOJ's annual strategic plan, and I needed to be there to guide them. Paperwork had accumulated, and documents awaited my signature. I scrawled it blindly on the papers Sybil put before me, trusting her to not let me sign anything I shouldn't. She knew the bureaucratic side of my job better than I did.

"You look rested," she commented.

"A little time with my family does wonders for me." *And a little sleep,* I thought. I'd finally gotten my quota of eight hours last night.

Shortly before nine, I left the building with Colby and Moore in tow to cross Pennsylvania Avenue to the Hoover Building in sunshine, eschewing the underground tunnel that connected our two buildings. Easter Monday was quiet, a holiday for many government workers. The day was fine and promised to improve.

"Good morning, General Kelly." I was greeted by guards inside the street-level employee's entrance. The small lobby I entered looked out on a brick courtyard where a fountain splashed merrily in the sun. Park benches and spring-green ivy climbing courtyard walls contributed a bucolic flavor to the building's outdoor atrium. Twenty feet above the benches, a carved bronze inscription had been mounted, its quote attributed to J. Edgar Hoover.

"The most effective weapon against crime is co-operation…the efforts of all law enforcement agencies with the support and understanding of the American people."

That was precisely the tact I had taken with Charleston television viewers. I relied on their cooperation. Perhaps over the weekend, our eight-hundred number had yielded some leads.

I boarded an elevator for the director's office. The building's quadrilateral shape lent itself to errant wanderings. After months of getting lost and being forced to phone for an escort, I had finally learned my way around this labyrinth.

"Good morning, Ann," Bill Cavanaugh greeted, standing. He was alone in his office. "Wow! You look like the girl I met in the NYU dining hall."

"Don't I wish." I was secretly pleased. "Where are the others?"

"On the fifth floor. Waiting for us in SIOC."

SIOC was the acronym for the Strategic Information and Operations Center. It was a secure, impregnable situation room and functioned as a command center from which the Bureau directed major operations. It was the nerve center for the FBI during times of crisis, a twenty-four-hour watch post and information-processing center. The strategies for dealing with the aftermath of the 9/11 attack and subsequent high-level Homeland Security warnings were conducted from here. During the Iraq invasion, the Counterterrorism Section literally took over the specially designed command center.

Bill walked with me down the hall from his office to SIOC's entrance where large red letters warned RESTRICTED ACCESS. A video camera filmed us as a scanner read his thumbprint. The heavy, vault-like door opened automatically with a sucking whoosh. We stepped onto a pale green carpeted, elevated floor. The floor was raised to discourage the concealment of electronic bugs beneath it and to make it accessible to technicians who swept the underside twice every twenty-four hours in their vigilant search for bugs.

I walked into a vast, glass-partitioned space and thought of Merlin's crystal cave. Glass panels as reflective as mirrors divided SIOC into twenty separate work centers. In this place, nothing or no one could be concealed. Everything was out in the open. Everyone working within SIOC was visible to everybody else, voices were muted from one room to the next as lips moved without sound, and agents looked like actors in a silent film.

SIOC's operations were overseen by a duty agent from the largest command room, known as OPS1. Today, the duty agent supervised a team of intelligence research specialists who busily worked sophisticated computer consoles. Muted news broadcasts from foreign capitals beamed down simultaneously from high, wall-mounted monitors. The monitors that fascinated me most were those that transmitted live earth images from Big Brother, law-enforcement's newest surveillance satellites that circled the globe. Although maintaining a fixed orbit, the satellites could be tasked to spy on any given set of coordinates they were fed.

In times of crisis, the DOJ was guaranteed secure communications from OPS1 to the White House Situation Room. We could speak to Central Intelligence Agency directors in their headquarters at Langley with confidence our conversations wouldn't be overheard. Our network was linked to select military installations.

I passed a second, similar command room, OPS2, and a control room/engineering hub that housed the high-tech equipment that ran the center. The atmosphere was one of bunker-like isolation with no outside windows to distract us.

We headed for the conference room. Through invisible walls, I saw Ed Cross, Vernon Young, Guy Johnson, and another man I didn't know seated at a long table, engaged in conversation. Clocks set to various time zones covered the walls, and large-screen monitors could replicate transmissions from OPS1.

"Ann."

"General Kelly."

"Don't get up," I said as they started to rise.

I took my place at the head of the table.

"Morning, all. Guy, I'm glad to see you made it."

"I've brought good news."

"Well, let's hear it."

In here, anything could be said. Electronic emissions couldn't leave or penetrate the shielded room. This was one place where it was secure to discuss top secret material and information so new it hadn't yet been classified.

"Before we begin, who's our guest?"

Bill said, "Ann, this is Special Agent Hank Rava-nell."

I smiled. So that's who he was. "We haven't had the pleasure, but I do know you by reputation, Agent Rava-néll. I'm pleased to see you here, because we can use all the help we can get." I stretched my hand across the table and shook his enthusiastically.

Guy said, "Your trip to Charleston was not time wasted, General. Remember that old lady, Mattie Long?"

"Yes, of course."

"Remember she spoke of her nephew? Turns out he did see something, and with her encouragement, he met with me. The day before the fire—that would be Tues-day of last week—he saw a pickup truck driving slowly through the neighborhood, kind of cruising, as if the driver was looking things over. The driver and his pas-senger were white males. That's what attracted the boy's attention. The truck was a late-model Ford, dark green, and, guess what, the license plate was covered with mud. What the boy remembers in particular is there was a Confederate flag hanging in the rear window."

"They must have felt very sure of themselves to drive around a black neighborhood with that flag," Ed com-mented. "Or else they've got a death wish."

"How are you proceeding?" I asked.

"I've got NCIC searching the registrations of all Ford pickups reported stolen in South Carolina during the past two years." Guy referred to the National Crime Information Center where computer databases main-tained an inventory of stolen property, fugitives, and missing persons.

"I've pulled agents off other assignments and have

them canvassing Ford dealerships. We're also searching the state's vehicle registrations."

"Well, we've got the lead we've been hoping for, and
something good will come of it," I said, as much to re-
assure myself as the others.

To Ravanell I said, "I've heard about your pioneer-
ing work in the early seventies."

Hank Ravanell and his work in profiling were fa-
mous within law-enforcement circles. Ravanell was
a man of about seventy with white hair, a broad nose,
large ears, and mournful eyes. Perhaps eyes acquired
that forlorn cast after they had peered into the hearts of
serial killers like David Berkowitz and Jeffrey Dahmer,
as Ravanell's had. Forty years ago when profiling in the
Bureau got started, Ravanell had no models to work
from. He and his associates set about developing de-
finitive models to use in profiling assassins and serial
killers.

Ravanell, at that time a young agent with a background in psychology and physical-evidence collection,
developed a fifty-seven-page questionnaire, which he
used when conducting interviews with convicted mass
murderers like Richard Speck and assassins like Sirhan
B. Sirhan and James Earl Ray.

"I'm certainly not the first to use the tool of criminal profiling to assist in investigations," he said mod-
estly. "The earliest was that greatest of all detectives,
Sherlock Holmes. Or rather, I should say, his creator,
Sir Arthur Conan Doyle."

"First or not, your work is fascinating and a boon to
law enforcement."

Indeed, the Criminal Investigative Analysis Program was now considered the sexiest arena within the
National Center for the Analysis of Violent Crime,

and Ravanell was one of the Training Center's top instructors.

"Thank you, ma'am. Bill faxed me the Claiborne file and the church-arson files on Friday, and I've worked on them over the weekend. I had help from some of the best profilers at CIAP. We've reached certain conclusions."

I said, "We're anxious to have you shed some light on the type of criminals we're looking for."

Ravanell opened a leather folder and consulted carefully prepared notes.

"Let's take the case of Senator Claiborne's murder first. In a sense, it's an assassination, as Senator Robert Kennedy's shooting was an assassination.

"This is what I can tell you about the perpetrator. We can rule out schizophrenes and psychopaths. This crime was committed by what we call an 'organized personality,' that is versus a 'disorganized personality.'"

"I am familiar with those terms, but I'd like to hear their definitions from the expert. Tell me the differences."

"A disorganized personality is a person of average or below-average intelligence, socially and sexually immature, and there may be a history of psychological disorders. His work is sloppy, unplanned, and the crime scene will show what look like random acts of violence, although this individual often knows his victim.

"The organized personality, on the other hand, is someone of above-average intelligence, cunning, socially mature, and sexually functional. He may be married or involved in a committed relationship, and to all outward appearances, he leads a normal life. He may even be a respected member of the community."

"That is a frightening concept," I said.

"It also makes our job much more difficult," Bill observed.

"This is a composite of the type of individual you should be looking for. White male, age thirty-five to fifty, about six feet tall, intelligent and probably educated, highly motivated, religious or has been trained in religion either formally or informally, and is probably married with a family. His hobbies are hunting or rock climbing and outdoor activities."

He returned the clipped report to his portfolio as five pairs of eyes regarded him with astonishment.

"How in the world did you come up with all that?" asked Ed, whose Criminal Division had a history of harboring skepticism for the work of profilers.

"Maybe you'd better lead us through this description item by item," Bill suggested.

Guy and Vernon looked on, as intrigued as I. Yet I knew from experience those in law enforcement who disregarded the profiler's guidelines did so to their own detriment.

"Be happy to." Ravanell seemed not to take offense, apparently accustomed to skeptical attitudes.

"Okay, first item, white male. Our research shows most often the organized-personality-type criminal is a white male.

"Second, age. Your crime-scene report indicated the assailant entered through a second-floor bedroom window by scaling a tall tree. Anyone over fifty would probably not do that. I'm not saying it's impossible, just not probable."

"Well, if you've based the age on the ability to climb trees, why not a younger guy?" Ed asked.

"I'll get to that," Ravanell said affably. "The highly organized methodology of the crime, the way the scene was manipulated, indicates a mature, patient individual. Most males under thirty-five are hurried in their tasks. Again, gentlemen…General Kelly…profiles are not written in concrete. They are guidelines, but usually accurate guidelines. This is not a perfect science. Not yet."

"I must admit I'm intrigued by your theory of the manipulation of the crime-scene setting. I was there shortly after the body was discovered. I saw what you're referring to."

"I heard you were there, General Kelly, and you were instrumental in getting the investigation into the Bureau's hands," Ravanell replied.

"What I saw looked staged. The rooms were neat, too neat, nothing out of place. Senator Claiborne was dressed in his military uniform as if costumed. The Bible was marked at significant passages. To me, it seemed like a stage had been set. The killer was very much in control."

"Good point. Control is crucial to these organized types. They are control freaks. When we find this killer, we'll find a man who lives a structured life, lives in a neat house, has obedient children, is rarely absent from work, that sort of thing."

Ed snickered. "In other words, he's anal-retentive."

Ravanell replied coolly, apparently not letting Ed get under his skin. "I wouldn't characterize 'organized personality' that simply. Extreme anal-personality disorder will lead to compulsive-obsessive behavior—not murder."

"How can you predict his height?" Vernon asked.

"There were scuff marks on the tree he climbed. Judging by the distance between scuff marks, he has long legs, which suggests he is above average in height."

"Because he climbed a big tree with ease, you think he might spend his time outdoors, climbing or hunting. Deer hunters often climb into trees to watch for their prey. You know," Guy said, turning to the rest of us, "this is fascinating stuff."

"You're right on both counts." Ravanell grinned. "Then there's the fingerprint report that indicated the perp's fingers showed a type of scarring associated with a firearms accident. That, too, suggests an outdoorsman."

"The methodical way the crime was planned and carried out indicates we are dealing with an intelligent and motivated individual." I remembered I suggested the killer had watched Sam's house that night, had waited until we left, had known how to get inside and what he would do once he was there.

Ravanell continued, "The biblical references indicate someone who is biblically literate. Those are obscure passages, so this person knows his Old Testament well."

"Are you saying this guy could be a minister?" Vernon seemed shocked.

"Might be. Or a layperson engaged in religious activities, say a Sunday School teacher or deacon of his church. Yes, that is precisely what I'm suggesting," Ravanell replied.

"What's the status on interviewing Sam's dinner guests?" I asked.

"All have alibis," Ed answered. "Those people went home to spouses and families and were in bed asleep at the time of the killing. All are accounted for. Besides, what would their motive be?"

Bill spread his hands wide, then brought them together in a sharp clap. "What would anyone's motive be? Claiborne was so popular that, had he lived, he might have one day run for president."

"Maybe that was the motive. Maybe someone wanted to eliminate him as a contender."

"Now you're suggesting a political assassination."

Ed shook his head. "It was probably the gun freaks. Those NRA types. It amazes me how those guys can sucker folks into paying membership dues. All they care about is selling guns. If the gun industry wasn't earning profits of four billion a year, the NRA wouldn't give two hoots about anyone's Second Amendment rights."

"So where does this leave us?" I asked.

"Say," Ed interjected abruptly, "wasn't there some scandal a few years back involving the senator?"

"Scandal? Sam Claiborne?" I was incredulous. The two were incongruous.

"Well, not a scandal, but a trumped-up charge. Don't you remember the reports that got published in some of the syndicated small-town papers? The *Post* and the *Times* were too careful to fall for that rubbish, but a lot of the syndicates pick up and print from the wire services without checking. The story was that when Claiborne was still a general he was involved in a Gulf War syndrome cover-up. They claimed he knew the troops had been exposed to poison gases and lied about it."

"I do remember that." I reminded myself that for all of Edgar Cross' irritating ways, it was his quick wit that made him such a useful member of the Department and in brainstorming sessions such as these.

"I remember that, too," Bill declared, "although I'd forgotten about it. An investigative reporter for the *Post* who was trying to verify the charges discovered someone at the NRA had planted the stories and there was no truth to them."

"Maybe someone believed those stories," Ed suggested. "Maybe this guy never saw the retractions.
Maybe we got some poor slob, miserable with the
Gulf War disease, and he's out there and intent on
getting revenge."

TWENTY-FOUR

"LET'S REVIEW THE MURDER of South Carolina representative Daniel Rosen," I said.

Coffee cups littered the table. Cold air, required to cool the Center's equipment, blew from overhead vents. The combination of caffeine and low temperatures kept us going.

It was disconcerting to be sitting in this glass room, as if we were on a stage, and catch stares from curious technicians and agents as the morning progressed. Something important must be coming down, they'd say knowingly to one another, to get top directors and the AG in one meeting together.

Ed Cross, who as the head of DOJ's Criminal Division had ultimate responsibility for enforcement, opened the Rosen file and led off. "These are the findings of the forensic pathologists at Quantico. Incidentally, Rosen's body was released to his wife for burial this morning. She says their religion requires her to bury him right away, and Rosen has been dead already for…" Ed paused to consult the autopsy report. "Six days.

"As you already know, death was by gunshot to the head." He looked up to see our reactions. "The twenty-two-caliber hollow-point blossomed like a flower inside his skull, and then it boomeranged around causing a God-awful mess."

"All right." I was exasperated. "Tone down the rhetoric. How do they know for certain Rosen was already dead when the fire was started?"

"Because the docs say his lungs were clean. He wasn't breathing during the fire, ergo he inhaled no smoke or fumes." Ed looked pleased with himself.

"Have you discovered any connection between Rosen and the Mt. Zion Baptist Church?" I asked.

"None whatsoever. Rosen was a member of The Temple, a progressive synagogue, kind of like the way Unitarians are to Protestants," Ed reported irreverently.

Guy Johnson commented, "We've questioned Reverend Zeke Bell, and he says Rosen had never set foot inside his church. Bell didn't even know who Rosen was. A white man would surely have been noticed."

I asked, "Was the church set on fire in order to dispose of the body?"

"I don't think so," Vernon Young answered. "I've come to the conclusion Rosen's murder and the arsons were driven by the same motivation—bigotry and hatred. The fire was just a convenient dump site. We think the kill site was Rosen's car, which is still missing."

"Someone got to him while he was driving his car?"

"Yes, we think he was intercepted as he drove to the airport on Tuesday morning. He never made the flight that was to bring him here to D.C."

"Maybe someone nabbed him in the airport parking lot," Ed theorized. "Those places are so spread out. Say you've got a van following you, looking for a parking space, same as you. You wouldn't be suspicious. When Rosen gets out of his car, the van pulls up and someone grabs him."

"Guy, did you find anything in Rosen's personal

life to indicate his killer might be a family member or an associate?"

Guy shook his head. "We've questioned his family and friends, but haven't yet met with other state representatives. The state legislature is in recess. So far, everyone says he was the ideal husband and father, the good friend. Everyone we've talked to feels the same. He was a likeable guy.

"He only recently made enemies when he started promoting gay-and-lesbian rights and when he allowed state art funds to be used for that play. I've got a team of agents pursuing that trail."

"Vernon, what progress are we making with these church arsons? Bring me up to date on where we stand."

Vernon raised his left eyebrow thoughtfully. "We're making progress. Ever since the grant money came through to pay for patrols outside selected churches, the number of fires has decreased. That's the good news."

He rested his elbows on the table and leaned forward, gesturing with open palms. "Here's the bad. Wimbish and I got together over the weekend to brainstorm what we've been finding. It looks like we've got two sets of fires. We've got about a dozen fires from last year that were spread from as far west as Oklahoma to Richmond in the east. Those fires appear not to be related to each other nor to the ones we've been experiencing recently. Some, we've learned, were the result of accidents. In other cases, we've had crazies acting independently and for bizarre reasons. In Alabama we've had a rash of arsons attributable to one KKK cell, and we're making progress with our prosecution.

"There wasn't any real pattern among the church fires until about November–December. Then we started to see a different twist. In the last six months, we've

seen a cluster of arsons throughout Georgia, North and
South Carolina, Virginia, and Tennessee. All with iden-
tical signature patterns."

"Tell me about those signature patterns." I was
pleased with Vernon and what the NCATF was accom-
plishing.

"Okay, first there's the time factor. All the fires in
question were ignited anywhere from about midnight
to two A.M., whereas earlier fires were started at no
particular time—during the night, some at dawn, a couple even midday.

"A review of accelerants used in all the fires shows
the unrelated arsons were set with a variety of accelerants—gasoline, paint thinner, even charcoal. Whereas
each of the fires in this targeted area were accelerated
by kerosene—kerosene in great quantities. The foundations were literally soaked with kerosene. So were
the insides of the churches. That is another point of
departure. In earlier cases, there were few attempts at
break-ins to start the fires from inside the sanctuaries."

I turned to Ravanell. "What conclusions have you
drawn about the church arsonists?"

"I didn't personally review the arson files. I worked
with a group at ABIS, and they prepared case matrices
and then compared the data with the unsolved church
fires. Let me summarize what they found." He pulled
another sheaf of papers from his portfolio.

"They concluded there was a good possibility the
fires were masterminded but not ignited by the same
individual. Although the methodology in setting the
fires was the same, there were inconsistencies in the
execution of the plan, as though different individuals
were doing the grunt work."

"Explain what you mean."

"We have examples where kerosene was splashed high on outside walls, as though the can was being swung and waved about wildly. Then we've got other cases where the kerosene was poured in a straight, even line, like by a real meticulous kind of person."

"You can tell this...how?"

"By the burn pattern. The scarring of the wood is deeper where the accelerant has soaked in, and where kerosene is spread on the ground the earth is routed."

"Go on."

"I'd say you've got a master arsonist working somewhere out of northeastern South Carolina, and like the Claiborne perp, this is a highly organized and disciplined individual."

"Tell me why you say he's disciplined."

"Because, although he has the means to set as many fires as he wants, he doesn't rush. He doesn't go out and torch a couple of churches a night or over a weekend. He spaces them out, like he's waiting for some of the horror, and maybe the publicity, to subside before torching the next."

"Do you have a profile of this mastermind?"

"That wasn't possible. He's not the one actually striking the match, so to speak, so we don't have telltale scuff marks on tree limbs to indicate height, that sort of thing. We can say with certainty he is white, he is mature, and he possesses leadership qualities. He's able to sit back and plan, then order others to carry out his assignments."

"So this is a group?"

"Yes, ma'am, a well-organized group."

"I notice you've automatically assumed the perpetrator is a male."

"That's right. Our research shows women abhor

crimes like these, although there was one isolated case where a young female set fire to a synagogue, but she turned out to be a clinically disturbed adolescent."

God bless the women of the world, I thought. *How much worse would it be without us?*

"I do have a suggestion for you."

"Please. Be my guest."

"These 'organized personality' types are supreme egotists. Typically, they love to relive their triumphs. They get off on thinking they've put one over on law enforcement. These are the kind of guys who love to hang around where cops congregate so they can hear their exploits being described. We've had luck luring serial killers to gravesides where we've had microphones and cameras hidden and agents staked out. Usually, they'll make a full confession to the buried victim, discussing in detail what they'd done to him or her, sometimes even blaming the victim, like 'See what you made me do.'

"This strategy has worked with arsonists as well. I'd suggest you plant an article in a newspaper, something about how this is the six-month anniversary of the burning of Church X. Print a bright color picture of the blazing church. He'll really get off on that. It's almost as good as the real thing. Then have the place watched and see who turns up. It's hard for these guys to resist. They're drawn to relive their crimes. With them, it's a high. The truth is, they're often so clever, sometimes this is the only way we can apprehend them."

"That's an excellent suggestion, Hank. Vernon, I'd like to see this plan put in motion. Select a church in a good-sized town and a newspaper with wide distribution. See if you can get *USA TODAY* to run a piece. We don't want him missing the plant."

I turned to the topic that was most troubling to me

personally. "Guy, I don't suppose you have any leads on the man who tried to abduct me and the one who entered my hotel room?"

Guy hunched his shoulders defensively, a pained expression on his face. "No, we don't have a trace. The state car he stole was wiped clean. It looked like he took a bottle of spray cleaner and washed down the inside. There was so much dust and dirt on the outside, prints were obliterated. I'm sorry. I feel personally responsible."

"Well, you're not."

"It happened on my watch and on my turf."

"That kind of mindset is self-defeating and will rob you of objectivity. I need you to be clearheaded. Except for a false alarm in my building, there've been no further attempts to get at me. Thank God, so far, there've been no leaks to the press. I don't want my children worried, and Jack has enough on his mind just looking out for himself.

"What about the man in the coma? Is he awake yet?"

"No, and I check in with his doc every day. He's mending just fine from his wounds, and the neurologist thinks he'll wake up soon. We have an agent posted at his private room door."

"I'll tell Agent Moore. He'll be relieved."

I studied the men who worked for me. We'd been at this for hours without breaks or lunch, and we were all feeling the strain of failure. Bill Cavanaugh was thoughtfully quiet, but knowing him as I did, his brain was busily sorting and analyzing data like the most sophisticated computer. Vernon Young and Guy Johnson worked well together, and I could count on them to return to South Carolina and set in motion our plan to lure our arsonist to the scene of the crime. Hank Ravanell was a prize, and I was glad to have his help.

Only Edgar Cross appeared unfazed. Ed was an enigma, a career prosecutor with a brilliant record who hid behind a crass facade. I wondered if anyone had ever seen the real Edgar Cross.

As though he'd been reading my mind, Ed grinned wickedly. "Just for the hell of it, I ran Rakes' prints."

"Captain Rakes of Metro P.D.?" I was puzzled.

"The suspended Captain Rakes, whose ass is in hot water." Ed sounded gleeful. "Yeah, the guy really pissed me off."

"I hope I never get on your bad side," I said lightly.

"Not a chance. Not a chance. Anyway, I thought I'd take a look and see if Rakes had any burn scars on his fingers."

"Did he?" I knew full well what the answer would be.

"Naw. It didn't hurt to look." Ed confused me by smiling conspiratorially at Guy. "We've been saving the best for last."

"You do have something!"

"Yeah, we do. We got a match on the scarred print. The reason it took so long was when IAFIS turned up nothing, we ran it through the states' automated fingerprint systems. Now, we're not sure where this takes us, but I'll let Johnson tell you about it. It happened on his watch, as he likes to say." Ed's rhetoric rarely reflected his true feelings for he beamed proudly at the young SAC.

Guy, for his part, was chomping at the bit. "I told you last week we had an undercover agent cozying up to POSSE. Well, let me tell you how this all came about. We'd been hearing rumors of an organized paramilitary group, and when the opportunity came to get close, we grabbed it. Fellow in Myrtle Beach who owns an indoor gun range and gun shop decided it was time to retire. He was getting broken into every time he turned around, and his insurance rates were skyrocketing.

"Well, we got the Bureau to put up the money to lease the shop from him. He introduces our undercover agent to his steady customers as his wife's brother from Dallas who's going to run the shop for him for a while so he and the wife can do some traveling. Our agent calls himself Bud Starr. That's not his real name, but he won't let us call him anything else for fear of a slip-up. He's a likeable fellow, a man's man, and fits right in. He managed to get a rumor going he'd done time— nothing major, just a foul-up with the law—and if it wasn't for his sister's husband giving him this chance, off the books, he'd never get anything. So he's been able to get cozy with a lot of gun enthusiasts in the area."

"This is really good work," I commented.

"It gets better. AAG Cross said he had a match on the scarred thumbprint. Guess where it turned up?" He grinned like a small boy.

It took me a second to put it together. "The robberies at the gun shop."

"Absolutely, ma'am. How's that for good luck? Starr got word to us he's got something to report. We're meeting him at a safe house in North Myrtle Beach tomorrow. I was wondering if you'd like to be there."

Would I? "Wild horses couldn't keep me away!"

TWENTY-FIVE

BILL ESCORTED ME to Kimberly Riley's office. Riley was
one of the Bureau's artists, about twenty-five, quick,
bright, and talented. As I described the man who had
attempted to abduct me, she recorded the data into her
computer program. In no time, the image on her monitor
began to resemble the face of the bogus state trooper.

"Make the cheekbones a little sharper. Put hollows
under them."

She moved her mouse and a window appeared on the
screen. Highlighting her choices, she tapped the mouse,
and instantly the face took on a gaunt appearance.

"That's it," I cried. "That's him."

"Let's print it." The printer on her desk clicked and
whirred and spat out a black-and-white portrait of the
man who had tried to kidnap me on Thursday.

I held his likeness in my hand. It was uncanny. I
looked into that face and relived the panic I'd experienced as I struggled to get away from him. There were
the Mountie hat and oval sunglasses, the aquiline nose,
the long jaw, the high cheekbones, the full lips. Again
I was struck by a sense of familiarity; although, I was
positive I'd never seen this man before last Thursday.

I swallowed hard. "I'll keep this. Do you mind making another copy and walking it up to Mr. Cross' office?"

"I'll be glad to. Right away. What'd this guy do?"

"I'd rather not say. Thanks for your help, Kimberly."

"Anytime, General Kelly."

HALLE BURDEN WAS waiting at a corner table when I arrived at the Bistro Francais on M Street NW in the heart of Georgetown. There was a noisy café on one side of the restaurant, but Halle had chosen the quiet, formal dining room for our meal.

Halle had worked for Sam since he was elected to the Senate, and she'd been very close to him.

"How are you getting along?" I slid into my seat.

She shrugged. "Okay, I guess."

"How's Sarah?"

"Like you'd expect. She's distraught. She has no family left, except for her in-laws."

"It must be rough," I commented.

The waiter approached our table.

Halle ignored him. "Very. It's up to her friends to see her through. She likes you. I hope you'll call her."

I didn't need to consult my menu. Bistro Francais was a favorite restaurant of mine, and regulars knew the best item on the menu was the Minute Steak—grilled sirloin steak with herb butter, served with French fries. With the way I skipped meals, I could afford the calories.

"Of course I'll call her." I moved my fork and knife around.

Glancing up at the waiter, Halle said, "Bring me the Salmon Croquette."

"Have you examined the wine list?" he asked.

"None for me, thanks. Water's fine. Halle, you feel free to order a bottle if you wish."

"I'll have one glass. Make it a white burgundy."

As soon as he departed, she said quietly, "I've got Sam's computer. It's locked in the trunk of my car."

"We'll make the transfer after lunch. I'll have my agent take it to the best computer technician in the

Bureau. Deleted e-mails are his specialty. If there were any threats sent by e-mail, he'll find them. Then it's just a matter of tracing the Internet protocol address. Cross your fingers they weren't sent from an Internet café, because then we'll have zero.

"Ah, here's lunch. Let's enjoy ourselves, shall we?"

Halle gave me the first smile I'd seen from her face in a long time.

IT HAS ALWAYS bothered me as I dined in fine restaurants that my driver and agents were sitting outside in the car, hungry yet unable to eat their dinners until they took me home. When we pulled up in front of my house, I invited them in. Sam's computer was safely carried by Lauren Colby.

"I've eaten. Now you shall, too. Carlos, I've got a freezer full of your mother's wonderful Cuban casseroles. Come on in and we'll micro zap one. Or all."

"I never turn down food. Just let me call my wife." Moore reached in his pocket for his cell phone.

"Is there anyone you need to call, Lauren?" I asked. "You can use the phone inside if you wish."

We got out of the car, and I unlocked the front door and reset the alarm. I turned on lights, and we walked through to the kitchen, which, in my furnished, rented house, was the coziest room. I pulled a casserole at random out of the freezer and set the microwave oven on Defrost. Colby uncorked a bottle of Biltmore Estates Merlot. We settled at the kitchen table. Any one of these three people would take a bullet for me. I hoped it never happened. I suddenly realized how close we'd become. They were like family to me.

"This is a good idea," I said. "We ought to do it more often."

Colby filled our glasses. She'd been quiet, as if weighing some decision. "Actually, I've got some news we can drink to."

We looked at her expectantly, for Colby was always circumspect. She smiled shyly. "I'm getting married."

"Lauren!" I exclaimed. "That's wonderful."

"Who is he?" Moore asked.

Carlos said with mock severity, "He'd better be good to you, or he'll have me to answer to."

"His name is Tom. Same as your son's. He's one of my professors at Georgetown. He's twelve years older than me so we're anxious to start a family."

Moore said, "You're not leaving the Bureau, are you?"

"No. Of course not," Colby replied.

I wrapped my arms around her. "I hope your marriage will be as good as mine."

TWENTY-SIX

THE BEACHES AT Cherry Grove were broad. From its solitary location on a point of jutting land, the safe house commanded magnificent views of the Intracoastal Waterway on its front side. The back of the house, bowed like the prow of a ship, had sliding glass doors that overlooked a V-shaped deck, a broad expanse of sand, and the surging Atlantic. There was something almost mystical about the rain that splattered on the ocean. I expected to see the mast of some long-lost pirate ship come sailing through the mist.

The beach was deserted, rain pooling in walkers' tracks and rare tire ruts. The beaches were patrolled by jeep, and trucks drove onto the sand to collect garbage. As I stood before the glass doors, I saw a small black-and-white skunk brave the rain to scavenge for food. He scampered into garbage cans, finally coming up with some prize morsel that was partially wrapped in white paper. With lunch between his jaws, he disappeared under the boardwalk.

This was the wettest spring I remembered, and rain had dogged my flight from Andrews to the runways at Myrtle Beach Air Force Base. Guy Johnson had met my plane. He was starting to feel like an old friend.

I turned back into the room. The house felt wonderfully secluded, and for a moment, I wished I'd come here alone and for another purpose. I would build a fire in the massive stone fireplace that divided the living room from the dining area. I would brew spicy tea in the kitchen, and its aroma would fill the downstairs rooms. I would settle into a large, comfortable chair and open to the first page of a thick, intriguing novel, some old classic I was sure would not disappoint, like *Rebecca* or *Wuthering Heights*.

Later, as I was dressing to go out to one of the local seafood restaurants that lined the Grand Strand, I'd search through the library of compact discs that were shelved in the entertainment center. I'd find a reprise of Billie Holiday in concert, or Lena Horne, or Ella Fitzgerald, or maybe all three of those wonderful female vocalists together on one recording. I'd have a pre-dinner cocktail and listen to mellow, old blues tunes like "I'll Never Be the Same," "All My Life," and "Prisoner of Love."

Jack and I had fallen in love to those tunes on our first dates at the Algonquin's Oak Room and Café Carlyle. Reminded of him, I rewrote my fantasy to include his arrival in time to take me to dinner. We'd be relaxed and carefree. He'd have forgotten the horror of photographing U.S. all-terrain vehicles being blown up by roadside improvised explosive devices in Afghanistan. I wouldn't be tracking miscreants who burned houses of worship for kicks. When we went to sleep, side by side, I wouldn't dream of a friend's murder.

Guy Johnson brought me a mug of coffee. He had been in the kitchen brewing it while I was constructing my new life as a beach bum.

"Isn't this place something?" He gazed up at a vaulted ceiling that peaked twenty feet over our heads. Stairs to the second floor were hidden behind a wall, and a catwalk connected all of the upstairs bedrooms.

"Who does it belong to?" I asked.

"It's the vacation house of one of President Monroe's supporters. He's good about letting us use it this way. I'd love to be able to bring my wife and kids here, but, of course, that's out of the question."

"Has there been any change in the status of the man in the coma?" I asked.

"His doctor reports the swelling around his brain is improving and he should wake soon."

"Good, then maybe we'll find out who he is and who he works for."

"His fingerprints weren't on file. That means no arrests, and he wasn't in the military." Guy glanced at his watch. "Starr should be here any minute."

"How did he come up with a name like Bud Starr?" I wanted to know.

Guy shrugged. "Who knows? He's a bit of a character, as you'll see. Don't let his flamboyant style fool you. He's every bit as competent as the buttoned-up types."

At that moment there was a tap on the glass behind me, and I jumped, startled to see a man standing on the deck in the rain. Bud Starr was a cautious man. He had come in from the beach side.

Guy slid the door open. The smell of wet sand and salt air rolled in. "You're soaked. Get in here, man."

Bud Starr was drenched. His long, ponytailed hair was plastered against his skull. He wore a tan buckskin jacket with fringed sleeves that dripped rain. He was big and muscular and the closest thing to Steven Seagal I'd ever seen outside the movies.

His style was flamboyant, yet I wasn't put off. In fact, I felt a warmth toward him I couldn't explain. We introduced ourselves and shook hands.

Guy produced a towel, and Starr wiped his face and patted his hair. "I'm all right. A little rain won't hurt me."

"Get out of that wet jacket." When he had removed it, I carried it into the kitchen and draped it over the back of a kitchen chair. Water dripped onto the vinyl floor.

When I returned to the living room, there was my dream fire in the fireplace. The logs were gas, and Guy Johnson had turned them on. Bud Starr sat in a chair near the fire, rubbing his hands. He jumped up when he saw me.

"It sure is a pleasure to be working with you, General Kelly." He may well have been from Texas; there was a Southwestern twang to his voice. Or he might have been a master of dialects. I understood what Guy meant when he'd described Agent Starr as a man's man. What Guy didn't realize was Starr was a woman's man as well. There was an ineffable something about him that made you want to trust him, and that quality augured well for his success in infiltrating the militia group.

"Please sit down," I said. "You must be cold. Guy made coffee. Would you like a cup?"

"I'll get it." He moved away into the kitchen. His familiarity with the layout of the house told me this was not the first time he and Guy had rendezvoused here.

We gathered in easy chairs before the hearth. Already the fire was warming the air. Starr's jeans and Western boots were damp, and he stretched his long legs toward the yellow-and-orange flames that licked fake logs.

Gray light filtered through skylights where rain drummed. Lights were doused; we didn't wish to reveal our presence. Although the house was isolated from its neighbors by the contour of the land and the dunes, we were chancing nothing. From a car hidden by a scrub-oak barrier, two well-armed local agents watched the house. Rain pounded the deck, too, making the fire feel all the more cozy.

Guy said, "General Kelly was anxious to meet you and to hear your account of what you've been able to find out about the militia group."

I added, "Guy has told me about your setup at the firing range. Start at the beginning and tell me everything. What do you want me to call you? Bud Starr or your real name?"

"My name is Bud Starr, ma'am. To answer to anything else would be a fatal mistake and, one day, could cost me my life. Just like I grew a ponytail to do this job—" and he flipped up his ponytail with one hand "—I grew Bud Starr's persona. Bud Starr has been around. He's been in prison; he's tough enough to keep those Rambos out at Larry's Indoor Range and Gun Shop in line. Larry is supposed to be my brother-in-law."

I leaned back and sipped coffee. This was going to take time. I was prepared to give him all he needed. Starr, I sensed, was a man who wouldn't be rushed.

"Take this ponytail, for instance. Back in the sixties, it was the style of hippies, and no self-respecting man would be caught dead with long hair like this. Now, for whatever reason, it's the favorite of tough guys in the trades—the carpenters, the electricians." He shrugged his shoulders. "Go figure. I fit in, the way I dress, the way I look, the way I act. I have to walk a fine line. I have to be friendly, yet just a little bit tougher than they are."

"Is it working?" I asked.

"Oh, yes, ma'am. They're still testing me, but I'm gaining their trust."

"How do they test you?"

"Oh, they do things like, one day, they'll ask me a question about my past. Next day, they ask the same question but put a different spin on it to see if they get the same answer. That sort of thing. Like they're trying to catch me in a lie. I don't let them catch me. I'm always in the role, even now, and I never let down my guard."

"Must be a strain," I observed.

"Yes, ma'am. Undercover work destroys marriages. Some agents go bad. Turn to crime. Good or bad, most wind up being divorced by resentful wives who hate their guts. That's why I've never married. Wedded to the job, you might say."

"How long have you been doing undercover work for the Bureau?"

"Too long." He laughed, and I realized he'd been telling the truth when he said he never let down his guard. He wasn't going to let it down with me.

He seemed to realize he was still playing the game and it was not necessary here. "Fifteen years, ma'am. I know you're fairly new to Justice, so maybe you don't know how the Bureau goes about assigning agents to undercover work. They've got every known fact about me stored on a computer up there at headquarters— my physical characteristics, my skills and specialties, my hobbies, the cases I've worked, and so on. So when they're looking for an agent for a particular case, they sort through the computer files and come up with the best match."

"I hope you're the best match for this job." Could I take him down a peg?

Starr's ponytail bobbed as he nodded. "Oh, I am.

The best undercover agents are extroverts, like me, because we're comfortable around people and don't need downtime to get our heads back together like introverts do. You've got to be smart, so they check your college grades and your training records. You've got to be creative and able to think fast on your feet. You've got to be daring, ready to take risks, to move at a moment's notice—and not question your instincts.

"Then you're given special training—language and dialects, regional customs, things like how to read body language, how to respond to accusations. For example, suppose one of the regulars at Larry's starts mouthing off to me about how he knows I'm a cop because he's seen me with so and so or at such and such a place. The worst thing I can do is not respond. No, I've got to go after him, yell at him with something like, 'Why, you dirty, low-down son-of-a-bitch; that's a bald-faced lie,' and 'Let's go outside and I'll pound some truth into your ugly face.' Something like that. Go on the offensive."

His eyes, sharp blue, met mine. "Pardon the language, ma'am."

"I've heard worse. What makes you think you're earning their trust?"

"Well, they're starting to talk more freely around me. They're expressing their hatred for blacks and Jews and wondering where I stand. They say things like 'Us whites have got to stick together.' Or 'Wouldn't this be a better place if we could get rid of the niggers and the kikes?' The gays and the lesbians, and everyone else on God's green earth who is not a white supremacist or a skinhead, and don't I agree. The thing that pisses them off the most is an interracial couple. Let one of them see a black man with a white woman, and they're out choosing the tree limb they'll use for the lynching."

"Do you know if any of them has committed murder?"

"Yes, ma'am, I think some have, but I've got no proof. No confessions. I get the feeling what they're doing is on behalf of POSSE, like their leader picks one of them to do such and such job, and the next time, he picks someone else. It would be a shared guilt, if they were capable of feeling guilt. They're all in it together. It's a conspiracy."

"Do you have any idea how large their group is?" I asked.

"From what I hear whispered, it's big. See, the gun shop's got a seating area—chairs, couches, Coke machine. The guys like to hang around and talk. Lots of seasonal workers with time on their hands. Can't pour concrete in weather like this." He motioned to the rain.

"Then there's the after-three crowd, guys whose shifts end at three. They come in to shoot handguns and shoot the bull, if you know what I mean. I overhear a lot. I can be carrying on a conversation at the register and hear what they're saying across the room.

"So this organization rivals the American Knights of the KKK in size and scope. It's got members from as far away as Pennsylvania and Ohio."

"If it's so big, why haven't we heard about it?" Guy asked.

Starr chuckled derisively. "Well, for one thing, they don't have a membership secretary who goes blabbing on the radio giving interviews, like American does. They don't advertise themselves over the Internet, or with handbooks. It's all word of mouth, telephone calls, the mail. They exercise their constitutional right to privacy."

"Then how do they recruit?" I asked.

"It's members recruiting other members. In churches, high schools, the workplace. They get a feel for who is receptive, then test him, just like they're testing me. A lot of the members of the American Knights are also members of POSSE."

"We can subpoena telephone records," Guy said.

Starr spread his hands. "Whose?"

"You haven't learned the identity of the leader yet?" I asked.

"No, ma'am. Sorry, but that's a tough one. They call him 'The Commander.'"

"Yes, Guy told me," I said pensively.

"They're plenty secretive about him. I'm pretty sure he's got a military background. Maybe he really was a commander of troops. I'm sorry; I've got no name for you to run. I asked once if I could meet him, said I might be interested in joining their secret society if it would help us get rid of certain elements."

"And their response?"

"'You don't ask to meet him. You have to be chosen. Joining is by invitation.' Go figure."

"Do you have any idea where they meet?" Guy Johnson asked.

Starr smirked. "I know exactly where they meet. They've got a camp. That's what I came to tell you."

"For God's sake, why didn't you say so?"

Starr's smile was sly. "I was enjoying my conversation with General Kelly. Okay, let me explain how this came about. We've got lockers so when the shooters go onto the range, they can lock their jackets and personal stuff, like weapons, in a locker. I've got a master key. When I can, I go though their stuff. In someone's jacket pocket, I found a hand-drawn map. I took it to the copy machine in the office and made a copy. Put it back before anyone was the wiser."

Starr's dark hair was drying to a warm chestnut. I had to keep reminding myself this man was an agent. To me he seemed like just what he represented himself to be, a man who sold weapons to wild ponies like himself. He had an almost seductive way about him, and I wondered how far we could really trust him.

I was startled when he threw back his head and laughed, as if my thoughts were transparent, but he was referring to the directions to the camp. "The paper was actually labeled 'The Camp.' You'd think they'd know better. Good thing this so-called Commander doesn't know he's got guys so dumb they have to write down the way to his hidey-hole.

"So one dark night, I took a drive out there and did some looking around. I couldn't penetrate, couldn't even get close. I was stopped by a sentry and warned, in no uncertain terms, to stay away. He was armed with an assault weapon. That's how I know for sure this is the place."

Guy voiced his concern for Starr's safety. "I hope you used fake plates."

"I know better than that. I put the phony North Carolina plates on my truck before I went."

I asked, "Where is this place?"

"I'll show you. Let me get a map." He set his coffee mug on the hearth and got up and went into the kitchen where he retrieved a map from his jacket. He'd also found an ashtray and brought it back and lit up a cigarette. I presumed out at Larry's shooting gallery you didn't ask permission to smoke.

The state road map Starr produced was crisply folded like it was new; there were no telltale creases to indicate the section he'd found so interesting. He handed it to me. I unfolded it.

He sat back on his heels beside my chair and pointed. "Here we are, Myrtle Beach." A blunt fingertip touched the paper. Smoke curled up into my face, and I fanned it away.

"Sorry." He flicked the cigarette into the fireplace. "Every time I quit these things, I get assigned to a place where to not smoke is to stand out."

His fingertip skimmed over a red line on the map. "Okay. You take Highway Seventeen up through Wilmington. Then pass Camp Lejeune." He pointed to the marine base in Jacksonville.

The map was in my lap, and it collapsed and folded under the weight of Starr's jabbing finger. I righted and smoothed it.

"Keep going northeast on seventeen toward New Bern. It's about a two-hour drive from here. Now, there—" his finger stopped between two bright green splashes of color on the paper "—is where they've established a compound."

Guy Johnson was on his feet and peering over my shoulder. "They're sandwiched in between Hofmann Forest and Croatan National Forest. Nothing could be more desolate!"

"It's like no-man's-land," Starr affirmed. "Woods everywhere you look. There's a narrow river called the White Oak, and not much else."

"Jones County," I read off the map.

I thought about my father, who was so close by. An hour's drive would put me in Wilmington. He was packing the rectory and his study and preparing for his move to the bishopric in Raleigh. Yet it was for the best no one learned I'd been here, not even Daddy. For Agent Starr's sake, my meeting here in this safe house had to remain secret. Not even Sybil knew where I was. She thought I was in Columbia at Guy's office.

To Starr I said, "I grew up in Wilmington. I know this area well."

"Yes, I know you did," Starr responded.

Everyone knew. My life was an open book.

"I've been to the historic community in New Bern, the Governor's Palace, et cetera, but I've never visited those forests. In fact, until I saw them on the map, I wasn't aware of their existence. I just remember a drive through a vast wooded stretch of country before we reached New Bern. The night you were there, did you see any traffic into the camp, anyone coming or going?"

"Saw nothing, not even a hooty owl. The place was dead. That's why I was so startled when that sentry sprang on me from out of nowhere. He must have been wearing night-vision goggles to find me. The night was so pitch-black, I couldn't see my hand in front of my face."

Guy said, "Night-vision goggles? Those things cost a fortune."

"Don't cost a cent if you steal them," Starr retorted smartly.

"Larry's gun shop has been robbed often," I said. "What was stolen?"

"Handguns, ammo. Larry doesn't keep assault weapons. There've been no break-in's since yours truly has been on the job."

"That could be a coincidence." Guy's face was a blank.

I tapped the map. "Looks like just the place for a meeting of warlocks."

"It's just the kind of place you'd want for a secret camp, especially if you were building up an arsenal," Starr theorized.

Guy suggested, "Why don't I contact the SAC in Charlotte and have him send some North Carolina agents out to keep an eye on the place?"

"I want to talk to Ed Cross before any action is taken," I said.

I looked up in time to see Starr flick a disapproving glance my way. It vanished the moment I saw it. Let him think I was a wimpy bureaucrat who could not make a decision on her own. At this point, I felt the less Agent Starr knew about our strategy, the better, for his sake as well as ours.

Besides, this was not a job for local agents. This was a job for Special Ops.

TWENTY-SEVEN

AT NINE A.M. Wednesday morning, I left the fluted columns and classic grace of DOJ headquarters to enter the harsh ugliness of the Hoover Building. Crossing Pennsylvania Avenue, the sun beat down on my head with promises spring had arrived for good. It was exactly one week since Sam Claiborne's murder.

An enthusiastic group of tourists gathered around a plate-glass window that looked into one of the labs. Interest in the technical side of law enforcement was high among the half-million people who visited the Bureau each year.

In the ground-floor reception area, two-way glass was mounted so security personnel could surreptitiously observe visitors. My picture hung there, alongside portraits of Bill Cavanaugh and President Jefferson Monroe. I avoid looking at them when I could. My official portrait hung all over DOJ headquarters, in courthouses, and in U.S. attorneys' offices. Made me wish I had a different face.

The duty agent buzzed me into SIOC where I found the men tense and moody. Bill Cavanaugh, Edgar Cross, and the duty agent were gathered around sound equipment in OPS1. Screams and shouts and what sounded like a riot issued from the speakers. The men moved aside to make room for me. I raised my eyebrows questioningly as an angry voice shouted over airwaves, "You want an apology! You hear that, brothers?" Roars and jeers. "This nigger wants an apology. Well, here's your apology, nigger. I'm sorry we ever brought you to this country! I'm sorry we took the chains off your legs! I'm sorry we freed your worthless black ass!"

Faintly, in the background, among slurs and boos, singing and chanting could be heard. Bill filled me in. "We're listening to a live audio feed from a public radio station in Winston-Salem. There's an American Knights of the KKK rally in progress. They're showing off their numbers and trying to recruit more."

The threatening tone of the Klan was palpable as jeers and taunts turned into threats of violence. I felt uneasy, although I was hundreds of miles away and safely confined in the Hoover fortress.

Bill said, "The singing you hear in the background is coming from a coalition of interfaith ministers and church people who are confronting the Klan."

"Good for them," I replied. "Has anyone been hurt?"

Ed said, "Let's hope they got enough law enforcement on the scene to prevent that from happening. We got agents on the ground, observing, and a chopper making sweeps, but just to keep an eye on things. We got no jurisdiction to interfere if things get physical. Unless we're invited." His tone reflected his disgust with the situation.

"Well, anyone in his right mind would know what a threat this kind of rally is to public safety. Why on earth did Winston-Salem issue them a parade permit?" I was impatient.

"They've got a new mayor down there who's right of far right. The way I hear it, he practically gave them the keys to the city."

"Even so," Bill said, "the city has no choice but to issue

the permit. Otherwise, it's a violation of constitutional rights. Need I remind you of the right to assemble?"

"It's the right to assemble peacefully, Bill," I argued. "You know they can delay or cancel if it looks like they've got a group that'll get out of control."

Offensive language poured out of the speakers and into our ears. "Good God," I said.

"You'd think with our plunging economy and soaring unemployment rates, people would be feeling compassion for their neighbors and too busy looking for work to instigate this kind of trouble," Bill commented.

"You know what I think?" Ed speculated, "I think those bigots hate themselves. You know, inside, deep down where it counts. That's why they hate everyone else, too."

"Well, there's something I can do about this." I warmed as the blush of anger spread over my neck and ears like a red veil. It was all I could do to control my voice.

I picked up a phone from the console and dialed Lori Netherland's office on Indiana Avenue. Lori was an assistant AG who oversaw the Office of Justice Programs.

"Good morning, Lori. This is Ann."

"Good morning, AG. I bet I know why you're calling," she said somberly.

"Have you heard it, too?"

"Yes. PBS has been broadcasting it live, on and off. They say the townspeople are critical of the mayor for letting this go so far."

"I want to see a list of how much money DOJ is pumping into that town. We have an obligation to the taxpayers to spend their hard-earned money wisely."

"It's done. I thought you'd want that data. I've just been waiting for you to ask. I had a computer printout pulled for you. It's a record of all the grants they've been awarded with the dates they'll come up for renewal."

"Good girl! And thanks." I felt satisfied. Lori and I were on friendly terms and occasionally, when our hectic schedules permitted, met for a quick drink at the Willard. "Call Sybil and get on my schedule when their renewal applications come in, and we'll take a good, hard look."

"It's too bad my computer database doesn't include all their federal grants and contracts. Now, that would be some leverage."

"Don't worry," I replied before disconnecting. "I'll put a bug in the president's ear. He'll turn it over to Adam Kohn-Darby, and we'll soon see a list. Congress is funding one of those multi-million-dollar nutrition centers in Winston-Salem. There should be some red faces up on Capitol Hill when those obscenities get aired over national television. Thanks, Lori."

To Bill I said, "This stuff is turning my stomach. Let's go see what you've got."

"Jeff will make a backup of the tape." Bill gave a go-ahead nod to the duty agent. "I can't wait to show you what we've got for you, Ann."

He led the way through doorways cut in glass, into the conference room. Our high-level meeting was limited to Bill, Ed, and myself. What we were about to see and discuss was top secret, and the fewer people who knew about it the better. One of the things I admired about Bill, and Ed, too, for that matter, was they did not require an army of subordinates at their elbows in order to make the smallest decision.

Grainy black-and-white aerial photographs were

spread across the table. "Big Brother, our spy satellite, took these this morning," Bill said.

I slipped on my readers and bent to peer closely at the details of photos of POSSE's compound. "Hard to believe these were taken from two hundred miles up. Okay, let's see what we've got."

In the first series of photos, the camp itself was not discernible. At that point, the satellite had been approaching the area designated as thirty-five-degrees latitude and seventy-seven-degrees longitude. The Hofmann and Croatan National forests appeared as immense wooded areas that darkened the curvature of the horizon. Then the satellite moved into position directly over the campsite, and the forests became a black border that framed our target. The White Oak River cut through the canopy of trees, a shining silver ribbon unfurling toward the coast. Highway 17 was well-defined, a dissecting line between the forests, intersected by secondary roads that veered off to the west and east.

One secondary road led to the focus of our surveillance. A superimposed white arrow indicated the location. Then the camera lens had zoomed in to capture incredibly clear pictures. The tops of trees were as visibly defined as if one were seeing them from a low-flying airplane, and although tree cover obscured much of the campground, a large clearing opened up. In the middle of the clearing, a large white circle appeared.

"What's that?" I asked. "It's too big for a silo."

"We think it's a tent," Bill replied.

"And these?" I pointed to rectangular, flat-roofed buildings. "They look like those prefab corrugated warehouses. These down here, almost under the trees? Army barracks?"

"We believe that's exactly what they are," he said.

"What do you think they're keeping in those warehouses?"

"An arsenal," Ed interjected. "Probably enough weapons to start a revolution. That's what this is all about, isn't it? Overthrowing the government?"

The lawyer in me wanted proof. "Aren't you assuming too much?"

"Point of fact, we don't know what they're storing in those sheds," Bill said matter-of-factly. "Could be as harmless as farm equipment. We don't have enough evidence for a search warrant. The land is owned by a farmer named Mackie. Pays his taxes, no criminal record, and aside from having some weird ideas, we can't prove he's done anything illegal."

"What about planes and choppers, Bill? Are they flying surveillance?"

"They'd attract too much attention. We don't want the paramilitaries getting the idea we're watching them. We don't want them altering their behavior. If we get lucky, we'll catch them in the act of transferring arms."

Ed pointed to a detail on one of the photographs, running his finger along a clear swath that crossed the Mackie farm. "This is the Progress Energy power corridor. We sent some Special Ops techies out there this morning disguised as PE linemen. There's a string of utility towers that'll be useful for all sorts of possibilities. Their activities shouldn't arouse Mackie's suspicions because the linemen do this regularly. The power company gave us permission, and they'll cover for us should anyone ask. They even have their own service road, so our guys aren't trespassing."

Bill added, "We're sending in a communications

vehicle disguised as a power-company van that's equipped with all sorts of modern wonders."

"What's the strategy?" I asked.

"Well, for starters, they're eyeballing the place through high-powered binocs from cherry pickers. They've already reported back things are quiet, no one around. All those big storage buildings are padlocked."

"I trust they'll do nothing to arouse suspicion."

"Don't worry. These guys are good. They're out there climbing towers and checking lines. Or that's the way it'll look to anyone watching. What they're really doing is installing transmitters on the utility towers. We can't bug their buildings, but we can attach listening devices to the towers that'll pick up sound from a hundred-foot radius. They're installing video cameras with night-vision lenses that will scan in all directions. After the stuff is in place, we'll monitor the sound and pictures from here. Special Ops has set up a base nearby in the Croatan forest to monitor the activities from the ground."

I studied the photographs. "Is this everything?"

"All that could be shot before the satellite passed out of range," Bill said. "It'll be back over the site again at ten P.M. We'll meet back here to watch a live feed. You won't believe what that bird is capable of seeing after dark. It's equipped with heat sensors and night-vision lenses."

"I'll be here." I'd promised my children a long weekend. I was due to fly to New York first thing in the morning. I wasn't going to break my promise this time. The ten-P.M. meeting wouldn't interfere with my plans. I'd be home and in bed well before midnight.

I watched our reflections swim in glass like divers just below the water's surface. Then sudden movement in our direction caught my eye as the duty officer stuck his head in the door. "Guy Johnson's on the phone for you, Mr. Cross. Urgent, he says."

"Put him through on the speakerphone," I said.

"What's up, Guy?"

"General Kelly, you there, too?"

"Yes, Guy. Cavanaugh and Ed are with me. You said it was urgent?"

"It's a disaster. An explosion destroyed the gun shop in Myrtle Beach about twenty minutes ago. Right before it was supposed to open at ten."

I asked one word. "Starr?"

"We're pretty sure he was inside," Guy said solemnly.

TWENTY-EIGHT

"TELL ME WHAT happened."

"Like I said, a bomb went off at Larry's Gun Shop shortly before opening time at ten. Starr would have been there, setting up for the day's business. His car was parked out front. Or what's left of it. Agents checked his house; he's not there. I'm afraid they got him."

"So they were on to him," I said thoughtfully.

"Seems that way. I've got a bomb squad going through the wreckage. It's going to be hard to find a body in that mess. Damn, this really gets to me. It was only yesterday he briefed us."

"Well, if they've found him out, they know he's reporting to you, so watch your step." I wondered if they knew about my involvement. Probably so.

"I'm afraid I've got more bad news. I was about to call you when I got word about the explosion. Got a helicopter right out of Columbia for Myrtle Beach. Had to see it for myself."

"What's the bad news?" Bill asked.

"Huh? Oh, yes, sir, Director. We lost the man in the coma. Someone spirited him out of the hospital early this morning. He was still unconsciousness."

"What!" I'd been standing, pacing actually, and I had to sit down. Starr dead, our Charleston intruder missing. "I thought you had someone watching him."

"I did. The patient was unconscious, the other patients asleep; my agent left his post for only a moment, just long enough for a quick trip to the men's room. When he got back, the bed was empty. Our guy was smuggled out of the hospital right under everyone's noses. Nobody saw a thing."

"Someone was watching for his chance," Ed said.

"We turned the hospital upside down. He's gone." Silence. "General Kelly, I'm sorry. It shouldn't have happened, but it did. Just like the explosion."

"I can't believe this!" I exclaimed, frustration making me bitter. "How powerful is this militia group? They seem to be everywhere. First someone's able to steal a state car from the maintenance yard, then they get into my hotel suite. Now they pull a patient right out of his hospital bed. They had inside help for that one. They have connections everywhere! Listen, Guy, call me when you have something good to report." I broke the connection.

"Well, at least my investigation of that jerk Rakes paid off," Ed declared.

"More bad news," I groaned.

"No, this is a lead. Karl Rakes has got a crazy brother who's knee-deep into this paramiliterrorist crap." Ed had coined an appropriate name for the warrior groups. "Brother's name is Clifton. Lieutenant Clifton Rakes, USMC. Last served in Vietnam. Booted out with a dishonorable discharge."

"For what?" I asked.

"Failure to obey orders. I got his service record right here." Ed tapped a manila folder. "He crossed into the DMZ one time too many. Even back then he was a one-man militia, thinking he owed allegiance to no one!"

"Explain yourself," I said irritably.

"He refused to acknowledge the demilitarized zone. When the Cong ran for the DMZ, Rakes led his platoon in after them. This happened more than once. According to his record, Clifton Rakes was a very bitter little soldier. Openly condemned the government for thrusting young men into combat then not letting them defend themselves. In psychiatric jargon, they said he was crazy as a bedbug. He was relieved of his commission and discharged."

"That would make him how old now?" I asked.

"He's sixty-three," Ed replied. "He kind of drifted around in the seventies, and we don't know for certain what he was up to, but I've got a pretty good idea. Customs says he left the country several times for South and Central America. You know what that means."

"No, I don't. Don't play games with me. Let's have it. What was he doing in Central America?"

Bill answered, "After the Vietnam War, our soldiers were in great demand as mercenaries in foreign countries. Think about it. They were already trained to use the latest combat weapons. They were disillusioned with the U.S. for the reception they got when they returned home. They'd seen a lot of death. Most were sick of it, but there were others who could be bought. I think Clifton Rakes was one of them."

Ed continued the narrative. "Then in the eighties, he pops up in Wytheville, Virginia, as a wannabe preacher of some fundamentalist sect. That went on for several years, until he left town with the church's treasury. The Commonwealth wants him for grand larceny and fraud."

I thought about the biblical passages that had been notated and left on Sam's bedside table. All the evidence was leading to one man, and the pieces of the puzzle were too close a fit to be coincidental.

"Ann, he matches the general description of the man who tried to abduct you in Charleston. Same height, six-two." Bill looked at me thoughtfully. "We have a picture we want you to look at. Trouble is, it's almost forty years old."

"Show me." I studied a photograph of a U.S. Marine in his twenties wearing the smart dress uniform of the Corps. Face long and slender, chiseled cheekbones. "Now I know why he looked familiar. He looks like Captain Karl Rakes."

"Is this the man who tried to kidnap you?" Bill asked.

I stared at a face that might have been handsome were it not for his dead eyes. Pale gray, cold, and mean. Just like Karl Rakes'. "Looks like him, but I'm not positive. The man who grabbed me had on those mirrored sunglasses. I never saw his eyes. Sorry."

"We'll have an artist age the face in this photograph and compare it to the drawing they made."

"This explains a lot," I said.

"It explains why Claiborne's murder weapon disappeared from Metro P.D.'s Property Room." Ed shook his head angrily.

"His involvement explains why he didn't telephone us the morning of Sam's murder," Bill said.

I recalled Rakes' intransigence and sneering attitude.

"Thank God you happened along when you did, Ann. Otherwise, the case would have been bungled further than it's been," Bill said.

I stared unseeing at light reflecting off glass. "This is all conjecture. Where's the proof?"

"We'll get the proof." Ed thumped the photographs. "We'll get enough evidence for a warrant. Then we'll search those sheds, and I know what we'll find—an arsenal of illegal weapons."

"Are we all in agreement?" I asked. "Do we think Karl Rakes and his brother are connected to POSSE and they're responsible for the church arsons, Sam Claiborne's and Daniel Rosen's murders? And now Starr's?"

"It's what I'm thinking," Bill replied.

"My gut tells me they're the leaders of POSSE!" Ed said with feeling. "Remember, we got a scarred fingerprint from the break-in at Larry's Gun Shop that matches the one on Senator Claiborne's chair. When we catch up with Clifton Rakes, we'll find a man with scarred fingertips."

"Have you compared the latent thumbprint with the prints of this marine?" I asked.

"Got a fingerprint expert studying the ridges even as we speak. The computers are good up to a point; after that it takes the eyeball of an expert. A good fingerprint man can sometimes make an ID from the ridge."

"So you think the burn scarring on his finger occurred later, after he was off the radar?"

"I sure as heck do. It's him all right. I can feel it in my gut."

"I'm told you have good instincts, Ed. OK, report to me as soon as your fingerprint expert makes a decision. What about the other prints found in Sam's room?"

"Only what you'd expect. Sam's, the cook's, a cleaning lady's, his daughter's, people who had a reason to be there. I think Rakes wore gloves, then for some reason removed them."

"What about the prints from my hotel door and my apartment door?"

"None that couldn't be accounted for. Must've worn latex gloves."

Bill said, "On a hunch, I had Lejeune's records pulled. They've been experiencing thefts of heavy weapons. Sixty-six-millimeter antitank guns, dragon missiles, stingers, M-16s, and powder explosives."

"That blows me away." I was horrified and then realized the inappropriateness of my remark. "Theft right off the marine base!"

"When we get to the bottom of this, bet we find some skinhead marines who are members of POSSE helped relieve Uncle Sam of some of his deadliest weapons," Ed said bitterly.

"Lord help us," I uttered.

Ed offered the *coup de grace.* "Last but not least, there's not a trace of brother Karl."

TWENTY-NINE

"Barbara, welcome. I'm glad you could come on such short notice." I led Dr. Barbara Grant into my office suite.

"How could I resist dinner in your sanctum sanctorum?" Grant's smile was warm and sincere. Apparently she was giving me a second chance at friendship.

We passed through dimly lit rooms. Darkness pressed against windows, and the entire floor was amazingly quiet. Only a skeleton crew operated after hours. I was working late, trying to catch up on paperwork while waiting for the ten-o'clock meeting in SIOC.

"I've always wanted to see this place." Grant wore an attractive moss-green suit that brought out the green in her hazel eyes. Contact lenses substituted for her usual thick eyeglasses. I recognized her perfume as L'air du Temps with its light, floral fragrance.

"I'm glad you came. I owe you an apology. I behaved badly, and I was terribly rude."

"You were upset. I was to blame, too. I tend to forget professional people have feelings, just like anyone else who's lost a loved one."

I flashed her a look of gratitude. "Somehow I knew you'd understand. Thanks. I can promise it won't happen again."

"You're forgiven." Her sincerity touched her eyes. It was rare when I found a person I could trust, and I treasured those people. I promised myself in the future I'd treat Grant fairly and with kindness.

"I don't use this room often enough," I said. "Sybil, my assistant, has threatened to turn it into a file room if I don't begin to utilize it."

The dining room was not grand by any means, but its very existence spelled luxury. The food was prepared in the kitchen of the building's cafeteria, then reheated in a microwave in a butler's pantry. Sandwiches could be prepared here if necessary, and a refrigerator stored soft drinks, snacks, and frozen yogurt. It was the elegance of a bygone age that impressed visitors. Lofty ceilings and carved paneling rose high overhead, similar to the other rooms in my office suite. Depression-era murals of winged goddesses flying protectively alongside vintage aircraft were painted in thin, watery pastels. Some bygone artist had depicted war in an incongruously romantic and sentimental style.

"There's a rumor Bobby Kennedy roasted hotdogs in that fireplace," I said.

Barbara laughed. "I can see the Kennedys doing that. Marshmallows, too."

We dined on immaculate white linen, set with china and silver. Jan, the steward, in his snowy-white jacket, served our plates. The food was unpretentious—meat loaf, mashed potatoes, mixed vegetables, green salad, and iced tea.

"It's not fancy," I apologized.

"I happen to be partial to meat loaf," Grant said pleasantly. "The comfort foods have made a comeback."

"Let's have coffee in my office." I didn't want anyone to overhear our conversation.

Grant nodded. "Good idea." She lifted her briefcase off the floor and followed as Jan carried our coffee things on a tray. I shoved papers aside, and he set it on my desk, tactfully leaving and closing the door behind him.

Now we were solemn and all business. Grant retrieved the case file, a twelve-by-fourteen-inch-thick envelope, from her briefcase. "Would you like to see the results for yourself, or shall I summarize them?"

"I'd like to take a look at the file. Then I'll ask questions, if that's okay with you." I was trying to be respectful of her feelings, trying to curb my blunt, charge-ahead attitude.

"That's perfectly all right. I'll just enjoy my coffee while you read. Ask if you don't understand something."

The document was titled Autopsy Protocol and a case number had been handwritten with a black marking pen. It was a legal document file that hopefully would be used in court before long. The file contained the results of the autopsy, including the medical examiner's opinion, photographs, toxicology test results, X-rays and fingerprints.

I avoided the photographs. The X-rays were incomprehensible to me. I settled for reviewing the autopsy report.

Item one was titled External Examination. It included (a) a description of the clothing Sam wore, which, as I had seen, was his military uniform over pajamas, and (b) a description and identification of the body, which I did not care to read.

Item two, titled Evidence of Injury, was of interest. This was a lengthy, detailed description of the damage caused to Sam's head by a single bullet. Externally, (a) the barrel of the gun had been pressed directly against the frontal bone and fired, resulting in a starburst splitting of the skin. The exact cause of the formation of the stellar pattern was the hot gases that shot under the skin, expanding and ripping soft tissue. This could only occur when the barrel of a gun was pressed against skin over bone.

I struggled to remain detached. I had to be if I was to think this case through.

The internal damage (b) was described in great clinical detail, with the word cephalic referred to extensively, and although I didn't know the precise definition of the terms used, the gist of the explanation was the gun had been fired by someone standing over Sam as he sat. The bullet had entered through the frontal bone of the skull and exited the occipital bone, or at the base of the skull. I didn't wish to read about the damage to the brain. Suffice it to say, there was sufficient hemorrhaging and trauma for death to occur instantly.

Part three, the observations Dr. Grant witnessed regarding the central nervous system, or the head and brain, were more or less a recapitulation of item two.

There followed the results of the internal examination of the chest, abdomen, and pelvis, the weights, measurements, and condition of vital organs. In conclusion, Sam had experienced no breaking of ribs, and his vital organs—heart, liver, spleen, kidneys—were unremarkable for a man of his age.

I glanced through section five, Toxicology Test Findings, but, of course, Sam used no controlled substances nor was he taking prescription drugs.

The last item was titled Opinion, and I read it carefully. This was a summation of the official cause of death. Because it would be used in court, it was written in simple, easily understood terminology. Dr. Grant had written:

It is my opinion Samuel Louis Claiborne, a sixty-year-old male, died as a result of a gunshot wound to the head. The bullet, a .38 caliber, entered the front of the skull and exited at the base of the skull, avulsing the brain and resulting in massive internal hemorrhage. The cause of death was a .38-caliber gunshot injury to the head. The mechanism of death was loss of blood and shock secondary to traumatic hemorrhage of the brain. The manner of death was homicide.

I trembled with rage. How dare someone do that to my friend? How dare someone do that to a good person like Sam Claiborne? I considered our theory Clifton Rakes was the leader of the militia movement responsible for church arsons and murder. I wanted him! I wanted him so badly the desire was a hot flame in my chest. I was consumed by my hatred for this man who'd had the nerve to try to drag me into his car.

I hope we meet again soon, Clifton Rakes, or Commander if that's what your punk followers call you. This time things will be different. This time I'll turn the tables on you!

I looked up to find Barbara Grant studying me with a puzzled expression. "You okay?"

I wasn't okay. I'd never be able to handle this well. "Yes, I'm fine. You know I can't begin to count the number of times I've heard autopsy reports summarized in court, but this is different. It's different when it's your friend." I paused, grateful the coffee was hot and strong. "Actually, these autopsy conclusions are pretty much what I expected. No surprises there. I'm anxious to know if you found any prints on the body."

"We did," Barbara replied. "And we were able to

get clear impressions with photographic paper. There was a thumbprint on each eyelid, as you suggested. A thumb pressed first to one eye, then to the other. He was closing them, just as we thought. Trouble is, they were prints of that badly scarred thumb. Maybe of no use. I've turned them over to CID."

I longed to tell Barbara we'd had a break, that the scarred print had led us to burglaries at Larry's Gun Shop in Myrtle Beach. That an undercover agent had located a suspect militia compound. I looked into her intelligent, sensitive face and wished I could tell her Bill Cavanaugh and Ed Cross were suspicious of an ex-marine, ex-mercenary, ex-preacher named Clifton Rakes. That right now, bulletins were being issued to federal and local law enforcement to bring him in for questioning. Grant had a stake in Sam's murder investigation. She was a caring individual who had a right to know. Yet I couldn't tell her.

She said with feeling, "I respected Senator Claiborne for all he'd done. He was a fine senator and leader."

"You're right." A flash of memory tickled my brain and brought a smile to my lips. "What most people didn't know was how much fun he could be. He had a great sense of humor. Last New Year's Eve, we were all at a party. It was kind of a mixed bag as far as the guests were concerned. Politicos, media, showbiz people. Everyone had had a little too much to drink as we do on New Year's Eve. Anyway, Larry King came in, grabbed Sam, kissed him on both cheeks, whirled him around the dance floor. Everyone stared. Sam just grinned and said, 'Don't ask, don't tell.' He broke us up." A tear slipped down my cheek, and I wiped it with my fingertips. As time passed, the good memories would surface. They would be my comfort.

The red telephone jangled loudly. "My umbilical cord to the president. I've got to take this."

"Of course you do. I'll wait outside. Take your time." She refilled her coffee cup and carried it with her.

"Good evening, Mr. President."

"You're working late."

"Yes, sir. I have a meeting in SIOC at ten to view a transmission from our spy satellite. They've tasked it to fly directly over a suspect militia camp in North Carolina. This militia might be responsible for the church arsons and Senator Claiborne's murder."

"Well, that's good work. The faster we resolve these problems, the better. I'm just about hamstrung these days. I want Claiborne's murderer caught, and fast, and I want DOJ to prepare an airtight case. I don't want this weirdo slipping through our fingers because of some technicality."

"Yes, sir, I want him, too."

"Yeah. I know you do. I've got a stimulus bill pending that'll never see the light of day as long as my political enemies can keep the media focused on Claiborne's murder."

"I'll take care of it. Sir, did you by chance see news footage out of Winston-Salem about that Klan rally today?"

"Unfortunately, I did. Just sat down to lunch, and there they were on my TV set, screaming their vitriolic slurs. It was enough to turn my stomach. They're coordinating their efforts. Camp David on Sunday. Now North Carolina. They're well-organized. All they're making me do is dig in my heels."

"Yes, sir. That's what I thought. By the way, my department is taking a good, hard look at the grant money we're pouring into that city. In fact, I'm ordering an audit."

"Good idea," Jefferson Monroe said thoughtfully. "I think I'll have Adam see what they're getting from NIH and NASA. We have an obligation to see taxpayer dollars aren't finding their way into some hate group's coffers."

"Would you be willing to share that data, sir?"

"Don't see why not. It's public record. I'll have Adam fix you up. Good night, Ann. Let's set up a meeting with Alex Boyd. It's time we brought Homeland Security in on this militia business."

As the president's Homeland Security advisor, Alex Boyd needed a heads-up on the threat the militia might pose to national security.

The president took the bait, I thought gleefully as I reached to answer my chirping black phone. "General Kelly, this is Carol on the switchboard. There's a Father Matthew Phillips on the phone, and he says it's urgent he speak to you. Shall I put him through?"

"Yes. Yes. Connect him at once." My pulse quickened.

"Hello, Father Matthew." My voice had a calmness I didn't feel.

"Ann, thank God I've reached you. You can't imagine how hard it is to get through to you."

Matthew Phillips was replacing my father as rector at St. Andrews. There was only one reason why he would call: something was wrong with Daddy.

"What's wrong, Father Matthew? Is Daddy sick?" This conversation reminded me of the one I'd had a week ago with Sarah Preston, only now I was the daughter getting bad news about her father.

"I'm so sorry, my dear. Your father's had a heart

attack. I've been with him at the hospital all afternoon; otherwise I would have called sooner. I wanted to wait while they ran tests before calling you so I'd have something to report. Then I couldn't find your number, and the people who answer your phones kept shuffling me around. Otherwise, you would have heard from me sooner."

Spare me, I wanted to shout. My private numbers were on Daddy's Rolodex, and if Father Matthew hadn't been so upset, he'd have found them. "How is he? Tell me quickly."

"They've got him listed in critical condition, but there's hope, my dear. The doctors confided in me they think he'll make it. He received immediate attention, and you know that's crucial to surviving a first heart attack. He's resting now and stable. The catheterization showed a blockage, so they'll be doing bypass surgery at nine tomorrow morning. He wants you to be with him."

"Of course. I'll be there. Where is he?"

"The Cardiac Care Unit at New Hanover Regional."

I started to say I'd leave right away when I remembered the ten-o'clock meeting in SIOC. We should be through at ten thirty. I'd alert the airfield to prepare my plane for departure at eleven.

"I'll get there about midnight, Father Matthew. I'll have a car, so don't worry about meeting me. I'll go straight to the hospital."

"Anything I can do for you, just say the word," he offered.

"Well, if you'd tell the housekeeper to prepare my old room and two guest rooms, I'd appreciate it. There'll be two agents with me. Tell her I'm sorry but I'll have to wake her to let me into the rectory. It can't be helped."

"She won't mind. She's a good old soul. I'll do whatever I can to help. You know how I love your father. He's been my mentor and my inspiration for lo these many years. I'll see you in the morning, then."

"Yes. The morning. Don't wait up for me. I'll be late, but it can't be helped."

"Just come as soon as you can. We're holding a special prayer vigil at the church for him. Please call me if you think of anything else I can do."

"Before you go, Father Matthew, give me the number of the Cardiac Care Unit and the names of his doctors."

Matthew Phillips gave me the information and we said good-night.

Poor Daddy. I was afraid something like this might happen. He was seventy-two and shouldered such a heavy load, always putting his parishioners' troubles before his own. Suddenly I remembered Grant was sitting in my outer office.

"I've just had bad news," I blurted. "My father's had a heart attack. I've got to fly to Wilmington tonight!"

THIRTY

AFTER GRANT LEFT my office, I wearily climbed the stairs to my tiny hideaway to lie down and rest. I was hoping to nap but felt too keyed up to sleep. Wild thoughts tumbled around in my brain.

I imagined Daddy in an ambulance, stricken, frightened, so far from family. I had fleeting visions of the burned-out churches I'd visited, and the way Sam's lifeless head had lolled against the chair wing. I felt feeble and not up to the task of licking all these problems. Driven by a need for strength far greater than my own, I rolled from the bed and knelt on the floor and humbly prayed. *Why do I only turn to God in times of trouble?* My list of problems for Him to fix was as long as a laundry list. I hoped I could reach Him, as my father seemed able to do so easily. I asked for Daddy's safe recovery and that love would overcome the hatred in the hearts of killers and church arsonists. And my own.

Lastly, I prayed my children would understand when I called them in the morning to tell them I was once again canceling our vacation. It was better to wait until morning to make my call. By then, I'd have seen Daddy and could report firsthand about his condition. Maybe I was wrong to stand between my children and bad news, but I thought most mothers would do the same. I wanted them to have a good night's rest.

I'd notified everyone concerned about my emergency trip to Wilmington. The DOJ jet was being refueled and flight plans were being filed. Agents Colby and Moore had made quick trips to their homes to pack. Driver Carlos Perez would remain in Washington. The agents could take turns driving the car that would be waiting for me at the Marine Corps Air Station near Jacksonville, North Carolina. We made it our practice to land at military airfields whenever possible because they were secure, and commercial airports were not. From the Marine Base, the drive to the medical center would take about thirty minutes.

Rising, feeling stronger and spiritually renewed, I sorted through my clothes closet, pulling out a pantsuit and flat shoes. I took a quick, hot shower and changed into my practical outfit. An extra pair of khakis and a cotton sweater went into a duffle bag.

At nine forty-five P.M., I boarded my private elevator on the fifth floor of the Justice Building and rode to the underground garage and my waiting car. Agents Moore and Colby accompanied me. We would drive across the street and park in the FBI headquarters' underground garage. They would wait for me there while I boarded another secure elevator to the Hoover Building's fifth floor. DOJ's budget for next year included a request for an enclosed catwalk above Pennsylvania Avenue, linking my office to SIOC.

On the fifth floor of the Hoover Building, Bill stood waiting for me when the elevator doors opened. "Good. You're here. Come on. You just made it. We don't want to miss this."

He hustled me down the corridor and through the vault-like entrance to SIOC. The tension was palpable. Technicians, the duty agent, and AAG Cross were gathered in front of a huge glowing screen in dimly lit OPS1.

Ed turned. "One minute more and you'd have missed

this!" Excitement heightened his coloring and lifted his voice.

The duty agent said, "Listen up, people; we've got a live feed. Big Brother is passing over the compound. Watch closely, now."

Bill's shoulder touched mine as we stood with the others before the glowing screen. Computer operators tuned their equipment to the passing satellite, received its transmissions as their monitors flashed STATUS: LIVE messages.

The duty agent said, "That baby really struts her stuff at night. She's equipped with a telescope the size of a bus, digital cameras, and night-vision lenses."

"What if there's cloud cover?" I asked.

"She's got radar that can see through the clouds." He pointed. "Okay, General Kelly, she's passing over the forest now, just treetops. There…now…see that opening? We're over the compound."

I held my breath as the camp rolled into view. The screen projected an eerie green background, and moving objects stood out in black and gray.

"What am I seeing?" I asked.

"It's a caravan of vehicles. Keep watching. You'll get the hang of it."

I focused, trying to make sense of what I was seeing. Suddenly, all the pieces slipped into place to form a picture. The road into the camp was alive with vehicles.

"They're so close," I said. "It's as if I'm up in the treetops."

"We can get to within six inches," the duty agent explained.

"Amazing."

"Let's get a closer look," Bill Cavanaugh said. "Enlarge that tent section, will you?"

"Enlarge sector five," the duty agent instructed a computer technician. A window appeared on the screen, framing the area of the tent, tightening in on it. The tent image suddenly expanded.

"There are hundreds of men arriving," I commented.

Cars, jeeps, pickups streamed into the campground, were parked, their occupants climbing out and moving into the tent. I looked down on the tops of heads that were capped or bare-headed. I was able to identify articles of clothing: jeans, tee-shirts, overalls, camouflage fatigues—even sidearms and rifles.

"And more coming." Ed pointed to the never-ending line of vehicular traffic.

Bill said, "This is a lucky break. Looks like the whole damned militia is assembling, and we're capturing it on film."

"There's nowhere to hide, boys and girls; Big Brother is watching you," Ed sang merrily. "Looks like POSSE is getting ready to have a meeting."

A large truck pulled up in front of one of the warehouses. Two men hopped out of the cab.

"Uh-oh, get a look of that. What do you suppose is under that tarp, Ed?" Bill asked.

"Pull that tarp off." Ed was talking to them.

"Arms?" I asked.

"What else?"

The drivers of the truck merely walked toward the tent.

"Too bad," Bill said. "A photo of weapons on that truck would get us a warrant."

"Maybe the crew on the ground's got something. Special Ops planted a video camera on the main road. They've got a record of those cars and their plates. God, don't I wish we had a microphone in that tent!"

"What are our transmitters picking up from the utility towers?" I asked.

"We've got a technician listening to a live audio feed." Bill pointed through glass into OPS2 where a young woman wearing a headset was seated before sound equipment. "She's making a backup tape, and she'll alert us if she hears anything significant. Probably they're just picking up engine noises. The utility towers are just too distant from the compound for us to hear voices unless someone is standing under them."

Ed Cross said, "Well, let's hope a couple guys decide to go out for a smoke or a piss together."

"My, my, Mr. Cross, you do have a way with words." I laughed for the first time in days.

THIRTY-ONE

BRIGHT STARS PULSATED in a night sky so lucid it shimmered. I had napped in the lounge on the plane. Feeling groggy and worse for the short sleep, I stumbled across the tarmac to the waiting black car. As we sped through the night, shadowy trees and bushes rushed past our windows.

Not many miles in the opposite direction, the man we believed had killed Sam was conducting a meeting of paramilitaries, or paramiliterrorists as Ed Cross had referred to them. What evil plots would he hatch if he knew his arch-enemy, the attorney general of the United States, was a mere forty miles south of his camp, cruising along Highway 17 into Wilmington, with only two agents and an unmarked state trooper's car for protection? We'd wished to attract no attention to ourselves.

We drove directly to the New Hanover Regional Medical Center. The large campus was treed with immense willow oaks as I remembered, but in every other aspect it had changed greatly since I'd last seen it. Several new modern pavilions had been built. For as long as I could remember, the medical center had been in the throes of renovation or new construction.

As we turned off Seventeenth Street onto Medical Center Boulevard, the visitors' parking lot was on the left as it had always been. The main entrance to the eight-story, creamy brick building was reached by a circular driveway beyond a grassy knoll with a fountain in the center. The driveway was closed to traffic, for the entrance was being renovated. Although quiet at night, signs of a capital-improvement project were everywhere. A sign directed us to park at an alternate lot.

As Brad Moore maneuvered through a confusing maze around the complex, we saw construction trailers in parking spaces and heavy equipment that resembled dinosaur bones abandoned on the lawns.

The emergency entrance was well-lit and quiet. Moore parked between two ambulances, and no one seemed to mind or even to notice. "I'll go in alone. I won't be long." I left them to wait for me in the car and hurried up a long ramp toward automatic double glass doors.

I was expected, and a uniformed security guard greeted me as medical personnel stared curiously. The guard made friendly chitchat, most of which I didn't hear, as he escorted me to the cardiology unit. I felt a sudden and urgent need to find a ladies' room, but the urge passed by the time the elevator doors opened onto the fourth floor.

The lights were soft here as we walked the carpeted corridor. Walls were papered in mauve vinyl, and framed prints of pleasant scenes hung above polished oak handrails. The security guard walked with me to the nurses' station.

"This is Mrs. Kelly, here to see her father, Timothy Maguire."

The nurse looked up with bulldog leeriness from her charting task. "Mmm-hmm," she responded indifferently. "His doctor said it was okay."

She didn't seem to recognize me and apparently had no idea who I was, which suited me just fine.

"I'll leave you, then, Mrs. Kelly. It was a pleasure to

meet you, ma'am." The guard glanced at the nurse as if
he thought her a dummy.

The nurse left her paperwork reluctantly and came
around the counter slowly. "Okay, follow me." She was
wearing a pants outfit in white, and her hair was tucked
under a full cap. She walked like she had all the time
in the world, and I hoped she wasn't on the code team.
Determinedly I dogged her steps.

Through glass windows I could see sleeping patients, mostly elderly. Gleaming equipment recorded
vital signs and aided in the functioning of respiration,
sleep, and heartbeat. Monitors glowed and white running blips skipped across heart monitors. The complex
machinery that kept life going instilled fear in my heart,
and the rhythmic beeps they issued were as annoying
as a field of crickets.

My guide stopped to speak to another nurse who
was apportioning medications into tiny paper cups on
a metal cart. I looked through glass and open blinds
and saw my father's head propped against pillows. On
unsteady feet, I tiptoed into his room.

The nurse called sharply, "Five minutes only!"

Her bossy attitude, like the slap of a gauntlet, faded
into insignificance when I saw my father's face. I
dragged a chair over to the white sheets. His doctor
had warned me he would be asleep, sleeping medication
being administered by the IV pump inserted in a vein.

I slipped my hand under his carefully so as not to
dislodge the IV needle. "Daddy?" I whispered. He
didn't move. I looked up at the monitor and watched the
sketches of his heartbeat, not knowing whether what I
was seeing was good or bad. At least the line wasn't flat.

His face against the pillows was peaceful. Daddy
had a full head of hair, unusual for a man of his years.

At one time it had been wavy and auburn like mine. It was still wavy but had turned to yellow-white. My own hair would be that color one day. He needed a shave, and white stubble covered his cheeks and chin.

"Time's up!" the irritating nurse called from the doorway. I got up and leaned over Daddy, kissing his dry forehead. "I'll be back in the morning."

THAT NIGHT I DREAMT about the Klan. The dream was similar to nightmares I'd had as a child. I awoke sweating and remembered. It was 1970 and I was ten, living in Wilmington in the rectory with my father, sleeping at night in this very room. My mother was still with us. One sunny Saturday afternoon in May, Daddy and I had set off for a stroll to the Cape Fear River. I remembered the day was gentle and peaceful, so inconsistent with the turmoil that seethed all around us in the New South.

At Market Street we ran into a noisy crowd. Their excitement was a tangible presence on the street. Cars had stopped against curbs to free the center lane. Then a hush fell over the crowd. I turned to look where everyone was staring. A strange parade seemed to float down the center of Market, coming toward us. Tall figures wore long white robes with skirts that flapped around shoes and boots. Pointy hoods had cutouts for eyes. Their hidden faces only added to the terror I felt. Only one man had the courage to show his face. He was a pint-sized midget of a man, not much bigger than I, and dressed all in purple satin. He studied the crowd as he walked past, peering intently into each face as if to memorize it. When his pale, cold eyes met mine, I covered my face with my hands. Even at that young and innocent age, I knew I didn't want to be remembered by him.

At my side, Daddy went rigid, his grip on my hand tightening painfully. He pulled at me, wrenching my arm and dragging me away from the spectacle and back to the rectory. I couldn't help myself; like Lot's wife, I turned around for one last look. I knew who they were.

For months there had been talk in the church meeting rooms about civil unrest, demonstrations, shootings, and lynchings, talk that would stop the moment someone noticed me. That Saturday afternoon I heard Daddy speak in a tone I'd never heard before. He seemed to be cursing under his breath. "You can hide your faces, you cowards, but you can't hide your wickedness from God. He knows who you are. And so do I."

For weeks after that I had nightmares. Ghosts in long white robes penetrated my dreaming mind to threaten and chase me and make me afraid of the dark. My mother heard my cries and came to comfort me, her innate sweetness and goodness softening the harsh reality of those years. The newspapers and the TV news were filled with reports of the murders of "coloreds" who'd registered to vote and "whites" who'd helped them. Then the evildoers hit close to home.

A high-school student named Rufus Washington, who helped his father tend the churchyard and who was smart and occasionally tutored me with my math homework, was found hanging from a tree on the outskirts of town. I cried for days—for Rufus and for his father. Weeks later from my window, I saw old Mr. Washington out among the tombstones, leaning on his rake, his chin resting on his bib overalls. His son's murderers were never apprehended.

"When I grow up, I'm going to fix things," I'd whispered to the glass. "I'll bring the murderers of teenage boys to justice. People will be allowed to vote if they want to. I'll finish his work, Mr. Washington."

THIRTY-TWO

On Thursday morning I woke to sunlight streaming through windowpanes, and for a moment I didn't know where I was. For the first time in a week, my mood was light, and I felt a sense of well-being and a spirit of optimism. My father's surgery would be successful; we would apprehend and charge those responsible for the fires and for Daniel Rosen's and Sam Claiborne's murders. I added Bud Starr to the list of victims.

The rectory's housekeeper was a woman I had never met until I'd apologized for waking her late last night. Her name was Hannah and she had breakfast waiting for us in the breakfast room. In this large and sprawling house, there was a room for every purpose. A Queen Anne Victorian of brown wood shingles and intriguing turrets, it sat well back from the corner of Third and Dock streets behind a tall brick wall. Evidence of my father's packing filled the rooms: cartons, paper, foam peanuts, mounds of books heaped on the floor. I wondered if Daddy would miss this house, for he had lived here most of his life.

"I'm going to take a walk around the grounds." My hand was wrapped around a warm coffee mug. Colby pushed back from a plate of scrambled eggs and bacon, hash browns, and biscuits with jam, and moved to get up. "I'll go with you."

"No. Alone," I said firmly.

"It's too risky." She pulled on her jacket and stuffed biscuits into her pockets.

"I need to be alone." I needed time to contemplate the memories that had surfaced during the night. I was dressed in khakis and a cotton sweater with loafers, and I pulled on a jacket, for the morning was cool. There was dew on the grass that in an hour or two the sun would burn off, and the afternoon would feel summery.

Colby followed me off the back porch. "I won't intrude. I know how it is. You won't even know I'm around."

I paused, considering. Overhead, a wedge of wild ducks in search of a pond winged across a patch of sky. Moore and Colby were on the job; I had to respect that. "Okay. Just don't talk to me."

"Deal." Colby didn't intrude on my musings, content to trail along behind at a distance. She was a shadow in the background, and I soon forgot she was there as I yielded to childhood memories.

These days St. Andrews— the sanctuary, business office and Sunday School wings, the rectory, and the graveyard—occupied a full city block. When I'd lived here, one-quarter of the property was headquarters to Wilmington's Fire Department, with a large office building, fire station, and four engines. As a child, those engines had fascinated me, especially when the sirens clanged and one or two of the engines flew onto Dock Street with wheels barely touching pavement.

I walked alongside buff stucco church-complex walls and gazed up at blue slate roofs and a square bell tower. For a while, I sat in my favorite spot, St. Francis' garden, under the branches of a friendly old dogwood. Pink blossoms covered the tree, and azaleas and tulips and irises bloomed along stone paths. From the corner, St.

Francis blessed the birds and squirrels and the little girl who used to come here with a book.

Time to move on, I thought, getting up to complete my melancholy tour. I wandered to the old cemetery. Mossy, tilting tombstones with inscriptions dating as far back as 1729 cluttered a square of land enclosed by wrought-iron fencing. Early congregants rested eternally under crepe-myrtle trees with branches so thickly entwined by Spanish moss few leaves dared to grow. I remembered my old friend Rufus Washington and his sad caretaker father.

I passed the Daycare Center's empty playground, swings and slides awaiting children. I entered the sanctuary through doors located behind the chancel. The doors of St. Andrews were open during daylight hours to the public, being unlocked by a custodian at dawn and locked again at night by whoever was the last to leave. Tourists came here to admire the city's oldest church, and anyone who wished might enter to meditate. I looked up at the carved pulpit where every Sunday my father had led the service.

Suddenly I was reminded of Mt. Zion Baptist Church. I looked around, puzzled, the hair on my arms bristling as I grew alarmed. Hanging in the air was the acrid smell of smoke. It wasn't visible, but the smell was strong. Where was it coming from? Crossing the nave toward the narthex, the odor grew stronger. Shocked, I saw what I thought I'd never see in this church, yellow fire-scene tape.

The damage was minimal. The fire had been limited to the narthex. Flames had blackened the dark red carpeting and rutted through the pad, scarring the oak floor beneath. The few pieces of furniture had been removed. Streaks of soot stained the paneling, but all in all, the fire had been contained. The street doors were locked, a first for St. Andrews, but given the circumstances, not a surprise.

I hurried back to the rectory, Colby running to keep pace.

"What's wrong?" she called.

I didn't reply. The first of the daycare children were arriving by car in the circular drive, cherubs who waved to me as I rushed past.

"Hannah!" I called as I flung open the back door.

She rushed from the kitchen where she'd been packing china. "Yes, Mrs. Kelly. What is it?" Her kind face registered my alarm.

"There was a fire in the church! What happened?"

"Why, darlin', didn't no one tell you? The fire's what caused your poor pa's heart attack. We think some fool tourist dropped a burning cigarette on the carpet. Your pa came upon it and beat it out with his coat. The fire department came and finished the job, but the effort was too much for your pa's tired, old heart."

THIRTY-THREE

THE TELEPHONE RANG, all extensions throughout the house chirping at once, and Hannah excused herself to answer it.

"It's for you, Mrs. Kelly."

"Hello?" I thought it might be the hospital calling.

"Good morning, Ann; it's Bill. How's your father?"

"I'm leaving for the hospital now. They'll be operating in an hour."

"Then I'll make this quick. Remember the pickup truck Mattie Long's nephew reported seeing cruising the neighborhood before the fire?"

"Yes, of course."

"We think we've got a make on it. The video cameras filmed a dark green Ford pickup with South Carolina plates driving into the campsite last night. Better still, the truck had the dealer's name and Charleston stenciled on the rear. Guy Johnson is tracing the owner's name now. He'll have an arrest warrant by midday."

"That is good news," I said.

"The best news is our fingerprint expert ID'd Clifton Rakes by the ridge on that scarred thumb. He's our killer and the thief who stole weapons and ammo from Larry's Gun Shop. There's a warrant and an all-points out for him right now."

"You're not going to try to serve it on him at that camp?" I asked.

"No. They're too heavily armed. We don't want

another Waco on our hands. We've got the place surrounded, and we'll apprehend him when he leaves. They seem to be acting normally. They haven't hunkered in, so I don't think they suspect they're under surveillance."

"Good. Are you managing to keep all this away from the media?"

"So far, no leaks. Let's hope it stays that way."

"Thanks for the call. I've got to run."

"Good luck to your father."

DADDY'S SURGEON WAS with him in his room. We shook hands, and he introduced himself as Ron Feldman. Daddy was awake and never took his eyes off me.

I approached his bed and kissed him on the cheek. "How are you feeling this morning?"

He grinned. "Can't keep a good man down, sweetheart. I'll be running circles around all of you in no time."

"Of that I have no doubt." I smiled into his face.

"He's going to do just great, General Kelly. He'll pull through this like a champ. Won't you, Tim?"

My father gave his doctor a thumbs-up sign.

Dr. Feldman said quietly to me, "We've given him something to relax him. Don't be surprised if he slips in and out." He raised his voice and called to my father, whose eyelids were drooping, "I'll see you downstairs in about thirty minutes. You won't see me."

"How long will the surgery take?" I asked.

"We never know for sure until we get in there, but count on him being gone for hours. In fact, you can go home, if you want, and come back at about noon."

"No, I'd be a nervous wreck at home. I'll stay here." I laughed. "I'll be a nervous wreck here."

He started to leave.

"Dr. Feldman?" I called after him.

He turned and smiled knowingly. "I'll take good care of him, General Kelly."

FATHER MATTHEW CAME. He prayed in the chapel as Agents Colby and Moore and I wandered the corridors of the hospital because I was unable to sit still. I found a quiet lounge and used my cell phone to call my apartment in New York. Tom answered.

"Honey, I'm in Wilmington. Grandpa's had a heart attack, and I'm at the hospital."

"Grandpa's had a heart attack!" Tom shouted his alarm to Cathy and Ronnie.

"Mom!" Cathy cried over an extension. "Is it true?"

"Grandpa had a heart attack yesterday. I flew down here late last night, but he's going to be all right, my darlings, and I don't want you to worry."

"How can we not worry?" she asked. "We love him."

"I know you do. He loves you two so much. He's in surgery now. They're doing a bypass. I met his surgeon, and he seems very skilled, and nice."

"I want to come," Cathy pleaded.

"Me, too," said Tom.

"I know it will do him good to see you, but why don't you wait until tomorrow? He'll be in surgery and recovery for most of today and then not awake. Cathy, can you take care of the reservations? Use the credit card you use for school. If you have any problems, call Sybil."

"We'll take care of everything, Mom. Don't worry. I'll call Hannah at the rectory and give her our flight number and the time of our arrival."

"That's good. I'll meet you at the airport. Until then, my children, I love you."

"We love you, too, Mom," Tom said.

"Tell Grandpa we love him," Cathy said. "Mommy, take care of yourself."

"I will," I promised.

COLBY, MOORE, AND I had lunch in the hospital's cafeteria. I managed to eat a sandwich as strangers cast curious looks my way.

"I checked in with the head of security first thing this morning. Showed him my credentials, told him you were here and why. They've allowed us to park at the emergency entrance. We're down at the end of the row of ambulances. He thanked me for alerting him there was a VIP on the premises." Moore's eyes twinkled. "Guess he's grateful for the extra security."

"Your father is going to be okay." Colby patted my hand. "You want to go up and check his room again to see if he's back?"

"Yes, let's."

Dr. Feldman met us at the fourth-floor nurses' station. "He did just fine, General Kelly. He's really very strong. You can go in to see him, but mostly he's going to be out of it for the rest of the day. He should be fairly alert by about eight this evening. That would be a good time to visit with him."

"Thank you for taking such good care of him, Dr. Feldman." I turned to my agents. "You guys don't have to hang around in here. Hospitals are so depressing. Go on out in the sunshine, take a walk. I'm going to sit with him for about thirty minutes, then I'll meet you at the car. I won't be long."

Moore and Colby hesitated.

"Go on. I'm perfectly safe here. Look around."

The nurses' station was a beehive of activity as medical personnel moved in and out. Technicians busily rolled equipment, and nurses monitored patients.

"All right," Colby said. "If you're not down in thirty minutes, I'm coming up here after you."

"Agreed." I threw up my hands in mock surrender.

DADDY LAY MOTIONLESS in his bed. The monitors clicked and beeped and transmitted his vital signs to the nursing station. He looked serene and didn't seem to be experiencing any pain.

I lowered my head to his. "I love you, Daddy."

His eyelids flickered. "Love you," he mumbled hoarsely.

BRIGHT SUNLIGHT BLINDED ME as I stepped through the automatic glass doors onto the emergency-entrance apron. The sky was softly blue and cross-hatched with jet trails. Tall trees sprouted delicate spring green leaves. The noise of the construction was almost deafening as I looked around. Heavy earth movers graded and leveled the site of a parking garage. From behind enormous blue plastic sheets that covered the new wing came the buzz of drilling. Hammers banged. The grounds were alive with activity and confusion, with builders entering and leaving construction trailers and materials being unloaded from large trucks. At the same time, this was still a place that cared for the sick, and I was transfixed as an ambulance rolled up to the entrance, sirens blaring.

Paramedics scrambled out, yanked open rear doors, and lowered a collapsible gurney to the ground. Running with it in my direction, they called, "Move, ma'am." I jumped out of the way as a bloody body swathed in sheets rolled by.

I spotted our black sedan parked down at the end of

a row of ambulances. In the ambulance parked next to our car, a paramedic sat behind the wheel, while his colleague flung open the rear doors.

Through the open driver's window of my car, I saw Brad Moore slumped over the steering wheel, and for a second I didn't know what to make of it. Then knowledge hit me full force. Something was wrong! "Brad!" I called out in alarm. Leaning into the car, I saw the dark hole in his temple, the trickle of blood on his sideburn. Beyond him, Lauren Colby leaned into the dashboard, the black-tinted window behind her firmly closed. The dashboard was covered with blood. As was Colby's face!

I whirled around, screaming for help. The paramedic from the adjoining ambulance galloped to my side, a quizzical look on his face.

"They've been shot!" I screamed. "Do something. Get them inside!" I reached into my pocket for my cell phone.

"I'll take care of everything," the paramedic said, motioning to his partner. "Let's get you someplace safe." Taking my arm, he steered me toward the rear of the ambulance.

My mind was a jumble of confusion, and I moved a few steps before I protested. "I'm not hurt. Take care of them." I jerked my arm free, and my cell phone went sailing through the air and landed on the concrete. "Wait a minute! What are you doing?"

His grip on my arm tightened. He pushed me through the open doors into the back of the ambulance. I screamed, but at that moment, a pile-driver slammed down into the earth nearby, and my cry was lost in the noise of the ear-splitting blow.

The doors slammed shut. In an instant, the siren was wailing, and we were roaring away from the hospital at breakneck speed.

THIRTY-FOUR

THINK! THINK! I told myself as I gripped a side rail to keep from bouncing around inside the empty ambulance. *Clifton Rakes is behind this. That means they're taking me to the compound. He killed my agents.* Colby and Moore were friends. Oh, I'd make him pay.

Perhaps they aren't dead, I thought. *Perhaps they're merely wounded. Someone will find them soon. They'll get immediate medical attention, and they'll survive.* Who was I kidding? I'd seen the wounds. They were dead. As dead as Sam.

It was easy to figure out how Rakes' assassins had gotten to them. They'd never have been suspicious of paramedics. Someone dressed as a paramedic may have tapped on the car window. Moore would have opened it to speak to them, to find out what they wanted. They'd have had a clear shot.

I blamed myself. If I'd let them stay with me as they'd wished, none of this would have happened. They would be alive now. I'd be with them. I'd played right into Rakes' hands. I was filled with outrage. First Sam, then a South Carolina state legislator whose only crime was to fill theaters with laughter. Then Bud Starr. Now Brad Moore and Lauren Colby.

Moore had a wife and two small children. *Well, she's a widow now,* I thought harshly. *The kids are orphans. Damn you, Rakes.*

Colby would never know the joy of marriage. Never

know the joy of having children. She'd had her whole life ahead of her and so much to experience.

Well, I knew where they were taking me. I knew the place was surrounded by Bureau agents. *So okay, I'll find a way out,* I told myself.

I checked my watch. Two twenty P.M. We'd be at the compound in an hour. Maybe less. They were sure speeding. I hung on tight but still got bumped and jostled. No windows to see where we were going. The tiny window into the cab was covered on the cab side.

We're still in town, I thought. So many stops. Even with the siren blaring, we had to slow at intersections. They wouldn't want an accident. I pitched and rolled with every turn.

At one stop I grabbed the door handles and tried forcing the rear doors open. They wouldn't budge. Locked? Locked from the outside?

Then we slowed to a near stop, and the siren was abruptly cut off. We were pitched on a steep incline and drove down it. So they weren't taking me to the compound after all. Where were we? I waited for the doors to be thrown open, but they remained closed. Instead, I heard shouts, and the ambulance began to rock as someone banged and shoved at the sides. What on earth? We were in some sort of underground garage; that seemed clear. What were they doing? Then I got it. Covering the sides, installing panels, so no one could see this was an ambulance. Why? Because as soon as Colby and Moore were discovered, someone would remember seeing an ambulance parked alongside their car, and the search for it would be on.

I had to hand it to Rakes. He was not a fool. There were things I knew that he didn't. The Bureau was on to him. He was being watched. There was a warrant out for his arrest. Microphones and cameras were planted on utility poles throughout his compound. The road in was being watched. Bill Cavanaugh and Ed Cross would quickly figure out where I was. So all I had to do was stay calm and wait him out. I didn't want agents rushing in to the rescue. Someone would get killed. Maybe even me. No, I had to find a way to warn them to stay clear. I had to find a way to escape from Rakes.

Within minutes we were careening out of the garage and into the streets again. Eventually, we began moving at a steady, swift speed, and I assumed we were now out on the open highway.

Surely by now Colby and Moore would have been discovered. I'd left the rear door of the car standing open. Someone would see them. See the blood. I pictured them alive, breathing or on respirators, the bullets being removed. Skilled surgeons saving their lives. *Hold that thought,* I told myself.

Rakes had someone planted in the medical center, that was a certainty. Someone who reported all our moves to him. They had to survive. I just couldn't live with the guilt if they didn't make it.

I put myself in Bill Cavanaugh's place. He'd be the one to mastermind my rescue. Bill possessed a cool and analytical mind. I'd never underestimated him. *Where does that leave us?* I asked myself. First, there was the spy satellite. It would pass over the campsite again tonight. If I was out in the open, they'd see me. So I had to try to be out in the open at about ten o'clock tonight. If I couldn't escape sooner.

I wondered if Bill would risk flying airplanes or choppers over the camp. No. Too noisy. He might risk a single flyover by a surveillance-equipped HRT aircraft.

I pictured Bill and Ed getting the news I was missing. They'd rush to SIOC, listening and watching whatever the cameras and microphones were transmitting. Be in constant communication with the command post on the ground. They had to keep their distance until I got free. I remembered the way Rakes had used me as a shield when Colby was threatening to shoot him. That couldn't happen again.

As the ambulance sped to our final destination, I bolstered my morale by picturing a Hostage Rescue Team being deployed from Quantico at this very minute. The Ninjas would board helicopters and be flown into the nearest military installation in North Carolina, the Marine Corps Air Station near Jacksonville. From there, they'd be moved by marine transport to a location near Rakes' compound. That would attract no attention. Marine trucks in the area were a common sight.

It was up to me to escape. All I had to do was get away from my captors, make my way to the utility towers where my face and voice would be transmitted to SIOC. The message I had escaped would be relayed to the ground troops, and they would spring into action. Then, all I'd have to do was stay hidden until I was rescued.

Sounded simple, but how was I to get away from three hundred armed paramilitary soldiers? How did I know they weren't going to execute me at once, before there was any chance of escape?

THIRTY-FIVE

I RECOGNIZED CLIFTON RAKES at once as the man who had tried to abduct me in Charleston. He stood on the porch of a farmhouse with another man, whom I assumed was the farmer Mackie, the owner of this property. My captors pushed me toward him, powerful Israeli Desert Eagles that could blow me into a thousand pieces trained on my back.

Rakes watched with a contemptuous leer as I was thrust toward him. He stood at parade rest, his feet apart and his hands behind his back. He wore camouflage fatigues, combat boots, and a cap with camouflage markings. His eyes were hidden behind mirrored glasses again. I squinted up at him in the brilliant light and was determined to keep my cool. Casting my eyes right and left, I surveyed my surroundings. Mentally visualizing the aerial views of the compound I'd seen yesterday, I attempted to get my bearings. If I was going to get away, I had to know exactly where I was in relation to the utility poles and the power company's service road.

Off to the right, I saw the tent. Along the perimeter of the clearing, there were barracks and the warehouses we'd seen in the aerial photographs. The warehouse doors were open and wooden crates with military markings were being unloaded from the back of the truck we'd seen over satellite footage last night. *Contraband,* I told myself. Stolen weapons, ammunition, artillery, bombs. Like a deflated balloon, the tarp lay in a heap on the ground.

The air crackled with gunfire. Somewhere nearby was a firing range where Rakes' soldiers practiced their marksmanship skills.

I stepped onto the porch. I was determined not to let this man know how scared I was. To let him see my fear would be to play right into his hands. In the world according to Clifton Rakes, the game was everything, and making me cower and beg for my life was just what he wanted.

The best defense was a good offense. I seized his right hand from behind his back and turned it over, palm up. He was so taken off guard he didn't even struggle. I looked down.

"Scarred fingertips. You left your calling card. You killed Samuel Claiborne." I dropped his hand, revealed my contempt for him. I lifted my chin. "Take off those glasses. I want to see those eyes, the eyes of a cowardly murderer. No one kills a friend of mine and gets away with it. Remember that!"

Rakes threw back his head and laughed. A wave of his arm encompassed the house, the compound, his soldiers. "I hardly think you're in a position to do anything but beg for your life, little lady."

Still trying for the upper hand, I looked him over with cool appraisal. He was fit, didn't look at all like sixty-three. He was about a foot taller than me. At that moment I was awfully tired of looking up at people, especially people I loathed like Rakes.

He grabbed my wrist and pulled me into the house, his free arm making a shooing motion to the guards. He would need no assistance controlling a petite woman. The farmer didn't follow us inside but stepped casually

off the porch. We entered a farm kitchen that was pains-
takingly neat. There was no one else around. I rooted
myself to the floor.

"I want to know why you killed my friend!" I demanded.

Rakes relaxed a bit and even let go of my wrist.
"Knowing why won't change anything, little lady." I
had expected him to taunt me. He'd try to break me.
"Dead is dead."

I steeled my emotions, remembering my ice-maiden
rage. *A cool head will prevail,* I'd told myself on that
day, a day that seemed like eons ago instead of just one
week. "Then consider it my warped curiosity, but I've
got to know why."

Rakes pushed the brim of his cap up and down as
if massaging his scalp helped him to think. Across the
room, water dripped in the sink. The clap of gunfire
was muted. Outside the windows, the soldiers were visible. There were so many of them and only one of me.

Finally Rakes spoke. "If you had a brain in your
liberal head, the answer would be obvious. The last
thing this country needs is a nigger running things.
The Founding Fathers would roll over in their graves.
All those people are good for is slave labor. The Secret
Service keeps us at a distance from Monroe, but Claiborne was an easy mark."

I lifted my eyebrows.

There was no stopping Rakes now. "It's enough
we've had to put up with that fornicator in the White
House. Claiborne wasn't so bad in the Gulf. But the
U.S. Senate? No way. Once he backed the Brady Bill
and the Hate Crimes Bill, he showed his true colors as
the enemy of all freedom-loving men."

I played to his ego. "How in the world did you manage to get into his house?"

"Scouted his place for weeks. Couldn't believe my good luck when I saw him open his window. Knew the alarm had to be off. Ha! I even watched you leave his house, little lady, and you never had a clue I was there."

I inched slowly around the kitchen table. "Dressing him up in his uniform? What was that all about?"

"It sent a message, didn't it?" Rakes seemed to forget me. Gazed off into space. "A message that old soldiers do die." He chuckled to himself.

He's crazy, I thought. The table was between us now, but the way out was behind him. There had to be another door.

I kept him talking. "Why kill Daniel Rosen? He was basically a nobody. How was he a threat to you?"

Rakes' eyes sparked and his face turned crimson. I'd touched a sore spot. Rakes was homophobic. "We don't need that kind of gay-and-lesbian bullshit shoved down our throats. I've got grandchildren. D'ya think I want them exposed to that trash?"

I thought about my own children. I wondered if Rakes knew about them. *Of course he knows,* I told myself. I've always worried one of my enemies would hurt my children. I had to shift the conversation away from them. I remembered Ravanell's profile of the killer. "What do you do for a living, Commander?"

He seemed to mellow. He liked my calling him Commander. "I'm a high-school math teacher. Getting ready to retire. I'm also the youth group leader in my church."

This was spooky. Ravanell had been on target. "That gives you access to young, impressionable children, to recruit them for your hate group."

He pulled off his cap and threw it on the kitchen

table. "I teach them values and give them focus in lives they would otherwise throw away."

The scary part about this was Rakes believed every word he said and was incapable of seeing the perversity of it.

"You give them values by teaching them to burn down churches?" I edged past the humming refrigerator. There was a door into another room. I fixed my eyes on Rakes' face. "Are you responsible for the fire at St. Andrews?"

His grin was all the answer I needed. I turned and fled through the living room and had just gotten my hand on an outside door when Rakes caught up with me. He slammed me against the wall. He glared down into my face. "Don't ever try that again. My sentries have instructions to shoot you on sight." Then he grabbed my arm and dragged me down a short hall. He threw me into a room. I landed on the floor.

"You're too clever for your own good, little lady. You can just cool off in there."

I heard the key turn in the lock. I looked around. I was in a small, sparsely furnished bedroom. A window looked out toward the tent, but bars prevented my escape. Other people had been held captive here, and I wondered who they were and what had become of them. Were there other murders we didn't know about? Lynchings perhaps? The room smelled like fear.

I explored the adjoining bathroom, but it was windowless. There were no vents or trap doors.

I used the bathroom. Splashed water on my face and cupped it in my hands and sipped. I crossed to the barred window and looked out. It was almost four o'clock, and the camp was quiet except for the constant clap of gunfire coming from the firing range. Where had they all gone? What were they up to? I preferred to have them where I could see them. Finally, I lay down on the narrow bed and rested, conserving my energies for flight.

THIRTY-SIX

RAKES CAME FOR ME AT SIX. With my hands cuffed behind me, he steered me by the elbow, out of the farmhouse, and across the clearing.

The sun was cresting tall loblolly pines in the west. We were out in a clearing in a field. Around us, the air smelled of fresh pine and sun-warmed hay. A platform had been rigged, and I was led to it and forced to mount its rickety steps on unsteady legs. It was hard to maintain my balance with my hands cuffed behind me. I wanted badly to sit down, but there was no place to do so. I was forced to stand, on display. Rakes was exacting his pound of flesh. He put me on trial. My discomfort was his pleasure.

Assembled at the end of the platform were twelve men. Some wore camouflage fatigues and combat boots like Rakes. Others were dressed in denim. They had one feature in common: they all looked hard and mean with sunbaked skin and squinty eyes. I spotted a familiar face: Karl Rakes. So this was where he'd run to. Why was I not surprised?

Men armed with automatic rifles ringed the field. A crowd of about two hundred had gathered. The mood was ugly. More military gear, overalls, leather and chains like the lowest motorcycle gangs. "Hang the bitch!" they shouted.

I was perspiring profusely and could smell my own fear. *Don't let them get to you,* I told myself. *Remem-*

ber who you are and there is no way Bill Cavanaugh will let you die. I lifted my chin defiantly and stared over their heads. In the distance, pine trees were thick and dense. I searched the sky hopefully for a flyby, but the sky was empty, a defiantly gorgeous autumn sky.

My eyes dropped. Then I saw it. The top of a utility tower. My pulse quickened and my breath caught in my throat. *How far away is it?* I wondered. I tried to estimate one hundred feet. Would the microphones pick up from this distance?

Then Rakes spoke, and it was all I could do to keep a straight face. There were speakers mounted in the trees and Rakes was holding a microphone. His voice was amplified and carried easily to the transmitters.

"Ann Kelly, you're charged with crimes against the people. How do you plead?" He stuck the microphone in front of my face.

I said loudly and clearly, "You have guns aimed at my head, Clifton Rakes. Your own brother is a member of the jury. This is not a trial. I won't participate in this farce!"

I dared not lift my gaze for fear someone would see me looking at the utility tower and read my mind. I pictured SIOC. Bill Cavanaugh and Ed Cross would be gathered there with technicians monitoring the sound equipment, hanging on to and recording my every word. I had to make each word count. I'd tell them everything they needed to know.

"Why are you holding me prisoner in this compound?" I demanded indignantly.

"This is the Common Law Court. Here you will receive true justice. You are charged with the crime of aiding niggers to avoid jail for their crimes against decent white people. For helping them take away jobs from white men. Everyone knows niggers have no souls and are not true Christians, yet you sided with them against us when we purified their houses of devil worship. You're charged with consorting with Jews and assisting them in their plots to control our banks and our newspapers. You're responsible for the cold-blooded murder of Ronald Winchester!"

At the mention of this name, the crowd began shouting, "Hang her! Hang the bitch!"

Ronald Winchester had been a white separatist who was convicted of the premeditated ambush and murder of two federal marshals. He'd been sentenced to death and subsequently executed by lethal injection at the federal correctional facility in Terre Haute. Now I knew he had many friends among Rakes' men.

"Do you have anything to say in your own defense?" Rakes pointed the microphone my way.

"Don't do anything rash. It would be a mistake."

Rakes chuckled, and the crowd jeered with him. Rakes turned to the jury. "How say you members of the jury? Guilty or not guilty?"

Their cruel voices rang out as one. "GUILTY!"

"Ann Kelly, you are hereby sentenced to death by hanging at sunrise. May God have mercy on your soul."

Cold fingers of fear splayed my spine with his pronouncement. I was stunned with the realization these crazy warriors were going to kill me.

The crowd cheered, and I struggled not to panic. I leaned toward the microphone. "You have an arsenal here. Just don't shoot me!"

The crowd hooted and belly-laughed.

Rakes gave me a look that said I was demented and not worth his trouble. He took me back to the farmhouse, removed the handcuffs, and left me alone in the bed-

room again. My watch told me it was six forty-five. In
the bathroom I drank water from my cupped hands and
splashed it on my face, trying to wash away my fear and
tension. I stared at my reflection in the mirror. "How are
you going to escape from these crazy lunatics?"

THIRTY-SEVEN

I TRIED TO REST as my mind spun like a whirlwind. What was happening at SIOC? They had the compound surrounded, I knew, but if they tried to take the compound, I'd get killed. I had to break free of Rakes so the Hostage Rescue Team could storm the place. Somewhere out there they were as close as possible, watching and waiting for their chance to move in without endangering me.

I stood at the barred window and watched darkness slowly overtake the land. What a nice place this must have been once. A real, working farm, enclosed by two enormous forests. Porch lights flickered on, lights glowed from within the barracks, and through the trees, campfires and torches burned at a distance. Floodlights on tall poles illumined the parking area around the tent. The bursts of gunfire from the firing range grew sporadic, then died.

Sounds of revelry reached my ears: men laughing, calling to each other, probably drinking. Just when I thought I'd been forgotten, Rakes unlocked my door and reached for me. Jerking my arms behind my back painfully, he snapped the cuffs on my wrists again.

"Do you have to be so rough? You can't treat me like this," I complained so he wouldn't see how terrified I was.

"You ought to be glad you're alive to feel pain, little lady, 'cause in the morning it'll all be over." He slipped a noose over my head and tightened the knot around my neck. "Get the feel of it."

"Take that off me! Who do you think you're dealing with? I'm the attorney general of the United States. Do you think I got this far by being a coward?"

At that moment, I felt like nothing more than a coward, but I had to keep up my bluff. I had to keep up my courage. If he saw my fear, I was lost. I'd never make it.

"Not a chance. Get used to it. You and me's gonna have some fun, bitch."

What next? I glared at him. "The Gambinos and the Genoveses called me that, too. Guess where they are now? Dead or behind bars!"

For an instant I saw a flicker of something pass behind his eyes. Maybe he wasn't as cocky and self-possessed as he pretended to be.

He walked me out of the house and toward the tent. Some of the militiamen formed a gauntlet, and Rakes paraded me through it. They jeered and grabbed at me. Scruffy men, bearded and fat, or thin and clean shaven, some ugly, young and old. They wore jeans and flannel shirts, or tee-shirts with sleeves rolled around cigarette packs. I saw skinny farmers with leather faces and eyes narrowed into mere slits from years of squinting at the sun.

"Go home to your wives!" No way was I going to back down.

Hot tears seared my eyeballs, but I blinked them back. I consoled myself by thinking that not far away, somewhere out there beyond the stand of pines, the Ninjas and sharpshooters were crouched. Ed Cross was somewhere out there, too, in a command vehicle, all two hundred and fifty pounds of him, chomping on a Big Mac and reaching into a white paper sack for a second.

Mustard dribbled down his chin. I held that image, and it got me through the gauntlet as hands reached for me in a way that made me want to slap them if only my hands were free.

Rakes was really giving me a hard time. Each time I stumbled, he jerked the noose tighter and sneered sarcastically, "Just a taste of what you'll be feeling tomorrow morning, ma'am." The rough men all jeered.

Lifting the tent flap, he pushed me through. Spotlights blazed. He maneuvered me through the rows of stands. Men sat there, drunk and boisterous. *Am I to be their sport?* I wondered. The open, lustful looks I got from some of them unnerved me. Maybe they planned to hang me in the morning, but right now I was in imminent danger of rape.

Rakes sensed my fear. He pulled the rope short, showing me off, as men hooted and called slurs. As I stumbled past rows of them, I saw hot, feral faces with eyes that had died long ago. Rakes had only to say the word and they'd rip me apart.

Then the mood passed. Rakes seemed firmly in control. His men wouldn't make a move without his word. He thrust me down into a first-row seat and sat next to me. At last there was some slack in the rope. From a lowered head, I looked left and right. A man was raking a pit of dirty sand. Some sort of debris was being swept away. What new horrors did Rakes have in store for me?

The tent filled up. The men were noisy and impatient. They passed beer cans from coolers. Someone collected money.

The bagman reached Rakes. His tone was respectful. "You bettin', Commander?"

Rakes stood and fumbled in the pocket of his spotted

fatigues. He handed some bills to the man. "Red Devil." The bagman scribbled a receipt.

The rope was slack now. Out of Rakes' hands. I could take off and run. I wouldn't get far. They'd love to get their hands on me. Only Rakes stood between me and gang rape. He seemed to read my mind for he looked knowingly into my eyes. "You're the only girlie in the place, little lady."

At the exits, sentries were posted. They, at least, were sober. Powerful in fatigues, stance ramrod, automatic rifles ready to fire at Rakes' command. Let some of the members have their fun; Rakes' soldiers were on duty.

Suddenly, a cheer broke out. Two young men not much older than my Thomas ran into the pit from opposite directions. I did a double take. Over their heads they carried roosters. *Oh, dear Lord, no, not a cock fight,* I thought. Cock fighting was a despicable blood sport that had been outlawed decades ago. It was cruel and inhumane, and only twisted minds took pleasure in it. How could I expect better from these vile men?

"You ain't never seen nothing like this, little lady. Those cocks are the meanest bastards God ever made. Rip a man's throat out soon as look at him."

"Leave God out of this. It's men like you who are to blame. Cock fights are illegal!"

Rakes threw back his head and laughed heartily. I guess to him it was funny. What did a man like Rakes care about legalities? He broke the law each and every day. He made his own rules.

The bagman took the microphone and moved into the pit. Over loudspeakers, he introduced the two game-cocks as Red Devil and Satan, gave their weights and histories. Satan was a speckled fowl with white-and-gray feathers. Red Devil, Rakes told me smartly, was an Old English, black-breasted, red game rooster. As if I cared.

The handlers tossed their birds in the air. As I followed them with my eyes, Rakes commented, "They're being exercised. They love it. The handlers are called cockers, by the way."

What was with him? He was so caught up in this perverted shit, he thought I cared.

The crowd was already wild and the fighting hadn't even begun. Last-minute bets were being placed as more militiamen entered the tent, and the other bagman couldn't collect the bills fast enough.

In the ring the cockers held their roosters head high. Hands flew apart and the birds fluttered gracefully down into the sand.

"Will the contenders affix the gaffs!" The referee's voice broke over the hooting crowd.

Shiny metal devices were tied onto the legs of the cocks. Sharp spikes protruded from the devices. Miniature spurs. The birds kicked up their heels, testing the spurs, as lights from the rafters glinted off slicing steel.

"Get ready!" yelled the command over the speakers. The cockers lifted their birds, held them aloft overhead but well away from their own bodies to avoid contact with the razor-sharp spurs.

"Pit!" cried the referee. The crowd went wild as cockers teased opposing birds, using their own bird as a weapon to spar and jab, threatening thrusts at the other's head. Finally, when the birds and the audience were whipped into a frenzy, the fowl were dropped to the sand and the handlers withdrew.

The cocks sized each other up, engaged in their macabre dance, sidestepping and feinting. They parried like prizefighters in a ring. Puffed up, ruffled feathers intimidating. At first they seemed hesitant, as if their hearts weren't truly in this viciousness. Each seemed not to want to be the first to attack. Not the cruel bastards Rakes thought they were.

"Go, Satan!" someone yelled.

"Pop him, Red Devil!" came the answering cry.

Men, wild on beer and testosterone surge, cheered from the stands.

From my ringside seat, I had a better view than I cared to have. Satan initiated the first attack by leaping two feet into the air and throwing himself feet first at Red Devil. Red Devil jumped back, out of range of the stabbing spurs. Seizing his chance while Satan regained his balance, Red Devil flew forward, drove his feet into Satan, raked the spurs over Satan's neck and breast. Blood spurted.

The men chanted, "Blood! Blood! Blood!" and stomped their feet on the stands.

I couldn't bear any more of this and shut my eyes. Yet I couldn't shut out the sounds coming from the cockpit. The sounds I heard painted a picture of carnage. The soft slap as the birds threw themselves at each other. The thud when they hit. The rip of flesh, the splitting of bone, the popping of joints. Only death could separate Satan and Red Devil now.

Rakes grasped my shoulder and shook it. "It's over." Despite my loathing, my eyes flew open. Rust feathers mixed with white and gray fluttered down, broken wings hung limp and useless, and the sand in the pit was wet and red. My eyes snapped shut, and I willed my ears to be deaf. I couldn't block out the greedy crowd and their cries for more savagery. They were on their feet, stomping, and the stands shook under their weight.

After an eternity, it was really over. Then the jeering

became cries of triumph and groans of loss, swearing and oaths of getting even.

In the center of the pit, a heap of something that had once been alive lay dead or dying. I hoped for the birds' sakes they were dead. Like a pile of discarded, tattered rags, they clung together, mated in death, one bird indistinguishable from the other. Their long fight was over. Someone opened the tent's flap. A breeze stirred the air and ruffled beautiful feathers.

I felt dead inside—as dead as the birds. Something inside me hardened, some last remnant of softness crystallized into purpose. The torture of the innocents was symbolic of everything Rakes and his militia stood for. Looking at him, I felt such contempt and loathing; I realized on some level I had joined him. I wanted revenge. If I had a gun in my hands, I would shoot him between the eyes, like he'd shot Sam and Rosen and Moore and Colby. Never had I felt capable of killing another human with my own hands. I did now.

I was going to survive. I was going to live to fight Rakes on his terms. I was going to win.

THIRTY-EIGHT

RAKES SEEMED TO lose heart in tormenting me. Two men in suits coming through the tent's open flap claimed his attention. With a start, I recognized my old adversary from the Judiciary Committee, Senator Henry Carroll. Hope sparked momentarily until I realized with certainty, *He's one of them.*

Rakes must have read my mind for he turned. "Don't go getting your hopes up. Carroll's our banker."

Of course. Someone powerful had to be bankrolling the militia. Carroll, his hands guiding the purse strings of soft money sources, his conservative coalitions raising big bucks from questionable sources like the gun industry and Blackwater, was in a perfect position to funnel funds to Rakes.

Still, my heart sank as Carroll threw an arm around one of Rakes' soldiers.

Rakes scanned the bleachers, spotted his brother, Karl, and waved him over. Jerking me to my feet, he thrust me at Karl so hard I fell into him. Karl pushed me away like I was poison. Rakes jangled a key ring. "Here. Lock her up."

Karl grabbed my elbow and steered me through a flap in the tent's opposite side. The rope still dangled from my neck, its loose end trailing behind me, dragging on the ground. Karl ignored it and me, saying nothing to alleviate my fears. Rather than lead me to the house, he marched me into the dark line of trees that edged the clearing. Sweat popped out on my skin, chilling instantly in the breeze, causing me to shiver.

"What do you think you're doing?" I aimed for indignant, but heard my voice quake.

He laughed in my face. "It's not what you're thinking. I like my women young and sweet. A tough old bird like you doesn't tempt me."

The walk through the woods was rough going. With my hands cuffed behind me, I couldn't keep my balance, and I tripped and stumbled. Karl pulled me to my feet, mocking me. "What's the matter, Attorney General, can't keep up? Your cushy job up in Washington making you soft? Hurry up." He yanked my upper arm so hard I thought he'd jerk it out of the socket. "Cliff didn't say where to lock you up, but I've got just the place for you to spend your last night." He laughed wickedly.

What was he planning for me? My fears were quickly overwhelming my power to reason. Was he going to hang me now? Not wait until morning? I couldn't let him see how scared I was. "Where did you hide the murder weapon? The gun you and Cliff used to kill Senator Claiborne? You did take it from the Property Room, didn't you?"

Karl shrugged. "Of course I took it. Who else? That Property Room's a joke. The entire Metro P.D.'s a joke. They're all corrupt, you know, from the mayor to the commissioner and on down."

I remembered my training in negotiating. "I agree with you there."

Karl seemed not to hear. "Cliff and I had been planning that killing for a long time, ever since that damned traitor started pushing through legislation to deprive us of our rights. I couldn't wait to get away from filthy Washington. Talk about a cesspool."

"Cliff was the one who actually shot the senator, right?"

He stopped. "Yeah, but he couldn't have done it without my help."

"That makes you an accessory, not a murderer. It's not you who's facing a death sentence. Help me get away from here, and things will go easier for you."

"No way! Hey, me turn on my brother? Forget it."

We'd come to a small outbuilding, no more than a shed. In the dim light that shone down from a bare, low-watt bulb over the door, the sharp angles of Karl's face took on the look of a death mask. "You, Attorney General, are one more big stink in that cesspool. But no more. We've got plenty more scores to settle after you."

"Let me help you. My word carries a lot of weight. I'll help you get a deal."

"Deal? Me deal with you? Hell, no. Me and Cliff and the boys have got a job to do. Don't you understand? We've got our work cut out for us if we're ever going to clean up this country and make it a place fit for decent folk to live and bring up kids."

He gave the door to the shed a yank. Threw me in ahead of him.

"See how you like spending your last night here." He laughed eerily. "The condemned prisoner sleeping with the other condemned prisoners."

"Wait! For God's sakes, take these off." I fluttered my cuffed hands at him from behind my back. "I can't get my balance. You wouldn't want me to fall and break my neck and deprive all of you of your fun and games. The Commander wouldn't like it."

He seemed to be weighing my request, but I didn't

really expect him to go for it. He gave me another crazy laugh and I knew it was hopeless. Then he surprised me. "I suppose the condemned prisoner is entitled to one last request." Taking one of the keys on the key ring, he unlocked the handcuffs from my wrists. "Sleep tight." He stepped out the door and locked it behind him.

I rubbed life back into my numb wrists. Another solitary, dim lightbulb cast a shadowy luminescence inside the small shed. I heard the sounds of roosters, shifting, pecking, twittering. On my right, cages were stacked one on top of the other. The scratching came from inside. The gamecocks. They were terrified, like me, and backed away, into the far corners of their pens. Their glassy eyes regarded me with hostility and fear.

"I'm not the enemy." How could they know that? To them, all humans were the enemy. The humanitarian in me wanted to open the doors, to turn them loose and set them free, but they'd been trained to kill, and locked up together as we were, I couldn't risk it. I'd seen the damage Satan and Red Devil had inflicted on each other with their sharp beaks and talons.

We were separated by thick wire mesh, but on the will-to-survive level, nothing separated us. The birds fluttered in their cages and followed me with their eyes. Curiosity seemed to get the better of them. I was a new distraction as they waited for their turn in the pit. Were the games through for the night? Or were the militiamen simply taking a break? Would the handlers return for more victims? They were just boys; maybe I could rush them and escape when they opened the door.

On top of the nearest cage lay a pair of heavy suede gloves, long and cuffed, the gloves the cockers wore when handling the fowl. A rustle in the corner claimed my attention. Like so much discarded refuse, the broken bodies of the beaten were heaped in a pile. The smell of their bloodied and dying bodies filled my nostrils and made my stomach queasy. There was a small fluttering within the pile and a cry that sounded almost human. Those men had hearts of stone.

The rope still dangled from my neck. I reached up and untied it. Absently, my thoughts skipping from one futile plan to the next, I coiled the length of rope around my hand.

How to escape? That was my problem. I tried the door, even though I knew it was locked; I'd heard Karl turn the key. The door rattled but wouldn't budge, far too heavy for me to force. High overhead, just under the roof, a tiny window admitted much-needed fresh air. Maybe if I climbed up on the cages I could reach it. Even if I did, it was much too small for even my narrow shoulders to squeeze through.

I tried the door on the other side of the cages. Just a storage closet. Supplies, wheelbarrow, sacks of feed. Nothing useful as a weapon—not a shovel or hoe. Nothing. I closed the closet door as panic set in.

Outside, footsteps shuffled in the leaves. I pressed my ear to the door. Someone was out there. Someone was coming. The jingle of keys. Stretching on tiptoe, I grabbed the handler's gloves and hastily slipped my hands inside. The catch on the nearest cage door gave way easily. The door swung open. The frightened cock backed away into the deep recesses of his pen. I stretched gloved hands toward him. "Easy, fellow." I tried to sound calm as adrenaline exploded through my veins.

I grabbed him around the chest and pulled him out as he squawked. I took care to hold his wings down. If those strong wings got free, I wouldn't be able to control him for long. He was heavier than I expected. Eyes filled with terror, he hissed a warning.

"Easy, fellow." The key turned in the lock with a rasp.

I moved behind the door, the rooster grasped firmly in my outstretched hands. He was frantic with fear and struggled against my grip, managing to pull his wings free. They beat fiercely against my face. He screwed his head around and thrust his beak into my upper arm. Pain seared up to my shoulder like a flame, and I forced back a cry. My arms felt weak, and I knew I couldn't hold on to him much longer.

The door flew open. Karl Rakes' face appeared around it. "Cliff sent... Oh..." His expression froze, uncomprehending. Then his eyes widened and his arms rose defensively as he backed away. He didn't move fast enough. I threw the gamecock up, directly into his face. Wings fanned the air. In their coops, the other birds thrashed nervously. Sharp talons pierced Rakes' eyes.

His scream was a cry for mercy. The cock gave none. He was not through with Karl yet. All his pent-up fury was unleashed on Karl. In one powerful grip, his talons dug into Rakes' chest. He held fast, slicing into Rakes' neck with his beak. Blood spurted from the wound. Satisfied, the bird dropped lightly to the ground, strutted away, as if to say "That's that."

Rakes' bleeding eyes were blind. He stumbled forward, his hands outstretched. With every beat of his heart, blood pumped from his neck wound. He grabbed at it, clutching and choking.

Karl Rakes was losing a lot of blood fast. He tried to say something, but only a gurgling sound bubbled from his lips. If he was asking for my help, he was out of luck. Unable to stand, he fell to his knees and crawled aimlessly. I felt no pity. His bloody face reminded me of my last glimpse of Lauren Colby.

Lifting the coil of rope, I looped it around Rakes' foot, then tied the ends to the closet's doorknob. Quickly, I yanked the cage doors open, freeing the innocent. The birds hopped to the floor, scampered out the door, and scattered in the night.

I was out the door fast, slamming it behind me, turning the key quickly in the lock, pocketing it. All the while I prayed no one saw me.

Off in the distance, barrack lights and bonfires winked through stirring tree branches. Quarrelsome voices carried on night breezes. I ran in the opposite direction, pushed through dense foliage, sought the shelter of darkness.

Visualizing the camp as I'd seen it in satellite photos, I stopped to get my bearings. The farmhouse, tent, and barracks were behind me. I knew they lay in the northern quadrant of the property. The utility towers ran north-south, to the southeast side of the farmhouse. I tried to remember the direction Karl Rakes had led me, calculating the gamecock shed was southwest of the farmhouse. I'd have to cross the compound from west to east in order to find the utility corridor. The strong lights from the parking area provided me with a point of reference.

All was quiet, and I assumed Karl was too far gone to sound the alarm. I'd have a head start until his brother, Clifton, missed us and sent someone after us. I turned to my left and sprinted off in what I hoped was an easterly direction.

I plunged into the deep woods, grateful for the cover underbrush and small pines afforded me. I scarcely felt their scratches or slaps. They hid me from view effectively. The wound on my arm throbbed as it bled into my sleeve.

I tried to move without a sound, tried to prevent branches from swinging noisily as I pushed through them, but twigs snapped under my feet and leaves whispered, and the sound of my own breathing was a roar in my ears. I stepped forward gingerly.

Not all the militiamen were drunken revelers. The entertainment had just been a sop for the *hoi polloi,* the ignorant masses Rakes needed to form his power base. His soldiers were alert and sober, trained for war, expecting war. Sentries patrolled the grounds. Bud Starr had said he thought they were equipped with night-vision goggles. I had to be as cunning as a hunted animal.

Stealthily, I slipped from tree to tree, hiding behind the broad trunks of giant oaks. My night vision was good, and my eyes adjusted quickly to the darkness. For once I was grateful for my small size. It made me a smaller target. I developed a rhythm: duck behind a tree, watch, listen, dart to the next.

Close by, a bough slapped the air, and dry twigs crunched. I pressed against a tree, straining my ears as footsteps approached. *One of the sentries,* I thought. Where to hide? Under brambles, the broad outline of a fallen tree trunk. I dropped to my hands and knees and crawled to it. By now my hands were crisscrossed with scratches, and I felt welts rising on my cheeks. I rolled over the log and slithered down its back side, keeping my head low. To my ears, it sounded like a terrible racket.

The trunk was hollow, and I squeezed into it. Sawdust rained on my face. Never an outdoors woman, I feared raccoons and skunks, critters that lived in hollow trees. But not nearly as much as I feared Rakes and his men. I listened intently. No sound. Then I heard it. The sudden rush of exhaled breath, the shifting of a rifle, the scent of a cigarette. He was standing directly over me. I covered my mouth with my hands, too scared to breathe. His foot landed with a thud as he stepped over the log, the heel of his boot mere inches from my face. I didn't move until his footsteps faded away and I counted to one hundred.

I squirmed out of my hiding place and, crouched over, headed eastward again. Stars came out, but I had no talent for reading heaven's signs; the constellations formed no map for me. Again, I maintained my strategy of darting from tree to tree, until I ran out of trees and found myself in a broad clearing.

The power-line corridor! Overhead, I could see the dark stripes the power cables made as they cut across the starlit sky. Now all I had to do was move steadily southward until I reached the first utility tower.

I crept along the forest's edge, moving quietly but quickly under the low canopy of trees. Finally, I saw the skeletal utility tower glinting against the sky. Thank God for Special Ops. The microphones, cameras, and tiny transmitters they had mounted on the towers would transmit my message to SIOC. From SIOC, the message would be transmitted to the troops who waited on the ground.

I crept to the tower, turned my face heavenward, and spoke distinctly. "This is Ann Kelly. I've escaped. I'm heading south toward the service road. Have someone meet me there. Strike the compound. Now! Serve the warrants and bring those bastards in."

I listened for nearby sounds. When I heard nothing, I risked repeating my message. I felt certain my transmission was being received in SIOC, that Bill Cavanaugh was monitoring the situation and would relay my message to the ground troops nearby. A United States senator was about to be arrested for his participation in the covert militia's theft of weapons. Tomorrow it would be front-page news.

Maintaining my course along the forest's edge, I hurried down the hill in a southerly direction, following the power-line corridor. I had about a half-mile to cover before I closed the distance between the compound and the power company's service road.

A voice rang out. "Kelly!" I recognized the voice at once. Whirling around I saw Clifton Rakes silhouetted at the top of the hill. A tiny red dot danced on my chest, and I threw myself to the ground, covering my head with my arms. A crack of gunfire. A zing as a bullet whizzed by much too close.

Flinging a look over my shoulder, I watched Rakes advance toward me. I didn't dare stand up to run. Scrambling on knees and elbows, I squirmed over rough ground back toward the dense forest, hoping to hide until my rescuers caught up with him. In front of me, further down the hill, a line of shadows crept forward.

A barrage of gunfire erupted. Rakes shooting at me. The shadows shooting at Rakes. Me in the middle. Bullets pinged off rocks, singed the earth.

Suddenly, a snap and a pop overhead. A shower of sparks. Something cracked through the air like a whip, struck the ground just yards away. A severed power cable. A live wire.

Movement near me. I looked up. Rakes loomed over me. Apparently finding Karl dead had sent him over the edge. He seemed to think he was immune to HRT's bullets and seemed blind to the high-tension wire that writhed on the ground nearby.

"On your feet." Rakes' pistol was aimed at my head.

Rakes was obsessed with killing me. The man was clearly insane yet cunning, for he motioned me to stand between him and my shadowy saviors. I prayed a skilled sharpshooter was stationed in a tree behind him.

The live wire slapped the ground, sparking and sizzling.

"It's over," I said. "You're surrounded. Give it up."

"Then we'll die together."

As long as he was talking, he wasn't shooting.

"If the feds kill me, the Movement will be stronger than ever."

A sudden power surge flipped the cable into the air. Wildly, it whipped and arced closer to Rakes. I'll never know what possessed me to act so recklessly— maybe it was Rakes' confession he was willing to die for the pleasure of killing me—but I lunged for the cable, grabbed it around its thick, insulated cover, and drove the live end deep into his arm.

For an instant, disbelief registered on his face, then his features contorted as high-voltage current flowed through him and into the ground. The stench of charred flesh corrupted the sweet night air. Every muscle in his body contracted, and his lungs stopped breathing. When his organs started to cook, I flung the cable far away. Muscles rock hard, Rakes hit the earth like a fallen tree.

THIRTY-NINE

I WAS SURROUNDED by HRT agents. They pressed my trembling arms into a Kevlar vest and hustled me down the hill. Within seconds I heard a noisy drone in the distance. Steadily, the noise drew nearer and louder, and I recognized the telltale whup-whup-whup of helicopter rotor blades. We stopped to watch them pass overhead, a beautiful sight, Blackhawks outlined against the starry sky, lights blinking. If I could hear them, Rakes' soldiers could hear them as well. They'd be breaking out the arsenal, setting up anti-aircraft artillery. Powerful infrared search beams swept the ground as the helicopters sailed smoothly on course.

At the bottom of the hill, cars with headlights on high beam guided us home. I hit the service road at a trot, the Ninjas surrounding me, guiding me, pushing me on. My legs were limp, but their strong, young bodies formed a tight unit with me at its core, propping me upright, propelling me forward.

Figures, silhouetted in the headlights, ran to meet me. I recognized the bear-like shape of Edgar Cross lumbering toward me. I was never so glad to see anyone. My nightmare was over. The fear and humiliation I'd suffered at Rakes' hands surfaced with a burst of emotion. I didn't have to put up a brave front any longer. I threw myself into Ed's arms and surprised us both by bursting into tears.

Ed patted my back. "Ann, you done good. You done

real good, girl." He supported me as we walked to the car, and I was unashamed to lean on his strength.

He was helping me into the rear seat when the fireworks began. First, the sporadic pop of gunfire from the hilltop, then the high squeal of rockets, followed by a heavy and constant barrage of firepower. I was out of the car in a flash, standing with the others, staring at the sky, horrified and helpless. I watched as one of the Blackhawks took a hit. I felt my heart quicken when sparks flew and it began its spiraling descent.

The explosion was so powerful we felt the vibration under our feet. A flash split the night sky, followed by a terrible roar. The ground rocked as shock waves rolled, and the entire hill vaporized into a sheet of towering flames that could be seen for miles around. One by one, I counted three Blackhawks make it out to safety.

"Holy shit!" Ed exclaimed. "They wanted a war. Well, they got it."

A SWAT team rushed the compound. Anyone who managed to escape the explosion would be captured. I suspected few had. In the morning, aircraft would photograph a crater where once POSSE had assembled an arsenal.

POSSE was destroyed, but at a costly price. The pilots of the downed helicopter were dead. Sam was dead. So were Daniel Rosen and Bud Starr. Brad Moore and Lauren Colby were probably dead, too. POSSE was leaderless. It seemed fitting the militiamen who'd burned houses of worship had lost their lives in a catastrophic conflagration.

"Ann, you're shaking." Ed threw an FBI parka over my shoulders.

I hadn't realized I was cold, but my teeth were

chattering, and I wondered if I was in shock. I'd just killed two men.

We got into the car. "Now you're official." He handed me a steaming thermos of coffee. "I got to tell you, that message you sent was brilliant. You were sure cool, those jerks standing you up before their phony court, you feeding us the details about their arsenal."

Our car sped through the night, passing convoys of government transports heading to the scene, as we drove to the temporary command site on the edges of the Croatan National Forest.

"My agents?" I asked. "Did they make it?"

"The docs are working on them. We don't know yet." Ed shook his head sadly. "I've got a surprise for you. There's someone real anxious to see you."

"Who?" I asked.

"You'll see," he teased.

I felt safe in the backseat with him, and I knew from now on he would be my staunch ally, and I his. The others were right: when the shit hits the fan, Ed is your man.

The hastily assembled command post was a hodge-podge of utility vehicles, communication vans, Hum-vees, and transports, plus portable generators. Bright lights mounted in trees spotlighted the man who ran toward me.

With the sight of him, my lopsided world righted again, and I raced for his outstretched arms.

"Jack!" He squeezed me so tight I could scarcely breathe.

"My whole family is here." Daddy's voice and smile were strong. "I never thought I'd see you walk through that door, Jack." He reached up and shook Jack's hand.

We were gathered around Daddy's bed in his hospital room. Dr. Feldman reported he was recuperating better than expected.

"Are all of you co-conspirators?" I couldn't keep from smiling broadly. "How long have you known your dad was coming home?"

"Don't look at me," my father protested. "I didn't know."

"Dad wanted to surprise you," Tom said. "Cathy and I were sworn to secrecy. I almost spilled the beans last Saturday when you started to cry in Rumplemeyer's."

I leaned into the curve of Jack's arm. "Well, you surprised me, all right. You were the last person I expected to see. I thought you were thousands of miles away." Tears filled my eyes and I blinked them back. "I'm so glad you're home."

Then I reached out to hug and kiss my son. "I have you to thank for knowing what to do with that live power line." He and the others looked at me curiously. "You're an engineering student. You're the one who told me high-voltage power lines are insulated. That you can touch the cable and not be electrocuted."

Tom's grin was dazzling.

Daddy said, "As soon as I'm back on my feet, I'll be spending more time in New York on church business. We can celebrate most holidays together from now on."

I kissed his forehead. "The sleep sofa in the study is all yours. Now, if you'll excuse me, I want to go check on my agents."

I TOOK THE ELEVATOR down two floors to the Trauma Unit. One of my agents had survived the shooting; news of the other's demise brought tears of rage.

I got permission at the nurses' station to enter the

room. "Hello, Lauren," I whispered. She opened her eyes. Her pretty blonde hair had been shaved from the side of her head where the bullet had chipped off a chunk of bone.

Moore had lowered the driver's side window in response to the phony ambulance driver's frantic tapping. He'd shot Moore first. Colby's hand had flown inside her jacket for her Glock. She'd leaned forward to aim around Moore when the second bullet clipped her frontal bone, knocking her out cold. The shooter had been in a hurry, nervous he'd be seen, and assumed from all the blood she was dead. Miraculously, Lauren Colby had survived, and although she faced extensive reconstructive surgery, she would recover. Her marriage to the quiet man who refused to leave her bedside might have to be postponed, but she'd live to be a bride.

"Hi," she murmured weakly, and I could see she was in pain. Bravely and slowly, she whispered, "I've been hearing impressive reports about you, Ann. You missed your calling. You should have been one of us—an FBI agent."

I lifted her pale hand. "When some future president is smart enough to appoint you the Bureau's first female director, I'll sign up."

* * * * *

REQUEST YOUR FREE BOOKS!

2 FREE NOVELS
PLUS 2 FREE GIFTS!

WORLDWIDE LIBRARY®
Your Partner in Crime

YES! Please send me 2 FREE novels from the Worldwide Library® series and my 2 FREE gifts (gifts are worth about $10). After receiving them, if I don't wish to receive any more books, I can return the shipping statement marked "cancel." If I don't cancel, I will receive 4 brand-new novels every month and be billed just $5.24 per book in the U.S. or $6.24 per book in Canada. That's a saving of at least 34% off the cover price. It's quite a bargain! Shipping and handling is just 50¢ per book in the U.S. and 75¢ per book in Canada.* I understand that accepting the 2 free books and gifts places me under no obligation to buy anything. I can always return a shipment and cancel at any time. Even if I never buy another book, the two free books and gifts are mine to keep forever.

414/424 WDN FEJ3

Name _____ (PLEASE PRINT) _____

Address _____ Apt. # _____

City _____ State/Prov. _____ Zip/Postal Code _____

Signature (if under 18, a parent or guardian must sign) _____

Mail to the **Reader Service:**
IN U.S.A.: P.O. Box 1867, Buffalo, NY 14240-1867
IN CANADA: P.O. Box 609, Fort Erie, Ontario L2A 5X3

Not valid for current subscribers to the Worldwide Library series.

Want to try two free books from another line?
Call 1-800-873-8635 or visit www.ReaderService.com.

* Terms and prices subject to change without notice. Prices do not include applicable taxes. Sales tax applicable in N.Y. Canadian residents will be charged applicable taxes. Offer not valid in Quebec. This offer is limited to one order per household. All orders subject to credit approval. Credit or debit balances in a customer's account(s) may be offset by any other outstanding balance owed by or to the customer. Please allow 4 to 6 weeks for delivery. Offer available while quantities last.

Your Privacy—The Reader Service is committed to protecting your privacy. Our Privacy Policy is available online at www.ReaderService.com or upon request from the Reader Service.

We make a portion of our mailing list available to reputable third parties that offer products we believe may interest you. If you prefer that we not exchange your name with third parties, or if you wish to clarify or modify your communication preferences, please visit us at www.ReaderService.com/consumerschoice or write to us at Reader Service Preference Service, P.O. Box 9062, Buffalo, NY 14269. Include your complete name and address.

FAMOUS FAMILIES

REQUEST YOUR FREE BOOKS!

2 FREE NOVELS
FROM THE SUSPENSE COLLECTION
PLUS 2 FREE GIFTS!

YES! Please send me 2 FREE novels from the Suspense Collection and my 2 FREE gifts (gifts are worth about $10). After receiving them, if I don't wish to receive any more books, I can return the shipping statement marked "cancel." If I don't cancel, I will receive 4 brand-new novels every month and be billed just $5.99 per book in the U.S. or $6.49 per book in Canada. That's a saving of at least 25% off the cover price. It's quite a bargain! Shipping and handling is just 50¢ per book in the U.S. and 75¢ per book in Canada.* I understand that accepting the 2 free books and gifts places me under no obligation to buy anything. I can always return a shipment and cancel at any time. Even if I never buy another book, the two free books and gifts are mine to keep forever.

191/391 MDN FEME

Name	(PLEASE PRINT)	
Address		Apt. #
City	State/Prov.	Zip/Postal Code

Signature (if under 18, a parent or guardian must sign)

Mail to the **Reader Service:**
IN U.S.A.: P.O. Box 1867, Buffalo, NY 14240-1867
IN CANADA: P.O. Box 609, Fort Erie, Ontario L2A 5X3

Not valid for current subscribers to the Suspense Collection or the Romance/Suspense Collection.

Want to try two free books from another line?
Call 1-800-873-8635 or visit www.ReaderService.com.

* Terms and prices subject to change without notice. Prices do not include applicable taxes. Sales tax applicable in N.Y. Canadian residents will be charged applicable taxes. Offer not valid in Quebec. This offer is limited to one order per household. All orders subject to credit approval. Credit or debit balances in a customer's account(s) may be offset by any other outstanding balance owed by or to the customer. Please allow 4 to 6 weeks for delivery. Offer available while quantities last.

Your Privacy—The Reader Service is committed to protecting your privacy. Our Privacy Policy is available online at www.ReaderService.com or upon request from the Reader Service.

We make a portion of our mailing list available to reputable third parties that offer products we believe may interest you. If you prefer that we not exchange your name with third parties, or if you wish to clarify or modify your communication preferences, please visit us at www.ReaderService.com/consumerschoice or write to us at Reader Service Preference Service, P.O. Box 9062, Buffalo, NY 14269. Include your complete name and address.

SUSI1